ALSO BY SAM LEE JACKSON

The Jackson Blackhawk Series

The Girl at the Deep End of the Lake
The Librarian, Her Daughter and the Man Who Lost His Head.
The Bag Lady, the Boat Bum and the West Side King
They Called Her Indigo
The Darker Hours
The Colonel, the Cove, and the Dog that didn't Bark
Also
Shonto's Kid

The Man with the Lightning Scar

SAM LEE JACKSON

The Man with the Lightning Scar

Piping Rock Publications
3608 E Taro Lane. Phoenix AZ 85050
www.samleejackson.com

ISBN 978-1-7351654-1-7 (Print)
ISBN 978-1-7351654-2-4 (E)
Library of Congress Control Number 2021910469

To Carol, Amanda, Lance, Lily and Davis
all my reasons for living

1

The El Patron was quiet. The band had rehearsed, then gone home to rest before the nine o'clock show. I was sitting sideways on what had become *my* barstool, playing chess with my friend Pete Dunn who owned the *Thirteen Episodes*, the sixty-five-foot Sunliner that was moored across from and just down from my Tiger Lily. I had a half glass of tomato juice in front of me, but it had gotten warm. Pete had a Corona with a lime stuffed into it. Jimmy was behind the bar and Blackhawk sat across from me looking at Far Side cartoons by Gary Larson.

My eyes were just going back to the chess board when I saw Blackhawk stiffen. This was unusual because nothing ever bothered Blackhawk. He was looking toward the door. I turned my head and watched a man walk in. He stood a moment, letting his eyes adjust.

He was a tall slender man with dark hair and dark eyes, with his hair swept back like Blackhawk's. The most striking thing about him was the jagged scar that ran from his ear to the corner of his mouth. It was as if someone had drawn a lightning bolt on his face. When his eyes cleared, he was looking at Blackhawk. He walked over and sat next to him. He put his hand out. Blackhawk didn't move.

Jimmy came down and placed a coaster in front of the man.

"What'll it be?" Jimmy said.

"He won't be staying," Blackhawk said. Jimmy looked at Blackhawk, took the coaster, turned and walked away.

"Not very friendly," the man said.

Blackhawk just looked at the man. It wasn't friendly.

The man looked around. "Nice place you have here. I've heard all about it. A lot of our mutual friends have talked about it."

"We don't have mutual friends," Blackhawk said.

"A lot of people know who you are. I've heard you have a really good singer here. They say she's a beautiful woman."

Blackhawk leaned forward about an inch. "You don't know who I am now. If I think you pose any threat to that woman, any kind of threat at all, I will cut your head off."

The man laughed nervously. He held a palm out to ward Blackhawk off. "Whoa boy. I'm no threat to anyone."

"Why are you here?"

"Overcrowding," he said. "They are running out of space and they put me out on parole."

"I don't care about that," Blackhawk said. "Why are you here?"

The man took his time looking around. He looked at me. I held his gaze. "I could use a man like you," he said, looking back at Blackhawk.

"No," Blackhawk said.

"You haven't even heard me out," he said.

"No," Blackhawk said.

"We are talking a whole lot of money."

"No," Blackhawk said.

The man looked across at me. "Is he always this hardheaded?"

"No," I said. "Sometimes it's worse."

"Time for you to leave," Blackhawk said.

The man looked at him for a long time. He finally slid off his stool. He turned and walked to the door that led to the hallway out. He opened the door and turned.

"I will be back, Joseph," he said. He went out and shut the door.

I went over to Blackhawk and slid up beside him.

"Joseph?"

"There is no Joseph," he said.

"Who was that?"

"He tells people he is my brother," he said.

2

After the man had left, Blackhawk went upstairs without another word. He obviously didn't want to talk about it. Pete and I ended up driving back to the Marina and finished our game there. Now it was three days later, and I was cleaning stripers in the kitchen sink. Eddie had picked me up before dawn and we had spent three productive hours chasing a school of stripers across the main part of the lake. I don't know how he did it, but Eddie had an uncanny knack for knowing where to find them. He would motor to an area and within minutes we would be catching. Once they moved, he would find the new area and we'd start again. If you like to fish, it was heaven.

I wrapped and packaged about thirty pounds of fillets and put them in the deep locker to freeze. I cleaned up and scrubbed the counter down. I lit a scented candle to help get rid of the fishy smell. I zip-locked the entrails and walked them to the far reaches of the dock and dumped them for the seagulls. Diesel, the marina's dog, was lying in the sun and when I walked by, he perked up and followed me. Before I dumped the entrails, I selected a few choice heads and laid them out for him.

I went back to the Tiger Lily and took a shower. By the time I was out, Blackhawk was sitting on the oversized yellow couch. He had a Dos Equis in his hand, but his head was back, and his eyes were closed. I hopped back to the master stateroom where I slipped on a black T Shirt, a pair of cutoff jeans and strapped on my prosthetic. I slipped a Teva on my other foot. When I went back into the main salon, his eyes were open. I pulled a Dos Equis from the galley locker and popped it open.

I climbed up on a stool at the galley counter. I sipped the beer and waited.

Finally, he said, "I always knew the little shit would show up some day."

I made a noise of agreement. Nothing more than like a little hum.

"Oh shut up," he said.

"Of course," I said.

He closed his eyes again and sat there for a very long time. Finally, he sat up and took a drink and looked at me.

"This is going to be a problem," he said.

"How so?"

"I don't know. Not specifically. But, just knowing he is out there walking around makes me very uncomfortable. When his mom and my dad died, he was given custody of me. He was older than eighteen which made him legal. I wasn't. He had a job in a body shop, so he looked like he was being responsible."

"But he wasn't?"

"The body shop was a front for a drug runner everybody called Duke."

"How old were you?"

"Maybe fifteen."

"He got you involved?"

"He had me running drugs all over."

"What happened?"

"They got cocky. I pulled onto the street the shop was on and the street was filled with flashing red and blue lights. I turned down the alley, found a dumpster and dumped everything that would link me to the body shop. I went over the car, top to bottom. I drove home and went through the house with a fine-toothed comb. I ditched everything he had that was drug related. Then I made a sandwich, got a coke and went to my room and started reading. Two hours later the cops were at my door. They took me downtown and grilled me for five hours. I didn't give them a thing. While I was down there, they went through the house. Didn't find a damn thing."

I smiled. Not surprised.

"They put me in foster care and threw my brother in jail. He had been arrested and convicted twice before, so this was strike three. He drew a thirty-year sentence. I stayed in foster care until my eighteenth birthday then they marched me down to the Navy recruiter and signed me up."

I looked at him. "You sure don't seem to like that guy much."

"I had a lot of time to think in the Navy. After a while I realized that he didn't give one hot damn about me. He was just using me. If I hadn't gotten lucky, I would be the one in prison. He really is a cold-hearted bastard."

"What does he want now?"

"Don't know, don't care."

"You have any other siblings?"

"I don't have any at all. He and I share no blood. He was my stepmom's son from a previous marriage. Unless he's changed, which I'm sure he hasn't, he probably wants money."

"You want me to have a discussion with him?"

He smiled. "Truthfully, I'd love it. But no thanks. I just want him to go away."

"How old were you when your parents died?"

"Dad died when I was twelve. Had a heart attack. I guess he always had a weak heart, he just didn't know it. One day he got in the car to go to work, started the engine, slumped over and died. It was a half hour before my stepmom noticed the car was still in the drive and was still running."

I didn't say anything.

"When I was fourteen, Mom got breast cancer. Back then, that was a death sentence."

"Tough," I said.

"How about you?"

"Car crash. Killed them both instantly. That was before anyone wore seatbelts. I was in the fifth grade. Mom was a regular church goer. I saw one of the church elders come to the door and they took me to the principal's office. None of them wanted to look at me, let alone talk to me. I pretty much knew it was something bad."

"Life can change in an instant."

His cell rang. He answered, "Yeah." He listened a moment then said, "Hey, slow down." He listened some more. "I'll be right there." He stood up. He looked at me. "There's been a shooting at the club."

3

The parking lot was crammed with police SUV,s and flashing lights. I followed Blackhawk around to the back and parked beside him. We walked back around to the front. Detective Boyce was standing by the front door, writing in her notepad. A guy I didn't know was standing in front of her. She saw us. With the universal hand sign given to every dog everywhere when the master wanted it to stay, she finished writing, then came over to us.

She was looking at Blackhawk. "No one is hurt." She looked at me. It had been a long time since I'd seen her. This was no warm-hearted reunion. "It was a drive-by. As far as I can tell only one bullet hit the building. There was only one shot or fifty. Different folks heard different things. So far it was a white SUV or a gold-colored Laredo. We have a difference of opinion. Could be sending a message or just joy riders." She looked at Blackhawk. "You know of anyone that wants to send you a message?"

Blackhawk shook his head, "Where's Elena?"

"She's inside."

Blackhawk went through the door.

I looked around. There was a group of customers sharing stories excitedly. The police were getting in their vehicles and departing.

"Gang?" I said.

She shrugged. "No idea."

A police cruiser pulled into the parking lot and came to a stop. The back door opened, and Captain Mendoza stepped out. He looked neat, pressed and in shape, as usual. He stood for a long time taking everything in. Without acknowledging he saw us, he walked to us, his eyes roaming the lot.

He nodded at me. He looked at Boyce. "Whatcha got?"

"Not much," she said. "Elena has Rick's American open for lunch for the season. Some of that crowd were coming in when a vehicle ripped through. There were shots fired. Took all of five seconds."

"Any casualties?"

"Either by luck or intentional, but no."

"What kind of vehicle?"

"We're getting the usual clarity. Could have been a white SUV or a gold jeep."

"Jeep?"

"Laredo styled Jeep."

He looked at me. "Besides the fact that you are always here, what are you doing here?"

"Blackhawk was visiting at the boat when he got the call. I followed him."

"Don't go anywhere," he said. He turned and went to another patrolman.

"Don't go anywhere," Boyce said with a smile. She turned

her back and walked away. She would think it was funny if she walked away and didn't come back. I went inside.

The building was immense. It had a center hallway. There were three clubs altogether under one roof. The first one on the right, inside the door, was Rick's American. Elena had transformed it into a swanky, Bogart style nightclub complete with a sexy singer. All the lunch help was sitting at the tables. They looked at me expectantly. I kept moving. Further down the hall, and on the other side, was a smaller club that catered to the boot scooters. It had a bandstand, a mahogany bar and an enormous pair of longhorns above the bar. At the end of the hallway were the double doors to the main salon where Elena performed with her big salsa band. As I got closer to the double doors, I could hear Elena screaming, "I won't calm down!" I almost turned around and walked out. Then I heard Marianne's calmer voice. Marianne was the singer at Rick's. I pushed in.

They were gathered at the bar. No one was sitting. Nacho and Jimmy were behind the bar trying to be invisible. Blackhawk, Elena and Marianne were on my side of the bar. They all turned to look at me. Elena looked distraught.

"How many now?" she said. "How many shootings here?" She pointed at me. "First they were shooting at Jackson and shot my friend Boyce instead. Then they come bursting in here and grab me and everyone is shooting all over the place. And now, this."

"Now baby," Blackhawk said.

"Don't now baby me. Now baby, my ass," Elena said loudly and angrily. "I want to sell this place and move someplace safe." Blackhawk tried to take her in his arms, but she jerked away and stormed up the steps to the upstairs apartment.

"You want me to go up with her?" Marianne said.

Blackhawk was watching Elena. He shook his head. "I just want her to calm down, then you can talk to her." He looked at me. "You think this was random?"

"Don't know. Gotta treat it like it wasn't."

"Me too."

The double door opened, and Boyce came in. No one said anything as she came to the bar. She slid up on a barstool.

"Can I get you anything?" Jimmy said.

"No thanks." She looked around. "You all having a powwow?"

"Not really," I said.

She looked at Marianne. "Who's this little cutie?"

Blackhawk said, "Marianne's our singer in the new club. Marianne, this is Detective Boyce."

"First grade," I said.

Marianne offered her hand and Boyce shook it.

"So Detective, who did the shooting?" I said.

"Perps," she said. She was still looking at Marianne. "You like singing here?"

"Yes, I do."

"Hard to compete with Elena?"

"No competition," Marianne said with a faint smile. "Shakespeare in one room, Neal Simon in the other."

Boyce looked at me. "Intelligent too."

"Very," I said.

Boyce slid off the stool and started toward the door.

"If you find anything, you'll let us know?" Blackhawk said.

She looked back. "If it is your business." She went through the doors.

Marianne looked at me. "She always that hard-ass?"

"Sometimes worse. She's trying to impress you."

"Me?"

"You are the competition," Nacho said.

4

Blackhawk canceled the show for the night. He came up to me. "I want to show you something," he said. I followed him upstairs. We went to his office, which was down the hall from his and Elena's apartment. He fired up the surveillance equipment. He had it cued to a certain spot.

"Watch this," he said. He hit the play button. The footage was in black and white. It showed people coming up to the entrance and going inside. He fiddled with the dials and the view backed out. He pointed with his finger at the corner of the screen. Suddenly an SUV came ripping across the parking lot. A man was leaning out the back window firing a pistol. He wasn't pointing it at the building, he was pointing it behind him. Suddenly another vehicle came into view and went by so fast you couldn't tell if there was anyone shooting. In the blip of time it took I could see the passenger window open but I couldn't see anyone shooting. Blackhawk switched to another camera, one on the street, pointed toward the building. When the cars went by the cameras were on the wrong side, so there was nothing to be seen. There was chaos at the entrance and people were on the ground.

"What the hell was that?" I said.

Blackhawk shrugged. "What do you think?"

I looked at the blank screen for a time. "You give this to Boyce?"

"She was gone. I gave it to the other detective."

"So maybe you weren't a target after all."

"Won't make Elena feel any better."

"Probably not," I said.

I tried to catch Marianne to see if she wanted to go to dinner, but she was gone before I thought of it. I drove back to the marina. The shuttle was operated by a new kid named Teddy. He dropped me at the gate. Pete Dunn was sitting in the shade of his overhang on the bow of the *Thirteen Episodes*, sipping a cocktail and reading. It looked like a screenplay.

"Join me," he said as I walked up. I stepped aboard. "Fix a drink," he said. "You know where everything is."

I went into the main salon and moved to the galley. The air was cool inside. I fixed a quick dry Manhattan and, stirring it with my finger, went back out. I slid a deck chair out and sat. Pete put his finger on the page to hold his place and lifted his drink.

"Cheers."

"Back atcha," I returned. I looked at the screenplay. "Yours?"

He shook his head. "Student I had last year. He asked me to read it and make some observations. "

"Deadly," I said.

"Yeah, tell me about it. I had put it away, intending to get to it and forgot it. I just ran across it." He looked a little sheepish. "It was almost a year ago."

"Any good?"

"Not bad. But no one would buy it."

"Why not?"

He smiled. "Way too intelligent. Which is one way of saying, *boring*. The intelligent crowd at the movies is a very small demographic. No money in it."

"Maybe his next one will be a *Star Wars*."

"Maybe," he said. He was looking at me. "You look tired."

"Yeah," I said. I took a swallow of the drink. "I bought this place to relax. Read, fish, listen to music. I haven't been doing much of that."

"Take a staycation," Pete said. "Turn the phone off. When I first met you, you didn't even have a phone."

I stood, drained the glass and set it aside. "Exercise," I said. "I need to exercise."

"Never hurts."

I stepped out on the dock. "You want to talk, just holler," he said.

I saluted him and went down to the *Tiger Lily*. The boat was stuffy. I opened it up and cranked the air up to clear it out. I thought about another drink but decided against it. I stripped down and pulled on my old, faded yellow swim trunks. I put on the foot and slipped over the side. I was foundering at first, but after a while I got into a rhythm.

After the sixth trip to the buoy, I had found my breath and the blood was flowing. I did ten more then pulled myself out, toweled off and took a shower. By this time the sun was a faint reminder in the western sky. I slipped on a tee shirt, a pair of shorts and my utility foot. I took a bottle of Crown Royal Black up top and watched the sky.

I snapped awake when I dumped my drink in my lap. My phone said it was after one. I changed my trunks and went to bed. I had trouble sleeping but finally dozed off. When I woke my mouth was dry and sandy. I lay for a long time with a forearm across my eyes. It was still dark out.

I got up and drank a glass of water and went to the head. I started back to bed but diverted to the oversized couch instead. I sat with my head in my hands for a long time. Slowly I could make out the lap of the waves against the *Lily*. They became more urgent, then after a while I heard the drops of rain on the roof. It was almost depressing. No, it was depressing. I leaned back and closed my eyes and listened to it. It slowly built then became a torrent. It was a monsoon and soon it was coming in waves. There is something about being in a tin boat with the weather beating on you.

After a long while I got off the couch and started coffee. It was three fifteen. I turned on the radio and found some light jazz. When the coffee was perked, I made a cup and sat sipping it, thinking long deep thoughts about nothing. I listened to Art Pepper noodle his way around his sax and wondered why I had never attempted to learn to play any instrument. I was pretty good with handguns, but it wasn't the same.

The rain receded to a light drizzle and after a very long time I could see the sky beginning to brighten. I woke up stretched out on the couch, the half full coffee cup sitting on the floor. I swung my legs over and picked up the cup and gulped the cold coffee.

The rain was a bare spit. I slid my foot on and went out onto the bow. It was an eerie, dead wet world. I stood breathing the left-over cool night air. I heard a sound and leaned over and looked out on the lake. Eddie's skiff was chugging out into deeper waters. His old shoulders were hunched over, covered by an Army camouflaged cape. I wished I had gone with him.

I went in and grabbed my pole and a bag of frozen anchovies from the locker. I gathered up my tackle box and stepped out on the bow. I stopped. I stood there a long while. Finally, I went back in and put everything away.

5

I thawed a frozen English muffin and toasted it, browned a sausage patty and fried an egg. I put it all on the muffin with melted cheese and ate my sandwich. I cleaned up and went out and stood on the stern. Pete's place was buttoned up. There was very little activity at the marina. I stood there a long time, then went back inside. It had stopped raining and the sun was peeking out.

I packed a small bag, a small cooler and called for Teddy to come get me. I uncovered the Mustang, put the top down, put my Navy hat on and drove south to the 101, then east. I had decided to head to the Mogollon Rim. It had been a long time since I'd been there. I wanted to get out of the city and to smell the high ponderosa pines. The Mustang seemed to know where I wanted to go and soon I was zipping up the Bee Line Highway.

They had made improvements to the highway and now you had two lanes almost all the way up. By the time I pulled into Payson, I was hungry again. I stopped at the Knotty Pine Café and got a hamburger. I made it to go and munched on it as I drove up the rim.

The Mogollon Rim is a piece of God's artwork. You know you are going up but it isn't till near the top you realize you are zipping along the edge of a thousand foot drop off. The vista is spectacular. You wind around, drive through Kohl's Ranch, then through Christopher Creek and a few minutes later pop up on the top of the rim. A little bit further and the sign points to Woods Canyon Lake. This one is usually crowded since it's the first one, but I was counting on it being a weekday and being a little calmer.

It's a longer drive back to the lake than I remembered, but finally I pulled into the parking lot. There was a faux log building that trafficked in fishing gear, bait, beer, pre-made sandwiches, rental boats, gasoline and about anything someone would forget to bring with them.

I parked, put the top up and walked down to the shoreline. I stood and watched the lake for a long time. There was a slight breeze and the aluminum row boats gently banged each other. I took several deep breaths. The smell of wet pine was heavy. I went into the bait shop.

Behind the counter at the back was a young girl chewing gum and reading a Stephanie Meyer novel. I had read one but found it a little young for me. No one else was in the building. The girl set her book aside and looked at me expectantly. I spent a couple of minutes looking at the lures and bottles of the red eggs that are used to catch the trout. Finally, I picked up a Payday candy bar and set it on her counter.

"That be all?"

"Yes, ma'am," I said. "Is there a walking trail around the lake?"

"All the way around." She took my money and made change.

"Any idea how big the lake is?"

She looked at the wall. There was an overhead photo of the lake. "No, I don't," she said. "But people walk around it all the time."

I picked up my change and the candy bar. "Thanks," I said.

I went back to the Mustang and popped the trunk. I swapped my prosthetic for a running foot. I had a special one that wasn't the big running blade you see on TV. It was smaller, but manageable. I went down to the trail. I could have gone either way. I chose to the right and began to run.

In ten minutes, I reached the bend of the lake where the trail moved left, following the shoreline. Ahead of me, about a hundred yards, was a large flat boulder that had tumbled down the hill and landed on the shoreline. A man was sitting in a camp chair, fishing. He had a cooler beside him. As I drew closer, he got a strike and began working the fish through the water. He stood up and worked the fish up to the boulder. With a sudden movement he swung the fish up and onto the shoreline. I drew up and watched him. He deftly unhooked the fish and reaching into the water, pulled a stringer. He fastened the fish onto the stringer to join the half dozen others he had.

"Nice fish," I said.

He glanced at me. "Thanks."

"Is that a rainbow?"

"Cutthroat," he said. He dropped the stringer into the water and leaning down, picked up his beer can and drained it. He opened the cooler and dropped the empty can in. He fumbled inside and pulled out another beer. He offered it to me.

"Thanks," I said, taking it. I popped it open.

He opened one for himself and sat on the camp chair.

"Sorry, I only have one chair."

"No need to apologize," I said. I sat on the boulder, dangling my legs over the side. "You fish here a lot?"

He rubbed the gray stubble on his face. "Try to get up here when I can." He took a long pull on the beer. "Live in Mesa in one of those mobile home parks. Lot of old people. Got to get away from that once in a while."

I looked up and down the shoreline. "What makes this spot a better place to catch fish than say, down the way a little?"

He was baiting his hook with the little red faux salmon eggs the trout like to eat. He cast it out and snugged the line a little. He had an old-fashioned bobber. Round, red on top, white on bottom.

He looked at me, then said simply, "This is where the cooler is."

I had to laugh. He was watching his bobber, but every once in a while he glanced at my foot.

"What's your name, young fella?"

"Jackson," I said.

"I'm Larry," he said. He put his hand out and I shook it.

"Pleased to meet you."

"How'd you lose your foot?"

I normally have a story ready. Usually I say an industrial accident but there was something about this guy I really liked.

"I lost it to an IED."

He shook his head. "Marines?"

"Navy."

"Seal?"

21

I nodded. "How about you? You serve?"

He laughed. "Army. Company clerk at Fort Lewis."

"At least you have both your feet."

I emptied the beer and put the can in the cooler. "Thanks for the beer."

"Sure."

He looked back at his bobber. "Dammit," he exclaimed, yanking on the pole. He reeled it in. Empty.

"Good luck," I said. He waved and started baiting the hook again. I started jogging.

6

It was a couple of hundred yards before I really got my rhythm. The trail was dirt and rock, and uneven, worn smooth by thousands of hikers. There were only a couple of them on the trail and they gave way as I passed.

It was several minutes before I reached the end of the lake and wound about onto the back side. There was a string of fir trees that blocked the view of the lake for a short time, then it opened up again. I looked across the lake and stopped.

On the far side, Larry was standing with three guys. One of them had taken his fishing rod. When he reached for it, one of the others shoved him hard and he went backwards and sat heavily in the dirt beside the boulder. I began to run back toward them.

This time I wasn't just jogging. I ran flat out. I slowed to a walk fifty yards out to catch my breath. One of them was going through Larry's wallet. The other two had dumped his tackle box and were going through the contents. They didn't see me until I was right up on them. They looked up in surprise. They were young. Just punks causing trouble. They were drinking Larry's beer.

Larry looked up at me. He had a mouse forming under his eye.

"Well," I said. "If it isn't Huey, Dewey and Louie. Does Uncle Donald know what you are doing?"

The guy with Larry's wallet said, "Beat it, punk."

I stepped toward him and in the same motion hit him in the nose with the heel of my hand. Blood exploded down his chin, and he stumbled back. I followed and hit him again. He went down and rolled to his side. Without hesitation I kicked the nearest guy in the chest with my good foot, and he went off the boulder into the water. The third guy had a hunting knife in his belt, and he pulled it.

I stepped back and he took that as a sign I was frightened, so he moved forward. He was holding the knife up, pointing it at my face. I couldn't have gotten luckier. The hardest place to disarm a man with a knife is if he holds the knife down low.

In training, I had probably done a thousand reps of this move. I brought my hands up, as if to ward him off. He moved the knife in, and I hit his hand simultaneously with both of my hands and the knife flew out of his hand. It splashed into the lake.

The way it works is the right hand slaps the inside of the man's wrist at the exact same time as the left hand slaps the back of the hand holding the knife. It has to be quick and hard like the strike of a black mamba. The hand hitting the wrist keeps it from moving, while the hand hitting the knife hand smacks it real hard, which forces the fingers open and the knife goes flying.

It truly was fun to watch the look on the knife man's face. This guy stumbled back, then began running. The guy in the water began wading toward the shore. I stepped over and stood where he couldn't get out.

"Throw your wallet up on the shore," I said. He stood looking at me. Reluctantly he pulled his wallet out and threw it up on the shore. I stepped aside and let him climb out. He started after the other guy. I went over to the guy with the bloody nose. He was struggling to his feet. I pulled his wallet out and dragged him to his feet. I kicked him in the butt to get him going. He went stumbling after the wet guy.

I leaned down and picked up Larry's wallet and handed it to him. He took it with one hand while he dusted his seat with the other. He looked in it and put it in his back pocket. He looked after the disappearing punks, then looked at me.

"Thanks a lot. I could live with losing the money but getting a new driver's license and credit cards would have been a pain in the ass." He cocked his head at me. "What was that? Kung fu or something?"

"Not that fancy."

"Well, I appreciate it."

7

I was sitting in Blackhawk's office, my feet up on his desk and reading a *True West* magazine. I was studying an old photo of Alchesay, one of General Crook's chief scouts. He was considered one of the most handsome of the Apaches. I compared him to Blackhawk, looking for signs of Native American blood in Blackhawk. I wasn't seeing it. He looked more like a Roman statue. Except they always had curly hair and he didn't.

Blackhawk was ignoring me, as he was running numbers on the food costs for Rick's American. He was shaking his head.

"Problem?"

"I don't think I'm charging enough for the short ribs."

He glanced at the bank of monitors that occupied one side of his gigantic desk. He stiffened and leaned forward.

"Son of a bitch," he said under his breath. He pushed away from his desk and stood, then went out the door. I put my feet down and stood. I went around his desk and looked at the monitors. Sitting at the bar was the guy that claimed to be Blackhawk's brother. Behind him, seated at a table were two gunnies, the bulge of their pistols prominent on their hips.

Another monitor showed Blackhawk walking to the bar. I stood and pulled the Ruger from my back pocket. I jacked a shell in. I went out the door, through his outer room and down the hall. I moved quietly across the landing and halfway down the stairs till I could command the room. I sat on the steps and watched, the Ruger dangling from my hand. The Ruger had an infrared attachment and if I wanted to intimidate someone, I just had to push the button and center the red dot in the middle of their chest.

"I told you not to come back here, Delbert," Blackhawk said.

"I'm not Delbert anymore," the man said. "I converted. I'm Azeed Muhammed now."

"Whatever you call yourself, I want you to leave and not come back."

"Not very brotherly. I'm here to ask for help."

Blackhawk studied him. "I've got nothing for you."

"Mom would be very disappointed."

"The woman's been dead a long time and she's not my mother."

"Look, I think you and me could make a good team."

"I want you to leave," Blackhawk said. Nacho had been polishing the same glass ever since the three men had come in. Now he set it down and moved down by Blackhawk.

"Can't I even get a drink in here?"

Blackhawk waved his hand at Nacho. "Get him a drink."

"What'll you have?" Nacho said. He was about as friendly as Blackhawk.

"Bourbon."

"I thought Muslims don't drink," Blackhawk said.

"I'm not stupid about it," Azeed said. "I heard you are a stone-cold killer now."

Blackhawk didn't answer. Nacho poured two inches in a rock glass and sat it in front of the man. "Who said that?" he said.

"Guy I met on the inside."

"Who was that?" Nacho said.

"Said he worked with a guy named Emilio Garza who said he knew you very well."

He picked up the glass and saluted Blackhawk. He drained it and set the glass down. He looked up at Blackhawk. "I've got a big operation going and I need someone I can trust to watch my back."

"What makes you think you can trust me?"

"You were raised by Mom. If you give your word, you'll keep it."

"You aren't worthy to say the word 'Mom'."

"I'll pay you fifty thousand a week until the job's done."

Blackhawk shook his head. "Not for ten times that."

"You think about it." The man slid off his stool. With nothing more, Azeed went out the door followed by his two gunnies.

Blackhawk hesitated for a few seconds then turned and looked up at me. "Follow him," he said.

I went down the steps and pointed at Nacho. "We'll take your car," I said. His Jeep was not as conspicuous as my ruby red Mustang.

"It's out back," he said, vaulting the bar and following me.

He was parked in his usual spot and we jumped in and roared around the building. We were just in time to watch a pewter colored

Tahoe leave the lot and head east. Nacho expertly dropped in behind and followed. He put four vehicles between us.

"Is this really Blackhawk's brother?" he said, his eyes on the road.

I glanced at him. "Says he is. Blackhawk says there's no blood. Blackhawk's father married this guy's mother. She already had him when they married."

"What does that make them?"

"Damned if I know. Blackhawk says it doesn't make them anything."

The Tahoe swung down and got on the I-10, then got off on the 51. We followed at a respectable distance until they came off the 51 onto the eastbound 101. They exited at Pima Road. They drove north to Thompson Peak, then went west. They went far enough to start climbing the McDowell's.

We followed around for a while and it became more difficult to be unnoticed. The higher we climbed, the more expensive the homes became.

"Guy's got money," Nacho said.

Up ahead the Tahoe's turn signal started blinking.

"Go on past," I said.

As we did, I craned to look past Nacho. The Tahoe was pulled up to a gate that was slowly opening.

"Go up here and turn around." He did. "Pull over."

He looked at me and pulled to the curb. "Stay here a minute," I said. "Then we'll drive by and get his address."

I finally said, "Okay." He drove by the gate which had forty yards of driveway behind it. I noted the address.

8

I pulled into the marina parking and covered the Mustang. I turned and stood at the top of the hill and looked at the marina. The sun was sparkling on the water and there were boats running out on the main lake. Below was Old Eddie's River Runner and Pete Dunn's *Thirteen Episodes*. There was a new yacht moored at the end of B dock. There were two girls in bikinis lying on the bow.

There was a cool breeze from the southwest and it reminded me of the first time I'd been here. I had met the realtor lady at the parking lot, and on our way down, I had the shuttle driver stop so I could look at the view. There was a cool breeze from the southwest on that day. I knew the realtor lady was watching me from the corner of her eye. The driver dropped us at the gate, which happened to be open. Some of the slips were filled with simple fishing boats. Large price to pay just to drive down and get in and go fishing. Some of the other boats were larger. A couple of them were two stories. Back then, *13 Episodes* was named the *Moneypenny* and owned by a guy, I found out later, was a heavy weight in a drug cartel. But, my life was much simpler back then.

The realtor lady, whose name was Natalie, waved me aboard the *Tiger Lily*. I wasn't very impressed. Compared to some of the others it was small. About 65 foot. The first thing I noticed was that it held steady when I stepped aboard. A nice solid center. The paint was beginning to peel. Natalie unlocked the bow door. I stepped into a musty smell.

"It's been empty for quite a while," Natalie said. Her voice bright and cheery like all salespeople.

The first thing I noticed was an oversized yellow couch. I reached down and slapped it and a small plume of dust rose. "I'm afraid it'll need a good cleaning," Natalie said. "I have people that I've used in the past." I took that to mean it would be on my dime.

I went into the galley and turned on the water faucet. Nothing happened.

"The water and electricity have been turned off," Natalie said. "The last occupant got behind on his rent. Then one day he just just disappeared. Maureen shut it all down."

"Maureen?"

"The marina manager."

"Everything works?"

"If it doesn't, we'll have it fixed."

I walked through the rest of it. I stepped out on the stern. The fresh breeze off the lake was wonderful.

"How much," I said.

She told me. The reason I was even here was that the houses she showed me were way outside my budget. At least, the ones I wanted. She had been kind enough not to laugh. She also told me I had to get a cashier's check. She drove me to the closest bank. I gave the bank cash; they gave me the cashier's check. We signed everything then and there. She dropped me at the top and handed me the keys. I stopped at the marina office, met Maureen and rented a parking spot for the Mustang. The shuttle driver dropped me at my car, then followed me to the parking spot. I pulled my duffle from the trunk and he dropped me at the bottom. By the time the sun was behind the western mountains I had moved in, and the *Tiger Lily* was home.

Wrapped in a towel in the duffel was a bottle of Johnnie Walker Black. With no ice, I poured it neat into a jar that was the only thing in the cabinets. See? I'm sophisticated enough to not drink out of the bottle. I wiped the jar out with my shirt tail. Maureen had told me I would have electricity and water the next morning.

I took my drink out on the stern, unstacked one of the deck chairs and sat and watched the light fade. I sipped the scotch wondering what the hell I would do now. When it got too dark to see anything on the lake except the occasional boat light, I went in and slept on the bare mattress.

The next morning, I pulled everything from the duffle and laid it out on the bed. I put on my trunks. My swim foot was up in the trunk of the Mustang. I went without it. I dove in and took my first swim out to the buoy. The water was chilly and refreshing. I treaded water out there and for the first time in a long time felt like I belonged somewhere.

By the time I climbed back aboard, I had water and electricity. Maureen was good for her word. Good to know. I showered and shaved with cold water. Using my utility foot, I walked to the marina. It was deserted. As I reached the gate, I heard noise around the corner. I stepped over and saw an older guy on a tall ladder replacing light bulbs in the pole lights on the first dock. It was the only dock that was covered. I had asked Natalie what a slip over there cost, compared to mine. She said an additional $500. Too steep for me.

I made my way over to the worker and stood watching him. When he finally noticed me, he said, "Good morning."

"Morning," I returned. "Can you tell me when the restaurant opens?"

"Cook don't get here till nine. Opens at ten. Does mostly a lunch trade. You lookin' for breakfast?"

"That was the plan. Do you know of a restaurant close by?"

"There's one at Noterra, but that ain't close. I haven't eaten yet myself, you want to wait till I'm done with this, I'll be happy to whip up some eggs and such."

"You can do that?"

"I got the keys. I do all the odd jobs here, so Maureen lets me eat free."

"I'll be happy to pay."

"I'll be happy to take the money. For Maureen, that is. Hold on while I finish this."

Five minutes later, we were inside. He waved at the bar. Have a seat there." He put his hand out. "I'm Eddie," he said.

"Jackson," I said taking the hand. It was a firm hand that had done a ton of work and seen a lot of life. I sat at the bar. On the other side was a wide-open window that revealed the kitchen. Eddie went in and fired the grill and pulled eggs and sausage patties from the big locker.

When he finished we sat at the bar and ate. He had even brewed a pot of coffee.

"So you work here?" I said.

"I do the odd jobs. Maureen lets me slip my boat, use the restroom and the showers and eat two meals a day for doing the odd jobs she needs done. I buy my own beer."

"Sounds like a deal."

"You the new guy on *Tiger Lily*?"

"That's me."

"You like to fish?"

"I do."

"I'm going out in a bit. You can join me if you like."

"Love to. I just got here. I don't have a pole and tackle."

"You got any cash money?"

"A little," I said.

"There are poles and tackle in the gift shop. Get what you need. Get number 6 hooks and some clip-on weights. We'll be fishing for stripers and crappie using anchovies. Keep the price tags and pay later when the clerk comes in."

"Done," I said. I stood. I gathered the utensils and the plate. "What should I do with these?"

"Don't worry about it. I'll take care of it. Just go get your tackle so we can get on the water."

9

Now it was mid-May and the weather was balmy and beautiful. We were still a month or more away from the dreaded Phoenix heat. The winter and spring had been delightful. Blackhawk had not heard from or seen the guy calling himself Azeed. He was hoping the guy was out of his life. I had seen no indication that would be happening.

I was rolling a protective coating of elastomeric on the roof of the upper deck. I had done it when I first bought the boat, but it was time again. It is one of those miracle inventions that can be applied like paint, then turns rubberized as it dries. The trick is to not push it over the edge where it will run down the wall. You never see until it's too late. I only did it once.

I don't know what I was daydreaming about, but I was off in la-la land when I heard the dock gate bang shut. I lifted my head and looked down the long dock. Two men were coming. The one leading looked familiar. He was round. His head was round, his cheeks were round. He had on shorts and flip flops and from what I could tell his toes were round. The other guy was small and skinny. He wore work pants and a long sleeve shirt.

I stood watching and the round guy waved at me.

"Father Correa," I said out loud.

I stood, looking down at them, a smile on my face. Father Correa stopped and looked up, shielding his eyes. "Jackson," he said with a laugh. "Permission to come aboard."

"Come on," I said. "The front is unlocked. I'll be right down."

I pulled my gloves off and hurried down the steps. It made me smile to see Father Correa again. He ran a haven for displaced women, either pregnant or with little ones. Usually victims of domestic abuse. Women that would end up on the streets if it weren't for the good father. The other man was small, maybe five foot six and one hundred twenty pounds. He was dark and swarthy. He looked nervous.

I came in from the stern.

I remembered that every time I was at his place, he had a pot of coffee on. "Can I get you some coffee?" I said.

"Love some."

I moved into the galley and started rinsing the carafe. "Have a seat. Make yourself comfortable."

Once the coffee maker began to perk, I set out cups, sugar and creamer. I moved around and sat on one of the bar stools.

"How've you been?" I asked.

"Unfortunately, very busy," he said. "How about you?"

"Not so much." He meant unfortunately because he spent his time with the troubled girls.

He indicated the man next to him. "This is Sonny Tortelli. Sonny, this is Jackson. The man I was telling you about."

Sonny stood up. "It is a great pleasure," he said. "Father Correa sings your praises." He put his hand out and I stepped off the stool and took it. I looked at Father Correa and as usual he was beaming. He would beam in a tornado.

"What kind of trouble are you getting me into today?" I said.

"Oh, Jackson. You are so suspicious." He paused looking at the floor. Then he looked back to me, "However, I did bring Sonny here for a reason. Sonny owns and operates a dry-cleaning business that is just a block away from Safehouse. I'll let him tell his story."

The coffee pot beeped. I stood and moved to the galley and poured the coffee. "Help yourself to the cream and sugar."

"Black is fine," Father Correa said.

"Same for me," Sonny Tortelli said.

I handed out the coffee, then returned to my perch on the bar stool.

"Tell him what you told me when we talked this morning."

Sonny's hand was shaking slightly as he sipped his coffee. It took him a moment to get going. "I have a daughter. Annabelle. She has always been my joy. She is a beautiful, smart woman. The first in our family to go to college. She was going to be a teacher."

I noticed the *was*.

He set the coffee aside and pulled a photo from his shirt pocket. He handed it to me. The girl had her father's dark hair and eyes. She had the bright smile that goes with a posed picture. She was beautiful. He continued as I studied the picture.

"She has been out of school for two years now and she had her own place. As far as I knew, everything was good. Normal. No problems. Then she called me and wanted to come home for what she said was just a short time. She said her landlady was selling the house and she had to get out. Of course, I said yes."

"She came home and moved into her old room, but she was different. She didn't spend any time there. No time with us together. She would still be asleep when I left for the store and she would be gone when I got home. She would stay out until well after I had gone to bed. I tried to give her space, after all she was a grown up now. But how could she keep a job doing that. So finally, I tried to talk to her." His eyes filled with tears. "She wouldn't talk." He looked at Father Correa. "I finally lost my temper and I yelled at her. She was wasting her life. She didn't even respond. Finally when I wound down she said, "Are you done? That's all she said." His face was one of anguish.

"Sometime in the middle of the night, she packed up and left." He stopped, staring at the floor. I glanced at Father Correa. I frowned at him.

"She's a mature woman," I said to the little man. "Are you worried for her safety?"

He nodded.

"Did you call the police?"

"They said she was an adult and if I didn't have evidence that she was in jeopardy, there was nothing they could do. They said she probably just decided to leave." He sadly shook his head.

"I don't know what you are asking me to do," I said to Father Correa.

Father Correa put his hand on Sonny's shoulder. "Show him what you found."

Sonny stood and dug into his pants pocket. He came up with a very small manilla envelope with a metal clasp. He opened it and poured the contents into his other hand. He reached over and I put my hand out. He placed a very large diamond in my hand. I'm no expert but it sure looked real. It was huge and sparkled in the light.

"Hey, Jackson," a voice boomed from the dock. It was Pete Dunn, my neighbor. I stepped to the door.

"Come on in," I said, closing my hand around the diamond.

He came in, looking around in surprise. "Hey, sorry. I didn't know you had company."

"It's alright," I said. I introduced him to Father Correa and to Mr. Torelli. I handed him the diamond. He whistled.

"Know anything about diamonds?" I said.

"Only you shouldn't give them to someone soon to be an ex-wife." He looked at me. "Is this real?"

"I don't know." I looked at Torelli. "Have you had this appraised?"

He shook his head.

"So, we're not sure it's genuine. Where did you get it?"

"When Annabelle moved out, I searched her room to see if I could find anything that would tell me where she went. It was on the floor under the bed. She must have dropped it."

Pete handed the diamond back to me. I handed it to Sonny Torelli.

Pete said, "I have an old college buddy that owns a jewelry store at Camelback and 32nd Street. He appraises jewelry for estate sales all the time."

I looked at Sonny Torelli. "You okay with that?"

"Yes," he said.

"Good idea," Father Correa said.

10

The jewelry store was on the west side of 32nd street, down the hill and south of the mountain preserve. It was next to an upscale restaurant named Hoolies. The jewelry store had a gilded sign that read "Leonidas Fine Jewelry." Pete had driven and as we parked, I asked if his friend was from Greece.

"His name is Silverstein, he's from Jersey," he answered.

The store was like so many other jewelry shops. Glass display cases covering three sides of the room, with room for salespeople to stand behind. We followed Pete's lead and he moved to the end display case. An attractive woman came over.

"Can I help you gentlemen?" she said.

"Would you tell Fred that Pete Dunn is here to see him."

"Certainly, sir," she said brightly. She turned and went through a curtained door that led to the back. A moment later she returned. "He will be right out."

Sonny Torelli stood nervously watching the back doorway. Pete was looking a display of watches. I moved over by Father Correa.

He was looking at a display of diamond bracelets and rings.

He looked up at me as I came up. "What do you think?" I said.

"I think these could buy a ton of food for the kids that don't have any."

Hard to argue with that.

A short balding man came from the back. "Pete!" he exclaimed.

Pete was smiling as they shook hands.

"You finally come to buy some lucky girl an engagement ring?"

"Hardly," Pete said. "We need your expert opinion."

"You need to settle down with a good woman. That's my opinion."

"About diamonds," Pete laughed.

"Whatcha got?"

Pete turned to look at Sonny. Sonny handed him the small envelope.

Pete handed it to Fred. Fred opened the clasp and rolled the diamond out onto his palm. He looked at Pete quizzically.

"We'd like to know if it's real, and if it is, what is its value?"

"Give me a second," Fred said. He turned and went to the back.

We went back to studying the finery in the glass cases. It was ten minutes before Fred came back out. The diamond was back in the envelope and the clasp was open. In his other hand was a sheet of paper.

Fred looked at Pete. "Where did you get this?" Pete turned to look at me.

"With your permission," I said to Sonny. He nodded. I told Fred the story of Sonny's daughter and how he found the diamond. Fred listened attentively, looking from Sonny to me.

He rolled the diamond out on a velvet mat where it gleamed in the light.

"Well, the first thing I have to tell you, is this is very real."

"And its worth?" Pete said.

"Based on size, clarity and skill at cutting it, at auction I would put it at fifteen thousand dollars."

Sonny sucked his breath in. I think the rest of us did too.

"A buyer would probably offer ten."

"What would you pay for it?"

Fred smiled. "I'm afraid this is above my pay grade. But before you try to sell it, you need to see this."

He laid the sheet of paper on the counter and turned it for us to read.

He tapped it with his finger. "This is an alert the authorities circulate to jewelry dealers. This is about a jewelry robbery that took place two months ago in New York. It was all over the papers and newscasts. It was an exceptionally well-planned theft and the thieves got away scot free."

He tapped the paper again. "They estimate the loss at three hundred million dollars."

"Wow," Pete said.

"Yeah, but it was probably half to two thirds of that. It's typical to inflate these figures for the insurance companies."

"So, you think this is a hot diamond?" I said.

He looked at Sonny. "Can't prove it. I can tell you this. You go to sell this without provenance, you will be lucky to get pennies on the dollar."

"It's not mine to sell," Sonny said. "It belongs to Annabelle."

11

I was sitting outside of Captain Mendoza's office, biding my time, waiting to be summoned. He was letting me wait. I wanted to find out more about the jewel heist. Jimmy had googled everything the internet had to offer, which wasn't much, except for conflicting estimates of how much the thieves had gotten away with. If the police had clues, they weren't telling.

Boyce came out of Mendoza's office. She glanced at me but kept walking. I don't know what I did, but whatever it was, it must have pissed her off.

A few minutes later Mendoza came to the door and beckoned me in. He was as put together as always. Crisp shirt, nice tie, creased suit pants. Shoes gleaming. His hair was cut short. He had started as a patrolman and had worked his way up.

He waved at the chairs that faced his desk. I sat and he stepped around the desk and sat.

"You could have talked to Detective Boyce. We haven't identified the shooters. Based on the tapes Blackhawk provided, it appears they were shooting at each other. I could have told you this on the phone."

"Yes, I know that. This is about something different." I pulled my phone out and dialed up a photo I had taken of the diamond on the black velvet at Silverstein's shop. I handed it to him.

"Father Correa brought a neighbor of his out to the boat. His grown daughter had suddenly come home to stay a short time. They argued and she left in the middle of the night. He searched her room trying to get a clue as to where she went. He found that under the bed."

He took the phone from my hand and studied the photo.

"My neighbor at the marina, Pete Dunn, has a jeweler friend. He appraised that at fifteen thousand dollars. He had a flyer about the jewelry theft in New York. I'd like to know more about that."

"You need to talk to major crimes."

"Can you arrange that?"

Mendoza handed me back the phone. "You want me to make your lunch too?"

"The father's name is Sonny Tortelli. He's worried sick about his daughter. I'd like to find out if she's mixed up with the robbery."

He looked at me for a moment. He picked up the phone and punched some numbers. A moment later he said, "Hey Tom, it's Mendoza. I'm going to send a guy named Jackson over to you. He has information about the New York jewel heist." He listened for a moment. "I've worked with the guy before, he's a pain in the ass but he has valuable skills, and he does what he says he'll do." He listened again. "Thanks," he said. He looked at me. "Captain Newsome, second floor, west side."

I thanked him and went to the elevators.

Captain Newsome was behind his desk on the phone. He was a burly guy with a completely bald head and huge shoulders. He had a roll of fat on the back of his neck and a paunch. He appeared to be in his late fifties. He had the appearance of an aging bodybuilder. He was a little more rumpled than Mendoza, shirt with the top button undone, the tie pulled loose. I started into his office and he stopped me with a gesture and signaled for me to wait outside. There were no chairs, so I went back out and leaned against the wall.

After what seemed a long time, but was really, probably, less than five minutes, he hung up. He came to the door.

"Mr. Jackson?"

"Just Jackson," I said.

"Come on in," he said.

I followed him in, and he waved at a chair. His office was identical to Mendoza's but more cluttered. His eyes were flat and brown. Cop's eyes.

"What'cha got for me?"

I pulled my phone and dialed up the picture. I handed it to him. He studied it, then looked at me. "Get this off the internet?"

I told him about Sonny Tortelli. He never took his eyes off me.

"So you believe this guy?"

I told him about Father Correa. "I believe Father Correa believes this guy and I believe Father Correa."

He nodded slightly. "I know of Correa." He leaned over and shook the mouse on his laptop. His hands were big and meaty, but the fingers flew across the keyboard. He settled on something and leaned forward to read.

He looked up at me. "Four months ago, the Manhattan Depository and Safe was burglarized in an, their words, audacious robbery and the robbers got clean away even though an alarm was tripped. It says there were three men dressed as workers, yellow hard hats etc. The deposit boxes are secured in the basement. They disabled an elevator on the third floor, slid down the cables to the basement floor and using a powerful drill, busted through to the vault."

"How'd they get the tools in?"

"In garbage cans and heavy plastic bags. They busted into the boxes and made off with three hundred million in diamonds and jewelry. That included the diamonds that were scheduled for an annual show."

"What about the alarm?"

"The *Times* reported that the alarm was ignored even with a patrol car driving by. The building was considered burglary proof." He leaned back. "No way to prove your diamond was a part of it."

He watched me while I was thinking. "What's your part in this, Mr. Jackson?"

"Just Jackson," I said automatically. "Father Correa asked me to look into it for Mr. Tortelli."

"You a private dick?"

"No, just a friend. I've helped the good Father in the past."

"Mr. Tortelli file a missing persons?"

I shook my head. "She's an adult. He has no proof she's in danger. Could be with a boyfriend. This sounds like an inside job. How many people would know where and when all those diamonds would be there?"

He studied me coolly. After a long moment he picked up the phone and dialed. I could hear it answered on the other side. "How much can I trust this Jackson guy?" He listened to the answer. "Okay. Thanks." He hung up. He looked at me. He said, "Okay Jackson, Mendoza thinks you are okay so I'm going to trust you." He punched some keys. Satisfied, he turned the monitor around. There was a headshot photo on it. A man in his mid-forties with dishwater blond hair and small eyes. Other than that, his face was very normal.

"Wendell O'Malley," he said. "Worked at the Depository. Hasn't been seen since the robbery. The authorities there haven't disclosed this. I'm trusting you to keep your mouth shut."

"Yes sir," I said. "Can I have a copy of that."

"Hell no. I won't do that."

"I appreciate your time, sir," I said. I pulled my phone. "I have to call for my ride. Do you ever use Uber?" I held the phone so he couldn't see the face. I pulled up the camera. "What's the address here?"

He told me. I pretended to put information into the phone while I took a picture of his computer screen. I put the phone away.

"I appreciate all your help. If I stumble across anything, you'll be the first to know." I stood and left.

12

"I love that woman," Marianne said. "But I wouldn't want to cross her."

I laughed. We were in Blackhawk's and Elena's apartment. Marianne and Elena had just returned from a shopping excursion at Scottsdale Fashion Square. There were sacks and packages on the couch next to Marianne. Elena had taken hers to her bedroom.

"What did she do now?"

"Nothing she did. But when she walks into a department store, even one that caters to high end Scottsdale women, she walks like a queen. And they treat her like one."

"You've seen how the crowds downstairs react to her."

"Yeah, I wish I had half that."

I looked at her for a long moment. "You are a beautiful and talented woman yourself. You always play to a full room."

I think she blushed. She wouldn't look at me. "Thanks," she said softly.

I kept looking at her. Her gently streaked blond hair fell to her shoulders. Her eyelashes were long and natural.

"Would you like to go to dinner with me?"

She still didn't look at me. Finally she stuttered, "I don't know."

"I'd like to get to know you better, and you don't know me."

Now she looked at me. Her eyes were flecked with gold. "I've heard about you," she said.

"What have you heard?"

She looked across the room and hesitated. "I've heard you are a dangerous man."

I thought about that. I wondered what she had heard and who she had heard it from. Probably Elena.

"Unless someone is trying to hurt one of mine, I'm a pussycat."

Now she looked at me. "I've been told you are very protective."

The door opened and Blackhawk stuck his head in. "Hey," he said to me. "If I could interrupt you lovebirds, could I see you in the office?"

I stood and moved to the door. I looked back at Marianne. "How about that dinner?"

She looked at me with a cocked eyebrow, "Lovebirds?"

As I entered his office I said, "You sure as hell aren't helping me out."

Blackhawk waved me to the couch that faced his desk. "Drink?" he said.

I shook my head. "I think you pissed her off."

"She'll get over it. Besides, I think she likes you."

"She thinks I'm dangerous."

"You are. She gets by that, you are home free."

"This isn't seventh grade. Whatcha got?" I said to change the subject.

"I was looking at the property you followed Delbert to. It's owned by a corporation out of Las Vegas which is owned by another corporation out of Bahrain which is a dead end. I found that Delbert is on early release and doesn't even have parole."

"What's he up to, that he needs your help?"

"He doesn't need my help. He's just being an asshole."

"There must be something in it for him."

Blackhawk shrugged. "Nacho brought this in this morning." He picked up a copy of the *New Times*. He thumbed through it until he found the page he wanted. He folded the paper back and handed it to me. There was a half-page article accompanied by a picture. The article was about a drug bust.

"What am I looking at?"

"Read it," he said.

I read it. It was about the latest DOD. Drug of the day. It was something called actiq, a lollipop-shaped opioid 100 times more powerful than morphine. The article stated that the celebrity previously known as Prince and Tom Petty both had actiq in their systems when they died. I studied the photo. A man in handcuffs was being loaded into the back seat of a police cruiser. I looked up at Blackhawk. "What am I not seeing?"

"Nacho says this guy in handcuffs was one of the two that came in with Delbert the last time Delbert was here. He said he noticed the guy when he was in here because he looked like someone he had seen in prison."

"So you're thinking your brother is hooked up with the actiq people."

"He's not my brother, and yes, it would be just like him."

"How certain is Nacho?"

"He says he's certain but he's not. Not absolutely."

"Let's call Boyce and see what we can find on this guy."

"You call her," he said.

"No, if we want the information, you'll have to call her. I think she's upset with me."

"About what?"

"Damned if I know, but I'm sure I did something dire and nasty."

"Sounds like you. I'll have Elena call her."

"You object to me asking Marianne out?"

"Out where?"

"Out to dinner or something."

He shrugged. "I'm not her Daddy. You are both grownups." He laughed. "Or at least she is."

13

It took some doing, but Blackhawk finally got Elena to call Boyce. He told her to say the guy came in with a guy that was threatening Blackhawk and reference the *New Times* story.

"His name is Warren Ginakes," Elena said as she hung up. "They got him in an undercover sting. Three-time loser, so he's going away. She wanted to know who was threatening Blackhawk. I told her it was a guy who says he's your brother." She looked at Blackhawk, "But I told her he wasn't, and you threw him out."

Blackhawk looked down the bar at Jimmy. "Hey Jimmy, find out what you can on your magic phone about an ex-con named Warren Ginakes."

"Spell it," Jimmy said.

Blackhawk did.

Nacho put a beer in front of me and to be polite I had to drink it.

When we had come out of Blackhawk's office, Marianne was gone and she wasn't in the bar. Elena said she had gone home and no, she wouldn't give me her phone number. If she wanted me to have it, she'd give it to me herself.

I felt foolish, like I was in the seventh grade passing notes in study hall. I sipped my beer while Jimmy worked his phone. Elena went back upstairs. Nacho was sitting on his favorite stool reading. When he turned a page, I got a glimpse of the cover. *The Fountainhead* by Ayn Rand. It was a graphic novel. Better than nothing. I was impressed, his lips never moved.

My beer was half gone when Jimmy came down to our end of the bar.

Without preamble he began speaking. "Warren Thomas Ginakes. Thirty years old, born in Glendale, never graduated from high school. Spent three years of a five-year sentence in Perryville for drug-related felonies. Released early for good behavior. Went to Florence to complete his sentence for parole violations. Multiple. Became involved with the Ace Double Deuces while there. Thought to be one of their more formidable foot soldiers." He looked up. "I read the *New Times* article. The speculation is that he'll go away for a long time because of being a three-time loser. He was caught red-handed in an undercover sting."

"Does it mention any known associates? Anyone named Delbert or Azeed?"

Jimmy shook his head, "Nope."

I watched Blackhawk while he thought. Finally, I said, "You see this guy as a threat?"

He looked at me. "We were taught to assess everything, even if it only looked like a potential threat."

"What *haven't* you guys been taught?" Jimmy said.

I smiled. "What do we do now?"

Blackhawk thought about that. Finally, he said, "I want to know what Delbert's game is."

"You have an idea?"

He looked at me and smiled. "Thought maybe you'd find out. I'll pay for you to rent a little boring car so you're not as noticeable as your red hot-rod."

"Well, luckily, I wasn't doing anything at the moment."

Nacho looked up, "Just trying to get into Marianne's pants."

I shook my head. "Well, aren't you the suave gentleman."

I slid off the stool and drained the beer. Waste not, want not. "No time like the present." I moved to the door when Elena appeared above.

"Hey Jackson," she said in a loud voice. "Do you want to go on a double date?"

14

It was an old white Ford Escort. Older was cheaper. I drove it off the rental lot, through a Dunkin Donuts drive-through and forty minutes later I was parked a block down the street from the front gate of Delbert's lavish estate. Or somebody's lavish estate. It was a quiet street. I opened the box and selected a chocolate donut with chocolate icing and opened the large coffee. It was too hot to drink. I left the lid off and carefully placed it in a cup holder on the console. I slid down so my head was mostly behind the steering wheel, munched the donut and waited.

When I was a small child, my mother had admonished me more than once about my lack of patience. Black Mamba had drilled patience into me. I had spent hours immobile, either waiting for a target or just observing. The thing you learn is to slow your breathing and your metabolism but not fall asleep. It's a hard thing to learn but learn it we did. I had lain in an open field in a ghillie suit for two days one time. When your bladder filled to the point of pain, you just released and lived with the consequences. What you didn't do is move. Movement always attracts the eye.

I had been there for four hours; the coffee was gone, and I used the cup to pee in. Making sure there was no movement anywhere, I lowered the window and poured it into the street. Dogs do it all the time.

A half-hour later Delbert's car went past me and pulled into his drive. It had to hesitate as the gates opened. When I had first arrived, I had driven past, circled the cul-de-sac and came back to park. There were no cars outside the four-car garage. So he had been gone all this time. This probably meant he would be inside for a while. I settled down to wait. I had two donuts left. I wouldn't starve. I longed for a good long swim.

It was afternoon when the gates began to swing open, and the Tahoe backed out onto the street. I stayed low as it drove past. I couldn't tell who was in it. I took a slow ten count before I started the Escort, did a U-turn, and followed. The Tahoe was out of sight and I had to hustle to catch up. Once I got him in sight I hung back. He wound his way to the 101 and headed west. There were many lanes to choose from. I chose one that wasn't his and hung back far enough he wouldn't notice me. I was still close enough to close the gap if he decided to take an exit. We drove to the other side of the city, which in Phoenix is a very long way.

Just before the Glendale exit his right turn-signal came on. The stadium the Cardinals played football in loomed in the distance. Luckily, there was no game tonight, so the traffic was normal, if you want to call it that. After my time in Illinois, this was madness. I managed to make the same left turn light as the Tahoe. He went east into Glendale. It was trickier now. He drove to 55th Avenue and turned north and ended up at a park in the northeast corner. He pulled into a parking lot next to a playground. There was another vehicle parked there. A black Chevy. There was a picnic table under a small tree and two men were sitting on it.

I drove past. When I was far enough, I pulled into a driveway that sported a for-sale sign out by the street. A handful of solicitation items were stuffed into the front screen. I got out, got in the back seat, and unlimbered the old Nikon D60 and the 500mm telephoto lens. I looked through it and it was plenty. I wasn't going to need the AF-S teleconverter. The 500mm brought the men into sharp focus. I rested it on the open windowsill and began shooting. One of the guys rolled a doobie and lit it. They passed it around. Delbert had a dark bag at his feet. After they had talked a while and they had finished the smoke, he reached down and brought the bag to the table. He opened it and pulled out a gallon baggie. It was white and stuffed with pills. He handed it to the doobie roller and the guy handed him a black bag. Delbert pulled out a stack of stuffed zip locks. Delbert opened each plastic bag and pulled out cash. He counted it. So much for honor among thieves. They all stood and went to their cars. I waited until Delbert was moving before I backed out and followed.

He went straight back to his place. I figured he was in for the night, so I circled the cul-de-sac and headed back to the car rental return. Later I pulled into my parking spot and covered the Mustang. It was too late for a cart ride, so I hoofed it down the hill. As I went by the *Thirteen Episodes* the lights were on. The shades were drawn but evidently Pete was home.

I stepped on the bow and hollered. "Hey Episodes, permission to come aboard?"

A moment later the blind went up and Pete slid the door open. "Hey Jackson, come on in."

"Hope I'm not interrupting."

"Hell no. Just reading. I was just thinking about fixing a drink. Will you join me?"

"Sure. What're we having?"

"I was going to fix a Manhattan. Would you like one?"

"I'll just take a bourbon on the rocks."

"What kind of bourbon would you like?" he said, moving to the galley.

"Whatever you're pouring."

"Makers Mark okay?"

"Perfect."

"Grab a chair."

I leaned over and looked at his book, then sat in one of the chairs. *John Adams* by David McCullough.

Pete brought me my drink. He moved the book out of his way on the dark leather couch and sat down. "Glad you stopped by. Thought maybe you were gone again."

"No, I think I'm here for a while. John Adams, huh."

"Yeah. Much easier read than it looks. He was quite a guy. Washington was born to money; Jefferson was born to money, but Adams wasn't. It's interesting, Washington was tall and good looking and looked every bit the general and president. Jefferson was slender with a full head of hair and looked and acted the complete dandified intellectual. Adams was short and portly and plain and probably had a better mind than either of the other guys."

"Nobody thinks about those guys anymore. I'll bet you can't

find a high-schooler out there that can tell you a thing about any of them."

He took a drink of his Manhattan, "Sad but true. When I was teaching writing at Berkeley, I was appalled at how little the students knew of American history."

"I don't want to get depressed tonight. I'm depressed enough."

"What are you depressed about?"

I told him about Marianne.

"A double date?" he said.

"It's almost embarrassing. Passing notes in study hall. Find out if she likes me. Circle yes or no. That kind of thing."

"It's not that bad," he said. "In fact, I'd take it in a heartbeat. My love life is deader than a popcorn fart."

I laughed and finished my drink. I stood up.

"You like another?"

"No, thanks. I'm going to take a swim."

"Good luck with the girl," he said.

I swam out to the buoy and back three times, then pulled myself out of the water. I dried off, put on dry clothes, fixed a drink and went up top. I sat and watched the stars until my drink was gone. I thought about Marianne, I thought about Delbert, I thought about Eddie and how much older he was suddenly looking. I went down and went to bed.

15

I was at the El Patron by midafternoon. I had stopped at one of the last remaining film developers and paid him an extra forty bucks to develop my photos while I waited. I told him Detective Boyce of the police department was waiting for them.

"What now?" Blackhawk said.

"I'm going to show them to Boyce."

"She still upset with you?"

"Probably. If she isn't cooperative, I'll show them to Mendoza."

"Want me to come along?"

"Sure, if you want to. This guy is calling himself your brother."

It was a while before Blackhawk could break free, so it was an hour before we were walking up the steps to police headquarters. The sergeant at the desk sent word up to Boyce that we were there, and she kept us waiting for a half hour before we were cleared to go up. Blackhawk said she was probably busy. I said she was just busting my balls.

When we got upstairs her office was empty. There were chairs aligned along the wall, so we sat and waited. It was another fifteen minutes before she appeared. She walked by us without looking at us.

"Come on in," she said. We did. Blackhawk seemed amused.

She went behind her desk and waved at the two chairs that faced her desk. The last time I was here she didn't have an office. She must be coming up in the world.

"How's Elena?" she said, looking at Blackhawk.

"She's fine," he said. "The shooting rattled her, but she seems to be settling down."

"How's your little blondie?" she said looking at me.

"She's not my little blondie," I said. God, she could get under my skin. I could sense she was smiling without smiling.

"What have you got for me?"

I laid the envelope with the photos on her desk. She shook them out. She carefully picked them up one at a time and studied them. She reached for her phone and tapped out an extension number.

We could hear a phone ring in the far reaches of the outer room. It stopped abruptly. "Hey Danny, could you come in here a sec?" She hung up.

A moment later, Boyce's partner, Danny Rich came in the office. He nodded at us, "How you doin'?" he said.

We both nodded. "Whatcha got?" he said to Boyce.

She handed him the photos. "You recognize these guys?"

He took a pair of glasses from his shirt pocket and slipped them on. He studied the photos intensely. Finally, he looked at her. "Guy with the baggie calls himself Azeed Muhammad. Released about eight months ago. Serving under the name of Delbert Smith. The other guy is new to me. I haven't seen him before. The two sitting on the bench are Freddie Venuzuela and a two-time loser named Mickey Ebert. They are Ace Double Deuce."

I looked at Blackhawk. "Maybe we can see what Nacho can find out about Ace Double Deuce's connection to Valdez?"

"You think they're connected to Valdez?"

"Or Dos Hermanos."

"Either one, they are all dealers," Danny continued.

"But you haven't put them away?"

He looked at me. "Bigger fish."

"You think these photos will help?" Blackhawk said.

"Can't positively identify what's in the baggie," Boyce said.

"But it gives us new guys to watch." Danny said, looking at Boyce. She shrugged.

Boyce looked at me. "What are these guys to you?"

I looked at Blackhawk. He said, "Delbert Smith is the son of a woman my father married. He wants to be my brother."

"Wants to be?"

"Not a drop of blood. He's always been a loser."

"So why does he show up now?"

"He is trying to recruit me to help him with something. He says he can pay me fifty thousand a week to work with him."

"Jeez," Danny Rich said. "Where can I meet him?"

"Do it," Boyce said.

"Do it?"

"Get inside, report back to us."

"Can't do it. I'd kill him."

She looked at me. "What about you?"

"Cicero Paz is about as much fun as I want to have," I said looking into her flat cop eyes. Cicero Paz had been the kingpin of the drug trade in Phoenix and beyond. Captain Mendoza had assigned Boyce to undercover work, posing as a bag lady in the vicinity of Paz's headquarters, a bar on the westside called SanDunes. She kept track of all the comings and goings of Paz's gang. Mendoza had asked me to infiltrate the gang and watch her back. He asked me because he knew I didn't have to follow any rules and was willing to break a few to protect her.

"But you were so good at it," Boyce said. "I think you need to think about it."

16

I was sitting at the bar at the marina drinking a Dos Equis. Eddie was behind the bar substituting for the bartender that had called in sick. Except for me, the place was empty. The bar had large, garage-door styled windows that rolled up, and they were all open. The breeze was gentle and I could smell the lake. Sometimes it smells fishy, but today it smelled good.

"You hungry?" Eddie said.

"Hamburger sounds good."

A few minutes later he sat a plate full of hamburger and fries in front of me. He popped another beer.

"Been fishing lately?" he said.

"Not enough," I said. I didn't have to ask him. If he wasn't working for Maureen, the marina manager, he was fishing. He even fished in the rain if it wasn't too bad.

"I've got a freezer full of crappie," he said. "Would you like some?"

"Love it."

I was halfway through the burger when my phone buzzed.

"Jackson," I said.

"Jackson, this is Father Correa," his voice said in my ear.

"Hey, Father, what's up?"

"I've got Sonny Tortelli here with me. He's pretty upset. His daughter came back last night looking for the diamond. He denied seeing it and they got into an awful row. He's worried because she was sporting a black eye. Someone had been beating on her. He tried to get her to calm down and stay with him, but she took off."

"What can I do?"

"He followed her. He didn't think he could go to the police because they told him she's an adult and can come and go as she pleases. He knows that she won't complain about whoever hit her. He's feeling pretty helpless."

"Not sure what I can do. I've got a mouthful of hamburger. When I finish I'll be down."

It was an hour and a half before I parked down the street from Safehouse. They were in Father Correa's tiny office. Sonny Tortelli looked exhausted. His hair was disheveled and the bags under his eyes were dark.

"Coffee?" Father Correa said as I walked in.

"No thanks," I said. I looked at Sonny. "You going to be okay?"

He shook his head. "I'm just worried sick about Annabelle."

I hitched a hip on the small worktable the good Father had propped up against the wall. I had to move some papers. "Tell me everything that happened last night," I said to Sonny. "Tell me exactly what she said and did."

"I had a terrible headache," he said. "So I was home from the shop. I was lying down in the dark when she came in. She had her own key. She didn't expect me to be there. When I sat up, it scared her. I thought she'd come home to stay. But she just said, 'Where's my diamond?' I said, 'What diamond?' and she yelled at me, 'Where's my goddam diamond.' She never cusses at me. Never."

"Did she believe you?"

He shrugged. "She didn't want to. Finally, she stormed out. So I decided to follow her."

"Where'd she go?"

"Out in the northwest. Off of 99th Avenue, almost to Happy Valley Road."

"Did she see you?"

"I don't think so. There was no reason for her to think I would follow her. Finally, she pulled down a side street and parked at a big fancy house. It had a wrap-around porch and there were people there. None of them looked like people I wanted her to associate with."

"What did you do?"

"I drove on past and turned around and went home. When I went past, she was sitting on some guy's lap." He ducked his head and studied his hands.

"That doesn't sound like she's being forced," I said.

He didn't respond.

I looked at Father Correa. I shrugged. "What can I do?"

He shook his head, watching Sonny. "I have no idea," he said. "I always just thought of you as the miracle worker."

"I'm all out of miracles lately."

Sonny looked up at me. His eyes were miserable.

"Why don't you show me where this house is," I said.

He nodded.

We took the Mustang, and it was forty minutes before we pulled off the 101 onto 99th Avenue. Another ten minutes before we came to the street he had talked about, but we drove past it before he recognized it. I went a couple of blocks and did a U-turn.

I drove back and turned down the road. He pointed out the house. It was high end, two- story with a big veranda with pillars along the front. Wide front yard with decorative granite and professionally planted flowers. A long walkway led up to the porch. To the side was a retainage area designed to channel overflow in a hard rain. It was groomed with fine granite and stretched back past the house and the back area. Someone had planted new trees twenty feet apart down the middle of it. They were still pretty small. As I drove past I could see the back had a pool and a volleyball court and a basketball court. It also had horseshoes and on the west side was an open area with soccer nets on each end. I could hear loud music from the rear but could see no one. I turned around. I drove back past the house and pulled to the curb two houses away. This was still quite a distance; the properties were so far apart.

I unbuckled my seat belt and started to climb out.

"I go with you," Sonny said.

"No, no, you stay here. I just want to see what we're up against." He looked disappointed but he stayed.

There was no one around the front. The music was coming from the rear. At least they would call it music. To me it was a cacophony of chanting and badly rhymed words with a heavy drumbeat. To each their own.

The music was so loud the crunch of my feet on the quarter minus granite was drowned out. I turned the back corner before anyone noticed me. There were four young guys out on the volleyball court. They were engrossed in their game. The three sitting at a grouping of patio chairs turned to look at me. Annabelle made a fourth. The men sat in high backed patio chairs. Annabelle sat with her back to me. Her hair was long and glossy. She was sitting in what Nacho had dubbed a strap chair, a folding outside chair with intertwined plastic straps. They were alternately green and white. When she saw the other men look at me, she turned to look. She still had the mouse under her eye.

Without hesitation I walked straight to them. The boys on the volleyball court were shirtless and ripped and young. These guys were older. Not old, but certainly older than the volleyball boys. I hooked a chair from against the wall and dragged it to the table. I positioned it and sat next to Annabelle.

"Hey fellas," I said easily. Annabelle hitched away from me.

"Who the fuck are you?" the guy across from me said.

"A friend of Annabelle's," I said. I looked at her. "Someone been beating up on you?"

Her eyes slid to the guy that wanted to know who the fuck I was. I could see a flash of fear in her eyes. I was getting their best hard-ass stare. I almost wet myself.

Annabelle was staring at me also. I looked at her.

I handed her my card. Centered in the middle it had my name, Jackson, and a phone number, that was all. The number was the land line at the El Patron. "I'm here to take you home, if you want to go."

She shook her head, then looked past me. Whatever she was looking at had caught the other guys' attention also. I turned to look. Sonny Tortelli was coming around the corner.

17

"Papa," she said in a voice that was a cross between angry and frightened.

"Annabelle," he said. "I want you to come home."

"Papa, go away," she said. "I don't want you here."

"Annabelle," he said, he was almost crying.

One of the men stood and so I stood. "Last chance," I said to the girl. She shook her head and started to cry. I looked to Sonny and shrugged my shoulders. "She's not coming," I said. I moved over by him. I put a hand on his arm and tugged gently. "Time to go," I said.

He reluctantly turned, almost stumbling. We went around the corner of the house and I pushed him. "Go get into the car."

I stepped back around the corner with my phone in my hand.

"Say cheese," I said. I took their picture with all looking at me.

As I went back around the corner, I heard the main guy say, "Get that camera."

I stopped, then stepped back to the corner and flattened myself against the wall. A second later, one of the others, a big young guy came barreling around the corner. I hit him in the throat with a left, then followed with a chopping right to his cheek and temple. He went down on his face. I turned and sprinted to the car. Thank God Sonny had done what I told him and was in the Mustang. I jumped into the driver's seat and fired it up. I was spinning rubber and dust and rock before they made it around the corner of the house.

I got lucky on the lights all the way to the freeway. I headed east on the 101 and bailed out at 35th Avenue. I took Bell Road to the I-17 and headed toward Father Correa's Safehouse. No one was following. I called the good father and warned him I was dropping Sonny. I told him what had happened, and that Annabelle didn't want to come home. I dropped Sonny in front of Father Correa's. I warned him to not go home for a couple of days, then I headed to the El Patron.

There was a pre- happy hour crowd forming in the main salon and I had to take one of the three remaining empty stools at the bar. I had glanced into Rick's American as I came in, but no one was there. Elena was at the bandstand going over charts with her band leader. Nacho was behind the bar wrestling a new keg into place under the tapper. Jimmy was mixing drinks at the end.

Jimmy delivered his drinks and came over to me. "Beer or scotch?" he said.

"Beer," I said. I wanted the scotch, but something told me to go with the beer. He brought it and set it in front of me. I gave him a five. "Keep the change."

He shook his head, smiling. "Jackson, you know there is no change. There is no charge."

"Keep the five. I've got a job for you."

"Shoot," Jimmy said.

"I want you to get online and find out everything you can find out about a jewel theft in New York." I started to explain all the details I had.

"Hold on," he said. He went down to the register and got a small binder of lined paper and a pen. He came back.

"Okay, shoot."

I told him all I knew.

He nodded and jotted notes then moved down to the end of the bar and opened his laptop.

I sensed someone standing at my right shoulder. I turned. It was Blackhawk.

"I thought you had forgotten," he said.

"Forgotten what?"

He smiled. I could tell something was tickling him. "Our double date."

"What double date?"

"The one we are going on in an hour."

"No one told me about any double date."

"Sure, I did. You just forgot."

"I didn't forget. You didn't tell me."

"Well, I'm telling you now." He looked me up and down. "You can't go looking like that."

"I can't get to the boat and back in an hour."

"Go upstairs and take a shower. You can get clothes out of my closet."

"I'll look like a pimp."

"You saying I look like a pimp?"

I swallowed the remainder of the beer. "No, I didn't mean that. Somehow you carry it off." I slid off the stool. "Most pimps don't dress as nice as you."

"Just go," he said indicating the upstairs. So I did.

Their apartment door had a keypad lock on it. I punched the numbers and went in. As usual, the place was impeccable. I found a towel and washcloth in the linen closet and rummaged through Blackhawk's shirts. I found a dandy number that fit fine. It was black. Perfect. I was lacing up my shoe when Elena came in.

"Good," she said, giving me the look. She walked past and went into their bedroom. A second later she poked her head back out. "Marianne will be downstairs in a short while. I want you to be there to keep her entertained until I'm ready. We're going to Talavera at the Four Seasons."

"I'll bring my wallet," I said.

"You don't even have a job," she said, disappearing into the other room. I checked myself in the mirror and went downstairs.

18

Marianne wasn't there yet. Jimmy waved at me, so I went down to where he was. He turned the laptop around so I could see.

"These guys were pretty slick," he said.

"Yeah, three hundred million dollars' worth of slick."

"You know how they did it?"

"You tell me."

"Somebody told them where the diamonds were and when they would be there. The papers say they have a person of interest, but they don't name him. Sounds like an inside job. Street cameras show a van pulling up and parking on the street. It had signs that read ACME Construction."

"Shades of Wiley Coyote."

"Yeah, right?" He continued, "They all had coveralls and yellow hard hats. They all wore sunglasses and had beards and moustaches. They carried two galvanized garbage cans and four heavy plastic bags into the building. Nobody even glanced at them."

"Ballsy."

"Yeah. According to an Associated Press reporter that covered the robbery, they hiked up to the third floor, rang for the service elevator and when it came, they disabled it and slid down the cables to the bottom. That put them one wall away from the vault. They waited until the middle of the night, then blasted through the walls and busted into the boxes."

"Who was the reporter?"

"Guy by the name of Wayne Cosgrove. He's based in New York."

"Associated Press?"

"Yeah. So, I guess these guys loaded it all up, put it in the van and drove away." He looked across the room toward the double doors that led to the hallway. "Wow," he said.

I turned and looked, and Marianne had come in. She was in an off-the-shoulder black dress with a string of pearls around her slender neck. The dress was to just below her knees and she wore gleaming black stiletto heels. She didn't really look around, she just headed to the stairs. I met her at the bottom. She smiled and I felt lightheaded.

"They'll be down in a minute. Elena suggests we have a cocktail while we wait?"

"Sure," she said.

I took her elbow and guided her to a table against the wall. I seated her and took my seat. Jimmy was watching and I waved at him. He draped his forearm with a towel like the best of waiters and came over.

"Hi," he said. "What can I get you?"

Marianne smiled at him. "I'd like a cosmo."

He looked at me. "A gin gimlet," I said. He turned and went to make the drinks.

"What's a gin gimlet?"

"It's a conversation starter," I said. "It's basically just gin with lime juice and a twist."

"I guess you have to like gin?"

"It helps. You don't like gin?"

"Not much."

"I won't hold it against you. Your favorite's a cosmo?"

"When I'm out and want to feel sophisticated. Jimmy makes the best."

"And when you are at home and just lounging around?"

"I don't drink at home. At least not alone."

"And if you are not alone?"

"Is that your subtle way of asking if I am seeing anyone?"

"Must not be that subtle."

She laughed. Jimmy brought the drinks.

"Get you anything else?" he said.

I shook my head. I raised my glass and she clinked it with hers. We both sipped.

"So, are you?" I said as I set my glass down.

She was holding her glass up with both hands. She looked at me over the top. She didn't say anything, but her eyes didn't waver.

"You aren't going to answer?"

"So far it's none of your business."

"So far?"

19

The Four Seasons is nestled in the midst of a jumble of large boulders on the furthest north side of Scottsdale in what is known as the Troon area. The restaurant was billed as a Spanish steakhouse. After we were seated, the impeccable waiter took our drink order. Elena led off and ordered a G spot, which she eventually had to describe since the waiter didn't know what it was. Marianne ordered another cosmo. I ordered a Grey Goose martini and Blackhawk asked for a Glenlivet on the rocks.

Elena appeared to be a little irritated the waiter didn't know what a G spot was, but when the waiter brought it, she tasted it and smiled her approval. The waiter looked very relieved.

Blackhawk told him we would enjoy our drinks before we ordered. He backed away and left. "This is perfect," Elena said tasting her drink again. "I don't know why he said he didn't know what it was."

"Google," Marianne said. "He looked it up."

"That's cheating," Blackhawk said with a smile. "A bartender working in a place like this should know every drink ever made."

"You're a hard man," I said, sipping my martini. It was

delicious. Ice cold, the way I like it.

"How's your cosmo?" I asked Marianne.

She leaned forward and whispered in a loud conspiratorial tone, "Not as good as Jimmy's."

Elena smiled. "I'll tell him that."

The waiter circled back by. "Are we ready to order?"

Blackhawk said, nodding at me, "He and I would like another drink. How about you girls?"

They both demurred. "By the time you have the new drinks we'll be ready," Blackhawk said to the waiter. "In the meantime, bring us some foie gras, your jumbo shrimps and the seared scallops."

"Very good, sir," he said and turned to get the drinks.

We all picked up the menus and studied them.

The waiter returned with the drinks very quickly.

Elena ordered lobster bouillabaisse, Marianne ordered the 8 oz. fillet with horseradish crust and marsala mushrooms. Blackhawk ordered the Chilean sea bass, and I got the 20 oz. bone-in ribeye, rare to medium rare. Hot and pink in the middle.

The appetizers came out quickly. With one drink in us we settled into a mild comfortable state. I was looking out the window, marveling at the view when Marianne said, "How long have you boys known each other?"

I looked at Blackhawk and he had that bemused look on his face. I could tell he expected me to answer but it was Elena who picked it up.

"They met in the Navy."

"Were you on the same ship?"

"Not really," I said. "We were selected to go through a special boot camp. They divided us into ten-man teams and Blackhawk and I were on the same team. Are you an Arizona native or did you move here?"

"I was born in California but my family moved around a lot."

"I love northern California," Elena said.

"Why did you move here?" I said to keep the conversation going in the other direction.

"I was in a national traveling cast of *Wicked*. I was the understudy for Elphaba. The theater here, Gammage, out at ASU, was the last stop. I was dating a boy from here, so I hung around for a while. Then I got the job at the casino and learned to really like Scottsdale. So here I am."

"What happened to the boy?" I said, then was self-conscious because I was the one who asked.

Marianne looked at me coolly. "He didn't live up to my standards."

Elena grinned. "You go, girl."

I smiled at her. "You suppose I could get a list of those standards?"

"It's more like a book," she said.

Elena laughed. I looked at Blackhawk and he was enjoying himself.

Marianne looked at Elena. "I've got a question I haven't asked before."

"What's that, honey?" Elena said.

"Where did you get that Nacho guy? To look at him, he's very scary but when you talk to him, he is as gentle as a pussy cat. And funny."

Elena looked at Blackhawk. "You want to take this?"

"You're doing fine," Blackhawk said.

Elena shook her head in irritation, then she looked at Marianne. "Back in the day, the El Patron was not a classy nightclub like it is now. When Blackhawk came along it was still pretty rough."

"Did you know Blackhawk?"

"Oh, no. He just came in for a drink. Then he kept coming back. Me and all the other women noticed him. One day I was performing and when I finished, he stuck around. After the last set I was sitting with Rickie. Rickie Alverez owned the place and Blackhawk came over and sat down. It irritated Rickie and he asked what Blackhawk wanted and Blackhawk said, "I want to buy this place. Rickie said, "What makes you think it's for sale?"

"If it isn't it, should be," Blackhawk said. Then he named a price and Rickie almost swallowed his tongue. Then Blackhawk looked at me and said, "And your girl singer goes with the deal."

Marianne laughed. "Did you have a thing going with the owner?"

Elena smiled. "Not from that moment on."

"So where did Nacho come in?" At that moment they brought our food. After the waiters moved away Marianne repeated, "Where did you get Nacho?"

"A bunch of gang-bangers had come in and were doing shots of tequila and started getting rowdy. I was singing and they started making crude comments." Elena looked at Blackhawk. "Blackhawk came to their table and asked them to cool it and they stood up like they were going to attack him."

"How many were there?" I asked.

Elena shrugged, "I don't remember. Four or five," she said.

"Not enough," I said.

Elena smiled at me. "Anyway," she continued, "when they started acting tough, Nacho, who just happened to be in the bar, came over and stood beside Blackhawk and they shut right down. Fifteen minutes later they were gone, and Blackhawk offered Nacho a job." Elena reached out and took Blackhawk's hand. "Nacho told him he was a felon and was just out of prison. Blackhawk didn't care. He's been with us ever since."

She looked at Blackhawk. "Tell them about Juanita."

He shook his head, clearly uncomfortable. "They don't want to hear about that."

"Tell us," Marianne said.

Elena looked at Blackhawk for a long minute as he avoided her eyes. "Nacho was talking to us and he told us his mother was really sick and was in the hospital."

"She's Juanita?"

"Yes. He was upset. The hospital had just told him that Medicaid couldn't cover everything, and they would have to put her in a charity ward. Blackhawk got up and walked out. He went to the hospital and told them to send all the bills to him. Nacho became his brother for life that day."

I was looking at Blackhawk. He looked embarrassed. I had never heard this story. It explained a lot of things.

"How's your steak?" he asked.

"Great," I said. "Wonderful."

"So, this boot camp you guys were in, how long did it last?"

"A long, long time," I said.

"They're not telling you everything," Elena said.

Marianne looked at me. "What aren't you telling me?"

I shook my head. I looked at Blackhawk and I could see he was uncomfortable.

Marianne looked at Elena, who had taken a mouthful of food. She chewed and swallowed before she answered.

"Elena," Blackhawk said softly.

"He doesn't want me to talk about it. And I don't know much but they and the rest of their team did special jobs for the government."

"What kind of jobs?"

Elena shrugged. "I don't know, and they won't tell me."

I took a bite of the steak. It was tender and perfect. I took another drink of my martini. Marianne was looking at me. I couldn't tell what the look meant.

20

The next morning, I took my swim, then showered, fixed a mug of coffee and a bagel and went up on the sundeck. On my I phone I found three Wayne Cosgroves in the New York area. The second one I called was the reporter.

His voice was gruff and short. "Cosgrove."

"Mr. Cosgrove, are you with the Associated Press?"

"Yeah. What do you need?"

"I understand you wrote the article on the recent jewelry heist."

"You got anything on that?"

"I might have. Is this a landline or a cell phone?"

"It's a cell phone."

"A friend of mine is a Catholic priest that runs a safe house in Phoenix for young mothers that have suffered abuse. He has a neighbor that came to him about his adult daughter. She was grown and gone, but suddenly had come home asking to stay a few days. She wouldn't explain why. After a few days they had a row and she left in the middle of the night. The next morning when the guy discovered she was gone, he looked through her room to see if anything would tell him where she had gone. Under the bed he found a solitary diamond. We had it appraised by a guy that appraises estate jewelry. It appraised for fifteen thousand dollars. I showed a picture of it to a police Captain, and he told me about the robbery."

"How do you know this diamond was part of the robbery?"

"I don't. I'm going to send you a picture of it. Maybe someone on your end can identify it."

"Highly unlikely," he said.

"Yeah, I know. I've got another picture I'm going to send along. I tracked the girl down and I took her picture sitting with three guys. I'm wondering if you can identify any of them."

"Where are you calling from again?"

"Phoenix."

"What makes you think I would know them?"

"You know more about this case than anyone else. It's a long shot but if you don't mind."

"Send it along," he said and hung up.

I sent the photos to his number. I expected a response right away but didn't get it. I did some chores around the boat, walked down the dock to the marina restaurant and got some lunch. Eddie's skiff was gone so I assumed he was fishing. After lunch I walked back to the *Tiger Lily*. I stretched out on the over-sized yellow couch and tried to read. I couldn't help myself, I kept checking my phone to make sure I hadn't missed a call. I don't know what I expected to hear Cosgrove tell me. I thought about Annabelle and I thought about the mouse under her eye. I thought about Marianne.

After a while I drifted off to sleep. When I awoke my book

was on the floor and my mouth was dry. I must have snored. I got some juice from the refrigerator and took it up top. There was a nice breeze, and the *Lily* was gently rocking. I looked toward Eddie's and saw that his skiff was back. I remembered his offer of some crappie fillets. I drained the juice and rinsed my glass in the galley sink, then headed over to his old River Runner. He wasn't on board. I found him at the fish cleaning station. He'd had a good day. When I came walking up, he looked up.

"Hey boy," he said.

"You've had a good day," I said.

"I'm glad you are here," he said. "If it is okay with you, I'll send some of these home with you. I'm out of room in my locker. I've pushed Maureen's generosity about as far as I should."

"Maureen?"

"She's been letting me store some fish in her restaurant freezer."

"I'm happy to put some in my freezer. I'll warn you now, two or three may end up missing."

"You'd be doing me a favor."

I went into the marina store and got a plastic grocery bag. Eddie filled it up and thanking him, I went back to the boat. I cleaned up the fillets and bagged them in ziplocks and put them in my freezer. I took a shower and scrubbed the fish smell off of me. I caught a shuttle to my car and drove down to the El Patron. When I walked through the double doors, Azeed was sitting at the bar.

21

Blackhawk was across from him on the inside of the bar. He didn't look happy. He waved me over. I grabbed a stool, one removed from Azeed.

"It'll only be for a couple of days. Just till I figure out my next move," Azeed was saying.

Blackhawk looked at me. "Dipshit here did it again."

"What did you do?" I said.

Azeed looked at me. "Who the hell are you?"

"He's my brother," Blackhawk said. "My true brother." He turned to me. "He tried to peddle fake drugs and now he's got his whole gang after him."

"I didn't know they were fake," he said. "I don't do those kind of drugs, so I didn't know."

I looked down at his feet. A satchel sat there. He had one foot on top of it.

"Is the money fake too?"

He looked at me, his eyebrows arching. "Oh, shit. I didn't think of that!" He reached down and picked up the satchel. He sat it on the bar. He opened it and pulled out a random hundred-dollar bill. He held it to the light, looking at the watermark of Ben Franklin. He put it back and pulled another one. He went through several more. With relief he said, "They're okay." He put the satchel back at his feet.

I pulled the small Ruger, I normally carry, and pointed it at him.

"What if someone robs you?" I said.

He eyes widened. "Hey," he said. He turned to Blackhawk. "You wouldn't do that."

Blackhawk said, "I'm not the one that's doing it."

Azeed looked back at me, his eyes frightened.

I laughed. "You're safe enough." I looked at Blackhawk. "He's not safe here. They will be looking for him eventually." I put the gun away.

"Give me the satchel," Blackhawk said. "I'll put it in my safe."

Azeed looked at him. I could see him thinking hard. I helped him out.

"If they catch up to you and you have the money, they'll kill you. If you don't have the money, you can bargain."

He looked at me for a long time. He looked at Blackhawk. "How will I know you will give it back."

"You don't."

"What would Blackhawk do with it? And if you don't trust him why did you bring it here in the first place?"

He thought about that. Finally, he lifted the bag and handed it to Blackhawk.

"Where's Elena?" I said.

"She and Marianne are taking a spa day." He picked up the bag. "I'll put this in the safe. Be right back."

Jimmy came down. "You want anything?"

"Beer," I said. He moved away.

"Why does he say you're his brother?" Azeed said, watching Blackhawk go up the stairs.

I ignored him. Jimmy brought my beer. I picked it up and moved to the other side of the bar. Nacho came down the stairs and sat beside me. I had barely taken a drink when my .phone chirped. It was Blackhawk.

"Yeah?"

"I'm looking at the parking lot monitors. Delbert's got company and they don't look happy. Get him out of here. Take him out the back."

I took a large drink of the beer, said "Come with me," to Nacho and went around to Azeed. I grabbed him by his arm.

"Come on," I said. "You have company. Blackhawk says they don't look friendly."

He didn't hesitate.

"You have a car?" I said.

"I used Uber," he said.

"We're going out the back," I said. "We'll take your car," I said to Nacho.

They followed me. We went through the back-storage room and out the back door. Nacho was parked beside Blackhawk's Jaguar.

"Get in and buckle up." I looked at Nacho. "Get in the back, I'll drive."

"How'd they find me?" Azeed said.

I fired up Nacho's Jeep. I glanced at him. "That's dumb. You brought them here a while back. You think they forgot."

"Damn, this is a small back seat," Nacho said. I drove out the back way and headed north. I had no idea where I was going. I kept an eye on my rear-view mirror. After a while I pulled my phone and thumbed Blackhawk.

He connected. "Yeah."

"What kind of car were those guys in?"

"Looked like a red Rav 4. Why?"

"I'm looking at a red Rav 4 in my rear-view mirror. Where am I going?"

"Away from them."

"Duh!" I said, hanging up. "Hold on, I'm going to lose them."

I punched the Jeep and it jumped forward. Nacho had souped up the engine so there was no way a Rav 4 could keep up. I took the next two corners almost on two wheels. I made a lot of turns and ended up on I-17 heading north. I no sooner got on than I got off. They were nowhere in sight. I drove a while, keeping an eye on the rear-view mirror. Nacho was sitting sideways, watching.

I glanced at Azeed. "You have any idea where you can hole up?"

"I need to get out of town."

"It ain't going to happen today."

He shook his head. "I've got no place."

"How about you?" I said over my shoulder to Nacho.

"I just moved into a loft apartment at Virginia and Central. There are quite a few empties. Some are furnished. I know the manager. For a C note she'll look the other way for a couple of days."

It was a high rise called Park Plaza. The good news was that it had underground parking. If Azeed's friends hadn't seen us pull in there, which they hadn't, they'd never find us. Nacho had us wait in the car while he went in to talk to the manager. It was forty minutes before he was back. While we waited, Azeed wanted to talk but I told him to shut up. When Nacho got back, he was smiling, and he had lipstick on his chin.

He opened the door. "Fourth floor, in the back," he said. He looked at me. "You owe me a C-note and she wants a grand for a deposit in case he screws the place over."

"I've got the C-note, but I don't have the grand."

"How about you?" he said to Azeed.

"All my money was in that satchel."

"Satchel?" Nacho said.

"It's in Blackhawk's safe."

"Somebody will have to go get it," he said.

"Will she let us go in now?"

"I have the key."

"Let's get him in and you can come back tonight with the money. She'll probably like that."

The look on Nacho's face was priceless. He might as well have said "Ah, shucks."

22

Back at the El Patron, Blackhawk played the surveillance tape for me. First the parking lot, then inside the bar. That one he could enlarge, and he gave me a good look at the three guys as they came into the bar. I could see the moment they apparently saw us going out the back. They turned and rushed out. The outside monitor showed them running to their Rav 4, looking like the keystone cops. They jumped in and sped off the screen. Two of the guys were the two Azeed had met in the park.

"I didn't realize they were that close," I said.

"You're getting old," Blackhawk said. "You're beginning to slip."

My phone chirped.

"Jackson," I said.

It was Cosgrove. There was no chitchat. "You got that photo you sent me handy?"

"Of the diamond or of the guys with the girl?"

"The guys."

"Hold on, I'll pull it up." I fiddled with my phone until I found the photo. Blackhawk was quietly watching me.

"Got it," I said.

"I can't tell for sure," he said. "But the guy half turned, with most of his back toward the camera. I think his name is O'Malley. I think he was the inside man." I looked at the picture. The man was turning toward me when I snapped the photo. His face was in profile.

"Have you told the police?"

"I'm not that sure."

"Any of the others?"

"Never seen them before. The only thing I've seen on O'Malley is an employment photo. That's why I'm not certain. If he's in Phoenix, he's a long way from home. Left a wife and two teenagers behind."

"Can I get a copy of that photo?"

"Probably. It may take me a while."

"He didn't have any priors?"

"Squeaky clean," Cosgrove said. "Do you have anything else?"

"Not yet."

"Not yet? What's your interest in this?"

"Favor for a friend."

"You're not police. Are you private?"

"Not officially."

"You're playing with fire, buddy. If you come up with something else before you combust, call me." He hung up.

"Who was that?" Blackhawk said.

"Guy named Cosgrove. He's with the Associated Press and he did the article on the jewelry heist."

"What'd he say?"

I turned my phone around and showed him the picture. "He thinks this guy here," I tapped the phone, "is the inside man. But he says he can't be certain."

"Where was this taken?"

I told him about taking Tortelli out to the westside house.

"Maybe you should have a discussion with this guy. What's his name?"

"O'Malley. You want to tag along?"

"Sure. Nacho's watching Delbert and Elena's not performing tonight."

We took Blackhawk's Jaguar. I thought they might recognize the candy apple red Mustang. We arrived about an hour before dusk. Blackhawk pulled up in the driveway. No sense being subtle. We rang the doorbell three times. No answer. We walked around the house. No one was there. It looked like no one lived there. Looking through the windows we could see furniture but nothing that showed anyone stayed there.

"You want to go in?"

"If they did the heist in New York, they're pros. We won't find anything." We got in the Jaguar and backed out. As we pulled to the stop sign on the corner a black Chevy SUV rounded it. The driver was one of the other guys at the table with Annabelle.

"Turn right," I said. "Go down a half block and do a U-turn. Then pull over. That guy that just passed us was one of them. This street is a dead end, he has to come back out here." I twisted and looked out the back window as Blackhawk turned the corner. The Chevy pulled into the driveway we had just vacated. Blackhawk did as I suggested and we sat across the street for a few minutes until the guy came driving back out. He turned toward us. I ducked while Blackhawk fiddled with his phone. After he was a block down the street, Blackhawk pulled another U-turn and followed him. He led us to the Lake Pleasant Parkway. He turned north. He led us to the Carefree Highway and he turned west toward Wickenburg.

Before Wickenburg you would normally tee into the highway from Sun City. We didn't get that far. Blackhawk dropped back far enough to keep him in sight. Before we got to Castle Hot Springs Road, he turned north onto a dirt road. We followed. We didn't have to keep him in sight because he was churning dust. Unfortunately, we were too.

"Should've used your car," Blackhawk said bitterly.

Ten minutes later the cloud of dust went over a rise and then dissipated. We came to it and Blackhawk stopped. He looked at me. "Got a feeling. Walk up and look over the hill without being seen."

I got out and did as he said. On the other side and down below I could see the cloud of dust where the guy had turned off the road at a right angle. I couldn't see a road, just the dust. I jogged back.

I slid into the Jaguar. "Take the next right."

The sun was below the horizon, but we didn't dare turn the lights on. He started forward and avoided the ruts and holes as best he could. The Jaguar wasn't meant for four-wheeling. When we reached the trail we stopped.

Blackhawk looked at me. "What now, Kemo-Sabe?"

"No way we can Injun up on him, and I guess this little road probably ends out there somewhere."

"You know that was racist."

"It's a colloquialism."

"Awfully big word for a white-eye."

"Now who's being racist?"

The light was fading fast.

"I don't think he'll be back this way tonight."

"Think he'll stay out here?"

"This time of night. Who'd want to drive this road in the dark?"

"Indian logic?"

"I could get out and put my ear to the ground."

"Why don't you?"

"I'll get dirt in my ear. Besides, this Jag ain't no four-wheel drive. And I'm scratching it up."

"Arizona pinstriping."

"Having a cute name for it don't make it easier to rub out. Let's get out of here and come back tomorrow."

"We need a four-wheel drive."

"Jimmy's got a big honking F250. Jacked-up. All wheel drive."

"Think you can get the Jag turned around here?"

"Not without more pin stripes, which I'm sure you'll be happy to rub out."

Blackhawk's phone chirped.

He looked at it. "Nacho," he said.

"Yeah," he said into it. He listened for a moment. "We'll be there in about forty minutes, maybe longer." He disconnected. I was watching him.

"He's at the apartment where we stashed Delbert. He says the place is empty and a mess. There's blood on the kitchen floor."

23

We parked in the underground parking and took the elevator to Nacho's floor. Blackhawk led the way. I'd never been there. He rang Nacho's bell and the door opened. Nacho stepped back to let us in. The place was spacious and finely furnished. Expensive looking art was on the walls and the furniture was large to accommodate Nacho's size.

"Wow," I said. "Well done. Who would have thought?"

"Elena helped me," he said.

"Take us to Delbert's place," Blackhawk said. No chitchat.

We followed Nacho out. We went to the elevator and rode up.

Nacho led us down the hall. He had the key and unlocked the door. He pushed it open, and we followed him in. Blackhawk had his hand on the Sig Sauer on his belt. Nacho had been right. The place was a mess. The lamps were overturned and the bottoms pried off. The chairs had been slit open. The cabinets in the kitchen were opened and emptied. Not gently.

"Looks like your lady friend will need all that deposit money. I'll take the bedrooms," I said. "Nacho, why don't you go over the living room and the closets. Blackhawk, you take the kitchen."

I wasn't being bossy. I wanted Blackhawk to take the kitchen because he knew how. A kitchen had a multitude of places to hide something smaller than a breadbox. What we were looking for, I had no idea. Anything that might lead us to where he had gone. Or been taken. We knew the money wasn't there. There were two bedrooms. Both had been tossed but the bigger one had been used. The mattress was half off the bed. I didn't bother with the obvious. I stood for a long moment and studied the room. All the clothes had been pulled out and the drawers were either pulled out or on the floor.

There was a closet. It had nothing but empty hangers. Azeed hadn't brought anything with him, so he'd been in the same clothes all this time. The dresser had not been pulled out, so I pulled it out. Nothing was attached to the back. I got on my hands and knees and looked underneath. Nothing. I went through the room and the attached bathroom. Nothing. I went back out to the living room. Nacho was sitting on the couch and Blackhawk was still in the kitchen. I went in.

"Find anything?"

"Pizza boxes and delivery fast-food wrappers." He pointed to a corner. "Blood's over there."

I walked over to it and looked. It was smeared and on one side was the partial imprint of a shoe. "You see this?"

"I took a picture of it," he said. "Delbert's foot is smaller than that. He wears like a size seven."

"Tiny," I said.

"Like his brain," he said. His phone chirped. He thumbed it. "Yeah." He listened. He said, "We'll be there by then." He disconnected.

"Jimmy," he said looking at me. "Someone just called on the bar phone. Asked for me. Wouldn't give a message to Jimmy except to say it was important and he'd call back in an hour."

"We've got nothing here," I said.

He nodded and moved toward the living room.

"Are we going to call the cops?" Nacho said.

"And tell them what?" Blackhawk said. "That we were harboring a drug dealer they were looking for?"

"Well, since you put it that way."

It was dark, the downtown street illuminated with the spaced streetlights. We pulled out of the garage and headed to El Patron. Nacho stayed behind to soothe the manager.

Elena wasn't performing, but Marianne was. Blackhawk went down the hall to the main salon while I stepped inside Rick's American and stood against the wall and watched her. Her delivery was smooth and professional, but watching her made every man's pulse race a little bit. She was poured into a sequined dress that was slit up to mid-thigh. She wasn't doing anything really special, but her delivery was very sexy. Maybe it was because she was very sexy.

She looked at me and smiled. I felt the heat in my face rise. At the end of the song, the customers burst into robust applause. I readily joined. When she started the next number, I slipped out and went to find Blackhawk.

When I came through the double doors, I didn't see Blackhawk. I went to the bar and when Jimmy saw me, he pointed up. Blackhawk was up in his office or in their apartment. I climbed the stairs and went to the office first. He wasn't there, so I knocked on the apartment door. He opened the door.

"Come on in," he said. "We still have a few minutes to wait."

"If he's punctual," I said.

"You going back to the boat?"

"I'll wait for the call," I said. "Unless you want to get rid of me."

"Elena's already in bed," he said. "Let's have a drink."

"Be a fool not to."

He poured two scotches from his corner bar. He handed me one, then took a seat in the overstuffed chair.

We sipped our drinks and sat there, waiting. We had, long ago, learned to be comfortable with silence and each other. Just as I finished my drink Blackhawk's phone chirped. He answered. "Be right down," he said. He disconnected.

"Jimmy says there's a guy on the bar phone that wants to talk to me. The guy says he's Delbert. Actually he's saying he's Azeed but once a Delbert always a Delbert."

"Let's go see what ol' Delbert wants," I said.

24

The bar phone was an old-fashioned landline with a curlicue cord and pushbutton numbers. If you searched the internet for the El Patron, the number to this phone is the only number you'd find. Blackhawk and Elena had their own cell phones. A hundred people had Elena's number, very few had Blackhawk's. The phone was lying on the bar and Jimmy was mixing drinks. Blackhawk picked it up.

"Yeah?"

The bar was large and cavernous, and I couldn't hear the other end of the conversation.

"What's that got to do with me?" Blackhawk said.

I couldn't hear it, but I knew there was some major pleading going on.

"Why should I believe you? You haven't told me the truth in twenty years." He listened for a while. "Even if I did, what's in it for me?" He listened some more.

"Yeah, if I don't, I have it all." He listened again. This time for a long time. Finally, he said, "I'll think about it," and hung up. He looked at me with a wry smile. "The son of a bitch never changes."

"What's he saying?"

"He says he's being held for ransom. He wants me to bring the money to a drop and they'll release him."

"Who's they?"

"I'm betting he's ransoming himself. There's no doubt in my mind that if I showed up with a bag of money he'd shoot me in the gizzard."

"So, what now?"

The phone rang again. He let it ring. Jimmy turned to look at him.

"Don't answer this phone again tonight," he said. Jimmy nodded. He looked at me. "I'm going to bed," he said. "You staying here tonight?"

"I think I'll go home. Call me in the morning if you need back up."

"Will do."

I drove north on the I-17. There was something going on and at the flashing red and blue lights they flagged us off the freeway onto Greenway Blvd. They moved us to Nineteenth Avenue then up to Bell Road, then back to the Freeway. It made the trip home a lot longer. I parked in my spot and covered the Mustang. There was no shuttle this late, so I jogged down the hill and across the bridge.

When I stepped aboard the *Tiger Lily*, I checked the LED light that would be lit if someone had come aboard. It was hidden down low, where you had to lean and look in an improbable place to see it. It wasn't lit. The night was pleasant, so I opened the sliding stern door. I stripped down and climbed into the king size bed. I was asleep in seconds.

When I awoke, it was light out. I hopped into the galley and started a pot of French Roast and went back to the stern and slipped on my swim foot and my faded yellow trunks. I dove in and did six laps to the buoy and back. When I finished, I showered, toweled off, dressed and poured a large mug of coffee. I popped a bagel in the toaster and when it jumped up, I buttered both halves, then slathered it with peanut butter. I carried the bagel and my coffee up top and stretched out on a chaise lounge and watched the lake come alive.

I looked west and thought about the guy we had followed out into the desert. I thought about Annabelle Tortelli and the diamonds. What was that guy doing out in the middle of nowhere? I had no proof he had anything to do with the jewel heist. I wasn't positive that Annabelle's diamond was a part of it. Maybe one of those guys had given her a gift. Odd the diamond was a single stone, not in a piece of jewelry. The guy in the desert was a long shot. I could do a lot of driving and searching and probably for nothing.

And I thought about Blackhawk. While I was doing that my phone activated. I had turned it to mute before going to bed and now it was vibrating. It was Blackhawk. First you think it, then it happens.

"Morning," I said.

"The little bastard kept calling last night until I had to take the phone off the hook," he said with no preliminaries. "So I put it back on this morning and I just talked to him."

"What'd he say?"

"Said if I don't bring the money, they're going kill him. He says they are describing it as a very painful death."

"He expecting you to feel sorry for him?"

"Probably."

"So, what do we do?"

"He whispered he could hear them talking and they talked about a drop site. Said it was at third street and Roosevelt. Said it was a three-story abandoned building. Said it would be a day or so before the drop."

"That means one day at the most. Give them time to set up the ambush. I should be able to find it. I'm going to try to beat them there."

"Stay in touch. What about the diamond guy?"

"Probably a waste of time. He'll have to wait. Give me a couple of hours."

"Talk to you then."

I took the .45 caliber Kahr and a box of shells out of my bedstand. I stuffed them into a small gym bag along with a pair of jeans, a black tee and my lone running shoe. I had my utility foot on with a pair of shorts and a polo shirt. I called for a ride and met the new kid at the pick-up spot. He bounced me up to my parked car. I put the gym bag in the passenger seat and the car cover in the trunk. I drove to my storage unit and picked up two shotguns and a lightweight .22 caliber rifle with a scope and an eighteen-round magazine. It would shoot as fast as you pulled the trigger.

The drop spot was downtown. I found it. It was an old three-story building on a cluttered empty lot in the Roosevelt District. Some of the windows were boarded over. Some were cracked or broken out completely. I drove around it twice; the second time I wandered farther out, looking for vehicles that didn't seem to belong. I saw nothing unusual. It was early and the shops around the area weren't open yet. I had stopped at a 24-hour QT and bought coffee, a gallon of water and several sandwiches. I didn't know how long I would be waiting.

I parked the Mustang in the closest parking garage, which was at the Arizona Center. I stuffed the food in the duffle with the long-guns and ammunition and slung it over my shoulder. Grabbing the gym bag with my left hand, and the coffee with my right, I headed back toward the building. There was no one on the streets. I approached the building from an alley that was blocked by a blank-faced building behind it. I felt pretty certain I didn't have eyes on me.

All this didn't mean no one was there. I cautiously approached one of the broken windows and slid an eye up on a corner. It revealed an empty room. I slowly and carefully worked around to the windows that would reveal the downstairs. All was empty. Not just empty, but dirty and a haven for spider webs. I went back to the alley side and carefully pulled broken glass from one of the windows and hoisted the bags and coffee and then myself inside.

I set the bags aside, pulled the Kahr and jacked a round in, then put it back in my holster. I pulled the automatic shotgun. It held seven shells, which I think was illegal in Arizona, but if I was busted for that, it was the least of my problems. I jacked a shell into the chamber and thumbed the safety on. I began to explore. I was most nervous on the stairs. There was a service elevator but there was no power. I wouldn't have used it anyway. As quietly as humanly possible, I explored all the rooms. What helped was the floors were covered with dust. I was leaving the only footprints. I was alone.

25

I decided to make my nest on the second floor, close to the stairs. If they came to set up an ambush, I would have the higher ground. I sat down against the wall at the top of the stairs but far enough back to not be seen until someone was halfway up the stairs. I sipped the coffee and pulled a sandwich to eat. It was sausage, egg and cheese and better than I expected.

The day dragged on. I had to utilize all my rusty waiting skills to keep from getting antsy. I started putting lists together. My all-time favorite Chicago Bears backfield. Of course, Walter Payton and Gale Sayers. The most entertaining quarterback was a guy named Bobby Douglas. Really before my time, but I'd seen him on film. A big bull of a guy who was better suited to play old-fashioned fullback than quarterback. He would throw the ball as hard as he could, no matter if you were ten yards from him or fifty yards from him. He would throw so hard it would blast through the receiver's hands and smash him in the chest, sometimes knocking him down. I remembered watching a film on Dick Butkus, the middle linebacker. He once said his favorite movie scene was in *Hush Hush, Sweet Charlotte* when the head rolled down the stairs.

My phone buzzed. I had muted it. It was Blackhawk.

"What's up?"

"Quiet here," I said. "Heard anything?"

"Not yet."

"If this is the right spot, they'll come here before they call. They don't want to give you the chance to get ahead of them."

"Unless they are stupid."

"There is that."

"I was talking to Jimmy," he said.

"Yeah?"

"He saw the Jag and asked what happened to it. I told him about our desert excursion."

"That'll all rub out. Just take it to a body shop."

"Yeah, I know. But what I'm telling you is that Jimmy asked where we had gone, and I described it and he said he hunts out there."

"Jimmy hunts?"

"Yeah, I guess so. I never knew it."

"Doesn't seem the type."

"He does have that honking big truck."

"Does he know what might be out there?"

"Says it's wide-open desert. He's hunted deer and javelina but mostly dove and quail."

"So where did that guy go?"

"Jimmy says there are some scattered small ranches. Mostly people wanting to escape the city. Live off grid."

"So, this guy went to one of those."

"I told him about the girl, and the guys she was with. I told him her dad was really worried."

"Yeah?"

"Jimmy suggested that he throw his hunting gear in the truck and go out there and nose around. See if he sees something."

"Does he know about the diamonds?"

"Not much. Said he wanted to scout that area for quail anyway."

"Think he'd be safe?"

"What do you think? You're the one that knows who these guys are."

"Well, not really. I think they think they're tough, but I'm not sure they're dangerous."

"Jimmy's not Black Mamba."

"Yeah. If he goes, tell him not to get too close. Tell him we are looking for a Black Chevy SUV. If he spots it, tell him to note where it is and come back."

I heard a noise downstairs.

"I think they're here," I said.

"Get out of sight," he said. "They'll call me. Wait till I get there."

"Got it." I disconnected and gathered my stuff. I backed away from the stairs.

26

Jimmy found the turn-off Blackhawk had described. He stepped out of his truck and looked around. He left the truck. He climbed into the bed, then up on the cab. He looked all around. He had on camouflage gear with a bright orange hunting vest and hat. He hopped down, pulled himself up into the cab and made the turn. It was dove season, so all this was legitimate.

A few minutes later he found the turn onto the smaller dirt road and he turned onto it. The area was familiar to him, but he hadn't been down this track before. He drove down the overgrown dirt path until he saw the fresh tire tracks turning off. He followed. The road was rough, and he bounced along, trying not to make too much noise. He wondered how the Chevy fared coming down here.

After a few minutes he saw the glint of sunlight on metal up ahead. He pulled off into the desert, winding around creosote and sage. He stopped. He took his binoculars and his shotgun. He stuffed shells into the loops on his vest. He got out and began making his way through the desert, stopping occasionally to listen.

When he got closer and could make out the structure, he put the binoculars on it. It was a water tank. Up on stilts and feeding a metal cattle tank below. He knew that ranchers leased the government land for grazing. He hadn't seen any cows. There were no other buildings. He walked back to the truck and headed toward the tank.

When he got to it, he saw a ladder going up the side of the higher tank. He pulled over and, again, left the truck running. He climbed the ladder and glassed the whole area. He mostly concentrated on further up the road and there saw some buildings in the distance. All he could see were the roofs. No vehicles. He got back into the truck and started forward.

In five minutes, he rounded a curve and could see the buildings. A house made of concrete block, painted off white, and two out-buildings. One had the black Chevy SUV pulled into it. He could see a dark pick-up truck parked at the side. He sat and thought. No harm in being a hunter. He pulled forward and parked beside the truck. He pulled his phone and quickly took pictures of the vehicles. He stepped out of the cab.

"Hello, the house!" he called. "Anybody home?"

No one answered and he started to call again when the door opened. A young man in a striped, button down shirt and dress pants stepped out. A good-looking guy. He was followed by another guy. This one carried more weight than he needed. His face was ruddy and round.

"What do you want?" striped shirt said.

"Sorry to bother you," Jimmy said. "I'm out dove hunting, and I haven't hunted here before. Are there any earthen cattle tanks out here? Someplace the doves would fly to for water?"

Striped shirt looked at the other guy, then back to Jimmy.

"You just passed one."

"Yeah, I know. But it's a metal tank. The water was low and the doves can't get to it. No place to perch."

"What are you shooting?" the burly guy said.

"Remington 870," Jimmy said with an easy smile.

"That's what my Dad used to hunt with," striped shirt said. "Can I look at it?"

Jimmy's alarm bells went off, but he decided it would be better to go along than to refuse. He took the shotgun down from the window rack and handed it to the guy, butt first.

"Any shells in it?" Striped shirt said.

"Not in the chamber."

The guy made a pretense of looking it over. He sighted it, aiming down the road. Then he racked a shell in.

"Hey!" Jimmy said.

The guy pointed the shotgun at Jimmy.

"Keep your hands away from your body." Talking to the other guy he said, "Check him over. Take his wallet and phone. Let's see who he is. Check the truck, too."

The chubby guy went around behind Jimmy and frisked him. Then he pulled his phone and tossed it to the other guy. He lifted Jimmy's wallet. He went through it, dumping stuff on the ground when he was through with it. Jimmy had two twenties and the guy stuffed those into his pocket. He handed Jimmy's driver's license to striped shirt. Holding the shotgun with one hand, striped shirt looked at it, then tossed it on the ground. He dropped the phone to the ground and stomped on it three times.

He looked at the other guy. "Move the Chevy and put his truck in there and shut it up." He waggled the shotgun, "Let's go inside." Jimmy hesitated, then moved through the door.

The inside was sparsely furnished. The room was a combination living area and kitchen. There was a kitchen table with a linoleum top and metal legged chairs.

"Take a seat, James," striped shirt said.

Jimmy sat down.

The guy moved to the stove. "Want some coffee?"

Jimmy looked at the man for a moment, thinking about this. "Sure," he said.

The guy set the shotgun on the sink counter and reaching to behind his back pulled a Star SS .380 pistol. He shifted it to his left hand. He held it casually. Jimmy knew there was little chance of getting to the guy before the guy shot him.

The guy took a coffee cup from the sink and rinsed it one handed. He wiped it off with a dingy dishtowel and filled it from the pot on the stove. He walked it over to Jimmy and set it in front of him. He didn't offer sugar or cream.

Jimmy took the cup and blew across the steaming coffee and took a sip.

"You know I'm just out here hunting," Jimmy said. "I'm no threat to you guys."

Striped shirt hooked a chair and reversing it, straddled it. "James, you are in the wrong place at the wrong time. Enjoy your coffee. I'm going to have to keep you for a while. We will be leaving, so in the meantime, enjoy the coffee.

Jimmy sipped it again. "Coffee's pretty bad," he said.

The guy smiled. "Yeah, he makes lousy coffee."

"You don't look like the kind of guy that would live out here," Jimmy said.

The guy waggled the pistol at him, "Shut up, James."

Chubby came in. Striped shirt said, "Take James into the other room and tie him to a chair. Make sure he's secured."

Chubby came up behind Jimmy and slapped him in the back of the head. Jimmy spilled the coffee.

"Get up," Chubby said. Now he had a pistol in his hand. Jimmy complied. They moved into what turned out to be a bedroom. It had two single beds and they both had been slept in. The guy went to a closet and pulled out a loop of yellow fiber rope, the kind that is used on boats. He waved Jimmy to a straight back chair and efficiently tied him. It hurt. When Jimmy was a kid, he and his brother would take turns tying the other one up, then seeing how long it took to get loose. He had learned to clench his fists and expand his biceps and forearms. The guy jerked the rope so tight, that didn't matter.

The guy left the room, shutting the door and Jimmy waited. When he was confident they weren't coming back in, he began to try to free himself. The rope was rough and tight around his wrists, which were twisted behind him. His legs were tied, individually, to the legs of the chairs. After five minutes of struggle, he was covered in sweat and no closer to being free. He forced himself to rest. He scooted himself closer to the door, hoping to hear the two men talking. He could hear the voices but not the words. At one point he did hear what he thought were the words "the girl," and another time he was sure he heard the name Elliot. He looked around the room, searching for anything that might help him. The place was bare. Jimmy realized the only thing to do was wait. Two hours later Jimmy heard the vehicles driving away. He knew it would be hours, if not days before Blackhawk would find him. He began to try to free himself in earnest.

27

One of the first things I heard was Azeed's voice. He didn't sound very distressed. "Should we search this place?" he said.

"What the hell for?" another voice said. "There ain't nobody here."

Another voice said, "You think he'll come?"

"I'll sell it," Azeed said. "If he don't, or if he don't bring the money, we'll go back to that fucking bar and tear it apart and shoot everyone in it."

"Why don't we just do that now?"

"You don't know my brother."

"Okay, call him."

Azeed said, "When he gets here, you two be in the other room, one on each side of the doorway. I'll be sitting here at the bottom of the stairs. When I start talking to him, you two shoot him."

"What if we accidently shoot you?"

"Don't be a smartass."

"So call him already."

I had checked all the loads on the shotguns, the rifle and my pistol. I had the pistol in my hip holster, one of the shotguns and the .22 rifle lying on the floor, close to hand, and the pump in my hands. Even though I didn't think they could hear me, I kept my mouth wide to silence my breathing. They were quiet. The next time they talked it was muffled. They had moved to another room. I sat thinking about how I would make a move. Then Azeed's tone changed. I realized he was talking to Blackhawk. Pleading. There was a space, then I heard him say, "He's coming."

I settled down to wait. For me to surprise them it would work better if they were preoccupied with Blackhawk. I looked at my watch. I figured it would take Blackhawk a good forty minutes to get here. I wanted to be ready when he walked in the front door and drew the shooters out.

It took more like an hour. While I waited, I thoroughly expected one of them to come upstairs, but they didn't. I finally heard Azeed say, "He's here."

"I thought you said he's smart," one of them said.

"He's my brother. He thinks he's safe."

"Is he?"

"Hell, no. If you don't shoot him, I'll do it myself. Now get out of sight. Don't come out before he's all the way in. I want to make sure he brought the money."

I peeked down the stair. Azeed had seated himself on the bottom step. We all waited. I heard the door open. Azeed stood.

"Where's the money?" Azeed said. He began to speak again but then said, "Who the hell are you?"

I heard Nacho's voice saying, "I'm the Roto Rooter man." From my vantage point I could see his feet as he took a quick step in. Azeed was pulling a pistol from the back of his belt.

Nacho slapped Azeed in the side of the head. Flat on the ear. A hard slap is as good as a hard punch. Azeed fell backwards. I came down the stairs, two at a time. One of the guys, the heavy set one, opened fire but Nacho had already jumped back outside. The guy was anxious. The shots chewed up the top of the doorjamb.

I fired the pump, then pumped it and fired again. Both men fell backwards into the room. As I reached the bottom of the stairs Azeed was struggling to his feet. I rapped his head again with the barrel of the shotgun. He went down again.

I dropped the shotgun and pulled my .45. I fired two quick shots toward the doorway. Then four more, two on each side of the door. One of the guys grunted. There were more shots. They sounded as if they were coming from the back of the house, or even outside. I rushed the doorway. Nacho was right behind me. I dove through the doorway and rolled to my feet. One guy was sitting on the floor, blood oozing from his side. He was pale as a ghost. Nacho reached down and took his pistol. He wasn't the heavy set guy.

I heard glass breaking from the room to my right. Blackhawk's head appeared in the broken glass of the room we were in. I almost shot him.

"He's going out the side on your left," I pointed. I started toward the room when the guy let off a burst and Nacho and I dropped to the floor. There was a three second delay, then another burst, only this one sounded like it was from outside the building. Then I heard Blackhawk's Sig firing. I went through the door and across the room. I could see Blackhawk outside. I scrambled out the window.

By the time I hit the ground, Blackhawk was at the corner of the building. He cautiously peered around it. I came up behind him and he turned to look at me. Just then a burst of rounds started chewing the corner of the building, showering us with shards and splinters. We both ducked, squatting down.

"God, I hate those things," I said.

"Yeah, when you're the one that doesn't have it. What now?"

"Why don't you run to that telephone pole over there and hide behind it, and while he's distracted, I'll shoot him."

He didn't even look at me.

He dropped flat to the ground and slowly peered around the corner.

I said, "An old Indian trick?"

"Old Indians are smart Indians. Smart Indians stay alive." After a second, he said, "He's moving."

I looked around the corner and saw the fat man a half block down the street, moving as fast as his round body could move. I pointed my pistol at him, but it was too far.

"Pow," I said.

Nacho came up behind us. I looked at him. "The guy's gone," he said. "Shot in the back. Went all the way through. Right through his gizzard."

"I didn't know you were versed in anatomy."

Blackhawk stood up and looked at me. "I guess you should've asked him to turn around. Nobody likes a back shooter."

"Would have been the decent thing to do," I agreed. "But I was in a hurry to save your ass. I stepped around the corner and went quickly to the front door. There was still Azeed.

Except there was no Azeed. Azeed was gone. So was the satchel.

I looked at Nacho. "Tell me there was no money in that satchel."

"All of it," Nacho said seriously.

I looked at Blackhawk and he was trying to look very serious. Then they both burst out laughing.

28

Jimmy had managed to bounce himself over to the door. Scooting around, he got one hand on the doorknob. The door was a cheap, hollow, interior door. It had no lock. The two guys had not expected him to be a problem anyway.

It was awkward, but he managed to turn the knob enough to release the latch and he scooted, working to get the door open. Twice he had it open and twice it shut on him. Finally, he had it opened enough to stay open. In a cross between a scoot and a hop he got into the other room.

With great effort he rocked himself over to the sink. He was guessing that the drawer next to the sink had the knives in it. When he finally got there, he found the handle to the drawer was higher than his bound hands. He scooted around to where he was facing it. He tipped forward to try to get his teeth on the handle. He almost tipped too far. He caught himself just before he fell forward. He tried again. This time he got a purchase on it. It didn't want to slide out. It hurt his mouth, but he worked it back and forth as much as he could. It would barely move. He was wearing his jaw out. He took a break, working his jaw back and forth to release the tension. When he was ready, he tried again. This time the drawer slid right out. Not very far, but it slid. He scooted as far back as he could and still reach the drawer handle. He got his teeth on it and pulled. It slid out a few more inches. He repeated that two more times and finally the drawer came out and fell to the floor. Spoons, forks and butter knives scattered all over the floor. There were two paring knives.

He sat for a long time, thinking, stretching his neck to see where the knives were. He rested. Finally, he started rocking, back and forth. When he had enough momentum, he threw his weight to the side and tipped over with a crash. It hurt. He lay there for a moment trying to figure out where the closest paring knife would be. He strained to see it. He started inching his way through the mess of silverware, feeling each piece. It took ten minutes for him to find the paring knife. Once he had it, it was just minutes for him to be free.

He climbed to his feet. He went to the front window and carefully peered out. The black Chevy and the dark pickup were nowhere in sight. He went through the house, looking out the windows. Nothing but desert.

Finally, he slipped out the back door and worked his way around to his truck. All four tires were flat. He looked ruefully at his smashed phone. He picked it up and tried to fit it together. Too far gone. He looked for his shotgun. It was gone. He climbed into the cab and pushed the number six setting button on the radio. A hidden tray dropped open and he took the .380 out. He hadn't been around Blackhawk all this time for nothing. He checked the loads and climbed out. He stood, looking around, listening. He went to the back and gathered his canteen. Then he began to walk.

29

On the way back to El Patron, my mind was occupied with Azeed and what to do about him, but when I pulled up to the rear of the club, Blackhawk was waiting and I could tell he was troubled.

"What's up?" I said as I climbed out of the Mustang.

"Jimmy's not answering his phone."

"Is he supposed to?"

"I told him to call me. I told him to check in."

"What do you get when you call him?"

"It goes straight to voicemail."

"It's turned off."

"Why would it be turned off?"

I shrugged. "Battery could be dead. Any sign of Azeed?"

"Delbert," he said. "No, but if the money's here, he'll show up."

"I don't like the idea of Elena and Marianne here with Az...Delbert and his cronies coming, loaded for bear."

"Not to mention, the customers."

"Let's move the money," I said.

"Where to?"

"Father Correa?"

"Why put him in jeopardy?"

"You're right." I thought about it. "Let's take it to the boat."

"The boat?"

"You remember the hidey hole you couldn't find?"

"Yeah, I still think you're lying."

"I'm not. If you couldn't find it, Delbert sure as hell won't be able to."

"Okay. I'm going to close the bar until Nacho gets here. I don't want Elena behind the bar."

"Your call."

We went in and up the stairs. The safe in Blackhawk's office was sophisticated and substantial, but a pro could get into it. He went to the safe and kneeling, pressed a series of numbers on the keypad. He turned the handle and the door opened. Azeed's satchel was stuffed into the bottom shelf. He pulled it out and opened it. He showed it to me. It was packed with bills stacked together held by rubber bands. He shut the door, sat the bag on his desk and opened a desk drawer. He pulled out a small spray bottle. He sprayed the keypad and wiped it with tissue. The smell of isopropyl alcohol filled the room. Blackhawk is a very cautious guy. The spray erases the oil from his fingers that might linger on the buttons. We have been known to use special lights to highlight the buttons that had been touched.

Downstairs in the saloon he looked at me. "I have to lock this up and tell the other two clubs the main saloon is closed. Pick me up out front."

I went out the back and by the time I pulled around front he was waiting. He had his phone to his ear. He disconnected and put it into his pocket. He slid in, tossing the bag to the back.

"Nacho will come open tonight."

Less than an hour later we were parking in my slot at the top of the hill. The marina wasn't very busy. The wind was up and that was driving boaters and fishermen off the water. Rather than call for a shuttle, Blackhawk and I hoofed it down the hill. He carried the satchel. We stepped on board the *Tiger Lily* and I switched off the warning light. I slid the bow doors open and went through the boat to the back and opened the stern doors to get the cross breeze.

"Okay, show me where the magic hidey hole is," Blackhawk said. I went into the galley and got a box of Ziplocks and a roll of tape. I motioned for him to follow me. I grabbed a flashlight as we went through my stateroom. We went out on the stern. There was an indoor-outdoor rug covering the whole floor. I moved the chair I usually sat in when I fished. I peeled back one third of the carpet to reveal a hatch door. I opened it.

"I found this," Blackhawk said. "But there's nothing down there except your engines and stuff."

I dropped down. "Follow me," I said. He dropped down behind me, bringing the satchel. The area was low, and you had to bend over to make your way. I worked my way toward the bow, with Blackhawk following. Midway through the boat I stopped.

"Look around," I said. "Look for something unusual." I handed him the flashlight. He shined it all around. Then he did it again more slowly.

Finally, he handed me the flashlight back. "You got me," he

said. I shined the light on the wall and reaching up, I pushed the top of it, hard. It came loose and water poured out. You'd have thought I'd poked a hole in the side. But as suddenly as it came it subsided. I brought the wall down and it revealed a space. I reached down into it and brought out a clear waterproof bag. It held wrapped bills.

"This is my cut and run money," I said. Anything ever happens to me, come and get it. I replaced it. I pulled a half dozen gallon Ziplocks, and we began to fill them with Azeed's money. It took eight one-gallon bags to hold all the bills. We put them together and Blackhawk wrapped them with tape. He made it a tight waterproof package. We carefully placed it in the wall and replaced the wall. We climbed back out.

"Where'd the water come from?" Blackhawk said as I replaced the carpeting.

"Just a small natural leak. Once it gets to a certain level it stops."

"Anyone that accidently pushed against that wall would think they're sinking the boat."

"Yeah, cool huh?"

Suddenly a voice came from the bow. "Hullo the Lily!"

We went in and I peered down the hallway. It was Eddie and Pete Dunn.

30

"It's open," I hollered.

They came in. Eddie was carrying a package wrapped in brown butcher paper. Pete was carrying a bottle of Crown Royal.

"Looks like a social visit," I said.

"Yessir," Eddie said. He moved to the galley. Pete set the bottle on the counter.

"You guys know Blackhawk."

"Of course," Pete said. He extended his hand. "Good to see you again."

Blackhawk shook his hand. "My pleasure. Whatcha got, Eddie?"

Eddie started unwrapping the paper. "Just saw you guys coming down the hill. Figured you might want some lunch." He opened the wrapper, disclosing fish fillets. "Saw Pete and invited him along." He looked at me. "You got any oil?"

"In the cabinet," I said. "What do we have?"

"Some crappie and some catfish."

"Catfish?" I grinned. "What? Were you slumming?"

"Not my fault they get on my hook," he said, looking through the cupboard. "You got Bisquick?"

"Under the sink," I said. "You going to make biscuits?"

"Can't eat fish without biscuits."

Pete came around the counter and got four glasses. He poured a dollop into each one. Blackhawk's phone rang.

He pulled it from his pocket and looked at it. He frowned. "Hello," he said tentatively. He listened briefly then said, "Where the hell have you been?" He listened again. A lot longer this time. He looked at me and mouthed the word, *Jimmy*. Eddie moved around the galley and found a cast iron skillet. He poured oil into it. He had brought a bag of seasoned coating. He rinsed the fillets, coated them and set them aside. He put oil in the skillet and began to heat it. I found the box of Bisquick and got a bowl out. Then I got out of his way while I watched Blackhawk.

"You sure you don't want us to come get you?" He listened. "You're sure?" He listened again. "Jackson and I are at the boat. Stop by on your way to town." He disconnected.

"What happened?"

"Jimmy went out to the area where we were. He pulled up to a residence out in the middle of nowhere and two guys put a gun on him and tied him up. They left, he got free and walking out, ran into some hunters and borrowed a phone. The two guys slashed his tires and he's waiting on AAA to come pull him to Discount Tire. He'll stop by here once he gets new tires."

"But he's okay?"

"Says he is."

"Where was he?" Pete said. "And better yet, why was he there? What's going on?"

"You remember the diamond you helped me get appraised?"

Pete nodded. Eddie looked at me.

"There's more to that story I haven't told you."

I told them the story about the diamonds, what Newsome and Cosgrove had told me and about Father Correa and the Tortelli's. They listened with interest.

"Father Correa okay?" Eddie said.

I nodded. "He's a tough old bird."

"Three hundred million?" Eddie said, then cursed as he got popped by the hot oil.

"Probably less but that's what they are reporting."

Pete took a drink. "I don't know why I worry about coming up with a screenplay. All I have to do is listen to you."

Blackhawk looked at me. "Jimmy said he took pictures of their vehicles and the license plates. But they smashed his phone."

"Did he pick up the pieces?" Pete asked.

"I don't know."

"If he did, there's a good chance the photos can be recovered. I've done it."

"You smashed your phone?"

"Not on purpose. Accidently dropped it off the balcony of a hotel five stories up. Hit the

"I'd like to know who the bastards are," I said.

Eddie dropped a pinch of the coating into the skillet. It popped and sizzled. He carefully laid the fillets into the skillet and turned to the biscuits. Only then did he pick up his drink. "Here's to Jimmy and all those like him." He raised his glass. We followed. Might as well get comfortable," Eddie said. "These will take a little bit."

We moved into the main salon and sat. There was a cross-breeze and looking down the length of the boat and out the stern door, I could see whitecaps on the lake.

"Tell me about the diamonds again," Pete said.

I told them how the thieves pulled it off. "Cosgrove, the reporter for the Associated Press identified one of the guys in a picture I took."

"A picture you took?"

"I guess I haven't told you guys everything. Let me back up." I told them about Sonny Tortelli following his daughter to the house in north Glendale and me surprising the guys on the back patio and snapping their picture. I told him about Blackhawk and me going back out there and running into the guy that was one of them and how he led us out into the desert.

"He lost you out there?"

"Not exactly," I said. "We quit chasing him. The sun went down, and It got dark, and we were in Blackhawk's Jag. Not exactly an off-road vehicle."

"Scratched the hell out it," Blackhawk said. "Going to cost me a hundred bucks to get it rubbed out."

"But, he didn't know you were following?"

"No. We noted where he went and came back. I didn't know this but Jimmy hunts there and heard us talking about the area. He offered to go out there and look around."

"What did they do to him?" Pete said, looking at Blackhawk.

"Jimmy took his bird-hunting gear and found a house out where the guy disappeared. He knocked on the door, pretending to be looking for cattle tanks. Birds congregate around water holes. One of them pretended to be interested in his shotgun and picked it up and turned it on Jimmy. They tied him up and after a while, they left. It took him a while to get loose. He was walking out when he came across some hunters. He borrowed a phone and called Triple A, then called me."

"Not the cops?"

Blackhawk smiled, "No, not the cops."

"He's coming here?"

"After he gets new tires. Probably be three hours, maybe more."

"Lunch is ready," Eddie said.

31

It was just over three hours before Jimmy showed up. The tire shop only had three tires that matched, and Jimmy had elected to wait until the fourth tire was delivered. He had paid extra for the quick delivery. By the time he stepped on board, Pete and Eddie had left. I had cleaned the galley since Eddie had done the cooking and now Blackhawk and I were up top waiting on Jimmy with a Dos Equis in hand.

Finally, we saw him coming down the dock. "We're up top," I called as he stepped on board. He went through the boat and up the steps.

"Grab a beer," Blackhawk said. Jimmy turned and went back down. A moment later he returned, beer in hand. He had chosen a Corona. He hooked a deck chair with his foot and pulled it over to us. He still was wearing his hunting clothes. He handed Blackhawk the *Discount Tire* bill.

"You get mistreated?" Blackhawk said, looking at the bill. He didn't blink at it and stuffed it in his pocket.

"Nothing terrible. My brother and I used to play *I can tie you up better than you can tie me up* games when we were kids. We were fascinated by Harry Houdini. No one was a better escape artist than Houdini. I'm not as flexible as I used to be."

"Amen, brother," I said. "They tied you up?"

Jimmy took a long drink. "You guys told me about the girl and her dad, but you didn't tell me they were going to take my shotgun and tie me up. I guess I got too close. Hell, I was just a hunter looking for waterholes."

"Well," Blackhawk said, "to be honest we didn't expect you to make contact." He looked at me. "Some of us didn't think they were dangerous. Tell us what happened." Jimmy shrugged and related the events with a grin.

"You have your phone now?"

He had on cargo pants and from one of the pockets he pulled the ruined phone. "This is all I could find. I don't think I left any out there."

"Who was your buddy that helped us unlock a phone that time?"

"Bill Brown."

"Is he still around?"

"Yeah, I could take it to him and see if he can retrieve the photos."

"Pete Dunn says he dropped his phone from five stories up and they saved his photos."

Movement caught my eye, and I could see Eddie coming down the dock. He looked in a hurry. When he came on board, I was standing on the upper deck on the bow end looking down on him.

"What's up?"

He shielded his eyes looking up. "I was just talking to the kid that runs the shuttle. He says that when young Jimmy there came down the hill, three guys at the top were watching him with binoculars."

"Hold on," I said. I turned and went down the steps. I dug my binoculars out of my stateroom closet. They were a really good pair of Nikons. I went back up and moved to an area where I could see the parking area.

Adjusting them to my eyes I said to Jimmy, "Did you see them?"

"Nope," he said. "But I wasn't looking either. Why would they follow me here?"

I scanned the area. I finally found them. They were under the overhang, in the shadows. Two of them looked like the guys I'd took a picture of on their back patio. I handed the binoculars to Jimmy. He adjusted the focus and stared through them for a long moment.

Finally, he said, "That's the two guys. I don't know the other one."

"It's intentional," Blackhawk said.

I looked at him. "They knew he would get free. They waited for him. They waited while he got new tires. And now they're waiting to follow him again."

"Why would they follow me?" Jimmy said.

"They want to know who you are. They want to know if you were really out there hunting and stopped at their place accidently. Or if you know something they want to know."

"What?"

"The three hundred million-dollar question," I said. "I told you about the diamond heist, right?"

"Not really."

So I repeated what I had just related to Pete and Eddie.

"Maybe you should've told me about that before I went out there," he said, emptying his beer.

Blackhawk shrugged. "Yeah, maybe so. I did tell you to be careful and not to contact anyone."

Jimmy looked up the hill. "Now what?"

"Maybe you could injun up on them. We need to talk to them. Find out why they're following Jimmy," I said.

"What if they don't want to talk to us?" Jimmy said.

"There you go with those racist comments again." Blackhawk said. He looked at Jimmy. "I'll persuade them. They don't know me or Eddie. We'll go palaver with them."

"Palaver?" I said.

"Articulate Indian word."

"I'll go get the skiff," Eddie said. "We'll go around and dock at the public dock then have the kid take us up to where they are. We'll get the drop on them."

"Just like Tonto. I'll be watching," I said. I looked at Eddie. "Go get your skiff."

It was fifteen minutes before Eddie pulled up to the stern of the boat. Blackhawk checked his Sig Sauer then climbed in and off they went. I kept the binoculars on the three guys. Ten minutes later they suddenly turned, walked over to an illegally parked black Chevy and climbed in. They didn't seem to be in a hurry. As Blackhawk and Eddie came into view in the shuttle cart, the Chevy drove away.

"Dammit," I said.

32

I slept late the next morning. I had pulled the blackout curtains so without looking at a clock I had no idea what time it was. I don't keep clocks in my stateroom, unless I have a reason to set an alarm, in which case I can use my phone. I figured if I wanted to know bad enough, I'd get up and look at my phone. As it turned out, it was just before noon.

I set up a pot of coffee, put on my swim foot and dove over the side. I did six quick laps out to the buoy and back. I climbed back aboard and toweled off. Out of habit, I felt my own pulse. I was pleased to find I still had one. I took a fast shower and scrambled six eggs. I took the eggs, half a bagel and a steaming mug of coffee up top. I sat in the shade of the Bimini top that covered the cockpit. The lake was alive with boaters. The marina bar was beginning to fill. I looked at my phone and saw it was Friday. I sat for a while watching the festivities. Every one getting ready for the weekend. I noted that Pete's *Thirteen Episodes* looked buttoned up. There was a pleasant breeze, and the air was warming up.

I was down to the bottom of my mug when I could barely

hear my phone chirping. I had left it in the galley. I would ordinarily ignore it, but I wanted more coffee. I pulled myself up and made my way down the stairs. By the time I got to the phone It had stopped.

I poured the coffee then looked at the phone. I had missed a call from Father Correa. I thumbed the call back option. It was picked up on the fourth ring.

"Hello," said a female voice.

"My name is Jackson," I said. "I missed a call from Father Correa. It came from this number."

"Yes, sir," she said. "Hold on please." It sounded like she had covered the phone with the palm of her hand. I could hear her muffled voice and a male voice in the distant background. After a moment she came back on the line.

"Here he is, sir."

What I heard next was something that sounded like Correa talking with a mouthful of cotton balls. "Jackson?"

"Father Correa. What's going on?"

"I'm sorry. You'll have to bear with me." There were strange noises in the background.

"Where are you?"

There was a long pause, then he said, "I'm at the emergency room at Saint Joe's."

"Are you okay?"

"Yeah, I'm okay."

"What happened?"

Again, the long pause. Finally, "Sonny brought his daughter to Safehouse. They were both very frightened. She looked like she was on something, so I put her in a room to sleep it off.

Sonny told me Annabelle had come to him, very frightened. She told him some men were coming for her. He said he couldn't think of any place else to take her, so he came to me."

"They followed them?"

"Yes. He said at first there was no way for them to follow him, but I no sooner got Annabelle settled in and they came in. They beat us viciously, asking where the girl was. I used to be able to take a pretty good punch, but they knocked me unconscious. When I woke up, they were gone, and the girl was gone. It was all I could do to call 911."

"How about Mr. Tortelli."

"He was still unconscious when the paramedics got there, and I'm told he still is."

"How about the girl?"

"I don't know. That's why I'm calling. The police couldn't find her. Can you look?"

"Where are you again?"

"Emergency room at St. Joseph's."

"It'll take at least forty minutes to get there."

"They're going to release me soon. Why don't you meet me at Safehouse. I've got Shonda watching the place till I get back."

"Shonda? Big scary black woman?"

"That's the one. Has a heart of gold."

"I'll head there."

I had to circle three blocks before I found a place to park. When I went into Safehouse, Father Correa's office door was closed and locked. There was a new windowed hallway door that was closed and locked. There was a doorbell button on the wall next to it. I pressed it. I heard a faint ringing.

A moment later I saw Shonda coming' down the hall toward me. She studied me as she unlocked the door.

"May I help you?"

Educated. Most people would say *can I help you?*

"My name is Jackson. I'm a friend of Father Correa's. The doctor has released him, and I'm supposed to meet him here."

"You look vaguely familiar. He's spoken of you. You can wait in his office."

"I'm wondering if I could see the room the Tortelli girl was in?"

"She's not there."

"So I'm told. I'd like to look at the room."

She shrugged. "Okay by me." She turned and started down the hall. I followed. We didn't have far to go. She unlocked the door to room number 112. She stepped in and held the door while I came in. It had a bed, a vanity with a small television on top. There was an open closet and a throw rug on the floor. The room was small but even so there was a straight back chair at the end of the bed. The room was neat as a pin. There was the faint odor of cigarettes in the air.

"When was the last time the room was cleaned?"

"I haven't had time."

I opened the vanity drawers. "Was there anything in here? Anything you tossed after the girl was gone?"

"She smoked. It is against the rules, but she did it anyway."

I looked at her. She looked just as she had the last time. Like the direct descendant of Shaka Zulu. "You find that odd?"

"They took her. She didn't want to go."

I leaned down and looked under the bed. There was a

cigarette butt there. I picked it up. It had a long ash on it.

"Were you here?"

"No, unfortunately. If I were, they wouldn't have taken her."

I believed her. "Do you still have her cigarettes and lighter somewhere?"

She shook her head. They weren't here.

I looked around again. "I'll wait in his office." She moved out of the way so I could get by.

33

Father Correa came in a half hour later. Just looking at him made me cringe. He was moving gingerly. I got up to help, but Shonda came bursting through the door and took him by the elbow. One eye was bandaged over. There were stitches on his left cheekbone, and the eye you could see was bloodshot and had a terrific, yellow-gray shiner. He tried to smile at me, and I could see his lip was split and he was missing teeth on the left side of his mouth.

Shonda and I helped him to the chair behind his desk. He sat carefully.

"You should still be at the hospital for a couple of days," I said.

"This man is right," Shonda said.

He looked at me with his good eye. "The girls need me here," he said.

"I can take care of things," Shonda said.

He slowly shook his head. "You have a family and a job. You can't stay here 24/7."

She didn't argue. "I'll fix you some tea," she said. She turned and left.

Jackson sat in the only other chair in the small room. "Tell me what happened."

Father Correa took a tissue from a box on his desk and wiped his good eye. "I had no warning," he said. "I was in the back cleaning the laundry room when the bell rang. It was Mr. Tortelli and his daughter. They both looked very frightened. When I let them in, I could tell the girl was high or drunk, I couldn't tell which. I took her back and put her in an empty room to sleep it off. Mr. Tortelli told me she had showed up at his dry-cleaning place and begged him to hide her. He said she said the men she had been with had been involved in a diamond robbery in New York and they were here to sell the diamonds. She said the diamonds turned up missing and they thought she had something to do with it. So she ran away as soon as she had the chance."

"That explains the diamond Mr. Tortelli found in her room."

"Yes."

Shondra came in with a steaming cup of tea and set it in front of him. "Can I get you something?" she said to me.

"No, thank you," I said, and she turned and left.

"Then what?"

"I had no sooner got her in a room and was coming back to the office when they come in."

"They had followed them?"

"Yes. Mr. Tortelli said no one followed them, but they did."

"When did you know they were here?"

"I heard Mr. Tortelli screaming. I know it's hard to talk about a man screaming but that's what he was doing. I rushed back to the office and before I could even react, one of them hit me in the jaw. Knocked my teeth loose. I was so stunned I just went to the ground. Then they beat me in earnest."

"Did you recognize any of them?"

"No. They found Annabelle and draggged her out. One of the other girls called the police. Mr. Tortelli was unconscious. By the time the paramedics got here, I was still so groggy I couldn't think straight. Once they patched me up, I called you."

"How is Mr. Tortelli?"

"He's still in a coma."

"Any ideas on where they would take the girl?"

He looked at me. His eyes were bleak and pained. "Somewhere no one could hear her scream."

I sat looking at him, then past him, then at the floor. Finally, I said, "Do you have the Tortelli's address?" He gave it to me.

"What can I do for you?"

"Find the girl. It seems that is all I ever ask you to do."

"I'll do what I can."

The Tortelli house was rather ordinary. It sat on a corner a few blocks west of Encanto Golf Course, one of the oldest public courses in the city. It was a single-story ranch with a carport and a large backyard. I cruised by it and turned the corner. It had an alley in the back. I went to the next street and went to the end of the block and turned back. I parked next to the alley and pulled the .38 Smith and Wesson from the center console. It had a clipped holster. I clipped it to my belt and pulled my shirt out to cover it. I studied the alley, then started down it.

The Tortelli house had a double RV gate but no evidence there had ever been an RV. The fence was block. I could see over the gate. The backyard was patches of grass interspersed with weeds. It hadn't been mowed for a while. There was a utility shed off to one side. There were no cars in the carport and when I had driven by, there had been none parked anywhere close. I watched the windows that faced the back. They stared back.

In one quick move I went over the fence. I hit the ground running and moved quickly to the house. I flattened myself against the wall. I gently peered through the window. It was the kitchen and it looked like it had exploded. I moved to the next window. It was a bedroom, and it also was in complete disarray. I moved back to the back door. I could see into the dining area and into a part of the front room. There was no one.

The door had a deadbolt on it. I looked around and spotted some fist-sized rocks that ringed a tree well. I gathered one up and went back to the door. Without hesitation I broke the window, reached through and unlocked the door. I pulled the .38 and let myself in. The place was a mess. Someone had gone through it pretty thoroughly. I went through the house quickly, just to reassure myself no one was there. Then I went back to the kitchen and began to look more closely. I didn't have to bother with the drawers and cupboards. They had already been yanked out, the contents scattered on the floor. Sometimes people will hide secrets in the kitchen. Money in the freezer, that kind of thing. Sonny Tortelli didn't strike me as that kind. I looked anyway. Places like the ceiling fan with the housing that covered the wiring. I selected a kitchen knife from the floor and pulled a kitchen chair under the fan. I loosened the screws and pulled the housing down. Empty. I looked at the cupboards to see if one was easier to move than the others. Nothing. I looked inside for new screws. Nothing. Finally satisfied, I moved to another room and started over.

Forty-five minutes later I had been through the whole house. I was standing in Annabelle's bedroom when I noticed something. Looking back from the doorway, I saw part of the wall, in a corner, that was different. I stepped over and looked closer. The walls in the room were not textured. It was plain painted drywall. Except for this one spot. You had to be at an angle, but if you were, you could make out a three- by four-inch spot where someone had cut out a piece of the drywall, then put the cutout piece back in place, taped it, caulked it and repainted. It was a good job, except the tape that held the piece in place had a slightly different texture than the rest of the wall. Looking straight at it, you wouldn't see the difference. Being at the door and at an angle, with the light coming through the window at just the right angle, you could see it. Hardly anyone would notice. Hardly anyone.

I keep a pocketknife clipped to my front pocket. I slipped it out and thumbed the button that snapped it open. I sliced the taped rectangle and pulled it free. In the wall a key was taped to the stud. I pulled it loose and looked at it. There was absolutely nothing on the key that identified what it was to. One step at a time. I decided to go back to El Patron.

34

It began to rain when I left the Tortelli place. It was a light rain, but it was rain. I couldn't remember the last time it rained. At one time the statistics said Phoenix got about 7 inches of rain a year. Lately it seemed it was about half that.

Drivers in Phoenix get a little squirrely when it rains. I pulled into the El Patron lot and saw two guys standing at the front door. There was only one other vehicle in the front lot. Not surprising because the place was closed until later. I parked in the second row and walked up to the two guys. One was Ray, the retired cop Blackhawk had hired as the new guard. I didn't know the other one.

"Mr. Johnson," Ray said to me. "I think Mr. Blackhawk is out right now."

The other guy was watching me. I nodded to him. "That's okay. I left a credit card on the bar last night. I'll just bop in and get it." I reached for the door handle and pulled it open. I started through, then stopped and turned back. "Oh, just one more thing," I said and hit the new guy just below his ear. He fell back against the wall and Ray snapped the back of his head with the sap he carried in his back pocket. The guy was out cold. I looked at Ray.

"They caught me by surprise," he said. "I had just got here when they pulled up. They stepped out with AR-15s and I didn't have a chance."

"Let's get him inside," I said. We dragged the man inside. "Where's Blackhawk?"

"There are three other guys. They are all armed. Blackhawk, Elena, Nacho and Jimmy are upstairs. Don't know if it's the apartment or the office."

"You babysit this guy, I'll go up." He nodded.

"Should I call it in?" he said.

"Not yet," I said.

I moved down the hallway to the double doors that led to the main saloon. I eased the door open. The room was empty. I went up the stairs two at a time. I moved quietly down the hall. I pressed my ear to the apartment door and heard nothing. I moved on down to the office door and listened. I could hear muffled voices. I gripped the doorknob and as the voices intensified, I turned the knob.

When I heard Elena yelp, I went through the door. Azeed had her by the arm. The other two had their guns trained on Blackhawk and Jimmy. Nacho was standing behind the desk. I put the front sight of my Ruger on Azeed. Quick as a rat he moved behind Elena. Everyone had frozen.

"Hold it!" Blackhawk barked. "Nobody do anything." He looked at me. "Delbert wants me to open my safe. I've tried telling him his money is not in there. He doesn't seem to believe me."

Azeed was jittery. The other two guys were not sure what to do. One of the guys had bad meth teeth and freckles. The other was covered in tattoos. He wore jean shorts that were barely high enough to cover his crotch. His calves were a mass of tattoos.

"So show him," I said. Blackhawk shrugged and moved to the safe. While all eyes were on him, I thumbed the infrared sight button on the Ruger. A red dot appeared on Azeed's forehead. Blackhawk blocked the safe keyboard with his body and punched in the key numbers. He slid the door open and stepped out of the way. Azeed let go of Elena and went to the safe. He went through it twice. He turned to Blackhawk.

"Where is it, you son of a bitch." He pointed his rifle at Elena. "Tell me, you bastard, or I shoot her."

"If you twitch, I'll put a hole through your head," I said.

"If he doesn't, I will," Nacho said, his hand coming up from the desk drawer. Blackhawk's Sig Sauer was in it. I smiled at Nacho. Now that's what I call a Mexican standoff.

One of Azeed's guys said nervously, "It's not here. Let's go." The two guys shifted their feet, uncertain what to do.

Azeed looked at Blackhawk, pure hatred in his eyes. He turned and went out the door. The two guys followed him. Elena sat on the couch.

"I can't take this," she said to herself.

"I'll make sure they are gone," I said. I went out and down the stairs. Nacho followed. By the time we got to the front entrance, they were loading the guy Ray had sapped into the back of their SUV. Ray was inside the door, watching. He had a Colt .45 in his hand.

"Everything okay?" he said.

I nodded. "You are going to need more help. As long as that asshole is out there, nobody here is safe."

"I'll see what I can do."

Blackhawk sequestered himself with a distraught Elena in the apartment. Jimmy was setting the bar up and Nacho and I could read the writing on the wall. We went home. Pete Dunn was sitting on the sun deck on top of his boat, except there was no sun. It had stopped raining.

"Time for a drink?" he called to me.

"Let me drop my bag and I'll come back."

"Fix a drink and bring it up."

I waved to acknowledge and went to my boat. I turned the alarm off and dropped my bag inside.

He had a bottle of Crown Royal sitting front and center. I poured a splash over a cube and carried it up. He indicated a chaise lounge and I pulled it over to him.

"Anything new on the diamond thieves?"

"You know Father Correa? The guy I told you about earlier?"

He nodded "Safehouse," he said.

"Yes, the Tortelli girl and her father showed up there. She was scared to death. She said the diamonds disappeared and the thieves thought she stole them. She was worried for her life."

"So what happened?"

"The bad guys showed up and beat the snot out of Father Correa. Broke some of his teeth, blacked his eye and pummeled him black and blue all over. They put Tortelli in a coma and the girl is gone."

"These the same guys we saw up top watching your young friend.?"

"Yeah, I believe so."

"How is he doing, the good Father?"

"Not good." I sipped my drink and looked out toward the lake. I looked back at him and he was watching me.

"What are you going to do about it?"

"Find them and make them pay."

"Let me know how I can help."

Just then we heard someone coming down the dock. They were blocked by the Sundowner next door. When they came into sight, I recognized the two men as the men that had been at El Patron with Azeed. They each carried a duffel large enough for an AR-15.

35

"It just gets better," I said under my breath. We watched them step on board the Tiger Lily.

"I better get over there before they tear the place up. Go get Eddie."

"What am I, chopped liver?"

"You're a writer and an intellect, Eddie was a forty-year Chicago cop. Have him bring his shotgun."

"Jesus, really? Are they the diamond thieves?"

I was hustling down the steps. I had to laugh. "No, this is a different problem."

"You are a busy boy," he said, following.

We stepped onto the dock and he went one way, and I went to the Lily. I could hear them tearing the place apart as I stepped onto the boat. I moved quickly through the sliding door which they had kindly left open and for the second time that day, I put the front sight on somebody. They were in the galley. There were plates and dishes on the floor, some broken. I hit the infrared button on the Ruger and a red dot appeared on the cupboard between them. One of them spun around, causing the other to look.

"Hey guys. How you doin'?"

They had made the mistake of leaning the AR-15s against the counter. Tattoos started to reach for his.

"Touch it and you are dead."

His hand stopped.

"So you are looking for Azeed's money?"

"It doesn't belong to Azeed," Bucky said.

"Who does it belong to?"

"Salvatore Mendez."

"Who's that?"

"He's the boss of Valdez cartel."

"I thought it belonged to Dos Hermanos."

"Valdez says it is theirs."

This was a surprise. I had run across the Valdez cartel a while back when Pete Dunn's boat was known as the *Moneypenny* and was owned by a Dos Hermanos cartel boss.

"I thought it was Dos Hermanos that Azeed ripped off. Now you say it's Valdez."

"Nobody rips off Valdez. Valdez just wants the money."

"You don't work for Azeed?"

"Would you work for Azeed? Azeed is a dipshit."

"So you think I have it here?"

"Azeed does."

"How did you find me?"

"Azeed told us."

"What did he tell you?"

He shrugged. "He said Pleasant Lake Marina and the name of the boat."

I studied them, switching the red dot from one to the other.

Finally I said, "Turn around and put your hands on your head." They glanced at each other, then complied. When they were turned, I stepped forward and picked up the rifles. Without turning my back to them, I moved back to the door and leaned them in a corner.

"Okay, turn around."

They did.

"Here's what I'm going to do. Go ahead and search. Just don't break any more of my stuff. In fact, before you begin searching, I want you to clean up your mess and put a hundred dollars on the counter to pay for what you broke."

"What if we don't have a hundred dollars?"

"Then I will shoot you in the leg."

Tattoo leaned down and began to pick up the broken dishes. Bad teeth hesitated, then pulled a wad of bills and counted off five twenties. He laid them on the counter, then started helping Tattoo.

"There is a broom and dustpan in the closet there. If you are thinking about making a break out the back, know that the hallway is only wide enough for one, so I can shoot one of you. If the other makes it over the rail, I can shoot him while he is in the water. I have two boat anchors stored. They will fit nicely onto your ankles. I'm in eighty feet of water here and I don't mind feeding the fish on the bottom. It makes for better fishing." I heard a noise behind me. I stepped to the side and glanced back. It was Eddie and Pete. Eddie had his shotgun.

I moved out of the way so they could come in.

"What we got here?" Eddie said.

I waggled the pistol. "These boys think I'm hiding a bag of money."

"Damn," Eddie said. "I wish I'd have known that."

Pete said, "If you had a bag of money, you'd have a better boat."

"Says the rich Hollywood guy," Eddie said.

I smiled. "Here's what we're going to do," I said to the two. "I can tell you I don't have the money, but you probably wouldn't believe me. And if I made you leave, you'd probably come back, so, I'm going to let you look for it." I waggled the gun again. "Go ahead. Start looking."

They slowly put their hands down, glancing at each other.

"Wait a minute," Eddie said. He handed Pete the shotgun and moved to the men. He expertly frisked each of them. He looked at me, "Clean," he said.

"Start looking. Do a good job. I don't want Azeed or Valdez to wonder anymore."

They turned and continued going through the cupboards. Much more carefully this time. An hour later they had searched the *Tiger Lily* from the top sun deck down to the engine room. They found nothing. I emptied their weapons, dropping the ammunition into the lake. I handed them back the assault rifles.

"You satisfied I don't have the money?"

"At least not here."

I was beginning to tire of them. "This is a problem between Azeed and Blackhawk. Just one word of warning. You or Valdez fuck with Blackhawk or anyone close to him, the wrath of an angry god will come raining down on you and you will not survive the storm. You may think I'm exaggerating, but I'm not. He is not someone to be trifled with. And he is my friend. Now get the hell out of here."

"Sure thing, boat boy," Tattoos said.

I smacked him in the face with the pistol. He stumbled back and I hit him again. He went down.

"Get him up," I said to Bucky. "Get him and his mouth the hell out of here."

Bucky set his rifle aside and grabbed Tattoos by the arm and dragged him up. As soon as he was steady, Bucky picked up his rifle. He helped him out onto the bow. They stepped off the boat and went down the dock. Tattoos was wobbly.

"Probably should have shot them," Eddie said.

"Hell Eddie, you know that's against the law."

"I forgot. You need anything else?"

I shook my head. "Appreciate the back-up."

He started to turn away, then turned back. "By the way, there's another guy at the top of the hill that spends an awful lot of time looking through his binoculars. He's always looking in your direction."

I looked up the hill. Bad angle. I couldn't see anything. "Thanks for the heads up."

36

"Marianne said yes," I said.

"You expected different?" Blackhawk said, studying the key I was showing him.

Elena came from the other room. "She said yes? Yes to what? She doesn't know you enough to marry you."

Blackhawk started laughing. I could feel my face coloring. "No, no. Just a date. Out to dinner."

"Where at?"

"Wherever she wants."

Elena was hooking on an earring. She went to the mirror on the wall, and tossing her mane of hair to one side, worked with it until she was satisfied.

"Take her someplace nice," she said.

"I will."

She studied herself. Fluffed her hair, then turned and went back into the bedroom. I looked at Blackhawk.

"Any ideas?"

He shook his head, still studying the key. "I don't think it's a locker key."

"Not a bus locker or train locker?"

"I can't say for certain, but it doesn't look like it to me. It looks like a regular house key. Plain and ordinary. Maybe to an ordinary lock." He handed it back to me. I took out my wallet and placed it inside.

"Is Marianne working today?"

He shook his head. "Don't think so."

"She's at Rick's," Elena's voice floated in from the other room.

Blackhawk's eyebrows went up. "Got the ears of a retriever."

"I heard that."

"Guess I'll head down and see where she wants to go tonight."

"Go someplace expensive," he said. "You need a loan?"

I laughed. "If I need any, I'll just raid your brother's stash."

He smiled. "I wish you would and if you call him my brother again, I'll punch you in the mouth."

I held up both palms toward him. "I hear you." I turned. "Tell Elena goodbye."

"Goodbye," her voice came from the bedroom.

I laughed and headed downstairs.

Marianne was sitting at the piano. Sheets of paper were stacked in front of her, and she was chewing on a pencil. She was alone in the room and was so lost in thought that she didn't notice me. I came up behind her and cleared my throat. She turned her head and looked at me.

"Oh, hi."

I leaned against the piano. "Don't let me interrupt."

She smiled. "Give me a minute to finish this."

"Take your time."

She turned back to her paper. A small furrow appeared between her eyes as she thought. Finally, her fingers moved down to the keys and moved gently across them. The notes were bright and yet soft in the large room. She hummed something and then turned to the paper and made a notation.

I studied her. Her face was smooth and compact and had that quality most beautiful women have. Everything was one millimeter toward beautiful rather that one millimeter toward plain. I've always found it interesting how all our faces have basic similarities, but we look so different.

A whisp of blonde hair had worked its way down to hang on her forehead. She chewed on her lip in concentration. She wore very little make-up. She didn't need it. She wore more when performing but her audience was several feet away. I was only four feet away. Her neck was slender and perfectly formed. It looked like Audrey Hepburn's neck. Elegant. She had on a worn and faded yellow pull-over short-sleeve shirt and a pair of jeans that were fashionably torn above and at the knee. Something I never got, but hey, I don't wear them. But any skin that showed was A-OK with me

The tip of her tongue poked out the side of her mouth. I wanted to bite her. She finally sat back and looked at me. Did I mention her eyes? They changed with the light. Tonight, they were bluish green and flecked with gold. They were direct. It was disconcerting.

"Sorry about that," she said.

"Nothing to be sorry about. You're working."

She glanced down at her notes. "You like Sinatra?"

"I play him almost every day."

"What's your favorite Sinatra song?"

"*It Was a Very Good Year*," I said without hesitation.

"You are peeking," she smiled, cocking her head.

"Only at you," I said.

She held my look. Finally, she said, "That's what I'm working on."

"A very good year?"

She nodded. "*When I was seventeen*," she crooned. She stopped.

"Go ahead and sing it."

"Come by and see my show. I sing it most nights."

"That's a date. Speaking of dates. Where would you like to eat tonight."

"I don't care. You pick."

"What kind of food do you like? Seafood? Steaks? Italian or soul food?"

"Soul food in Phoenix?"

"Sure. It's a big city. You'll find anything here. Ethiopian, Russian, Croatian, Portuguese. What I'm thinking is one place I've only been to a couple of times. It's called Chaz's. Chaz is the name of the chef and he only makes two entrées a day. You don't know what you are going to get until you get there."

"You have to pick one of the two?"

"He is an excellent chef and his food, no matter what it is, is delicious."

"Fancy place?"

"Not necessarily. It's in Scottsdale. Home of cowboy chic."

"Is there such a thing?"

"People in Scottsdale think so."

"That sounds good to me. I don't have to wear a cowboy hat?"

"Oh, no. Not at all."

"Sounds fun."

"Done," I smiled.

"Now get out of here so I can finish these arrangements."

"Yes, ma'am."

I started to leave and had almost reached the door when she said, "Wait a minute."

I stopped and turned back to her. She stood from the piano and moved over to me. She took my shoulders and leaned into me and kissed me. I was so shocked it took a nanosecond before I was kissing her back. It was a soft, tender kiss. One you want to last forever. They never do but you sure want them too. She finally pulled away.

"What time tonight?"

"Eight? Your place?"

She smiled, "Sounds good."

"Now you have to tell me where you live."

She did.

37

Chaz's was located on the southeast corner of Scottsdale Road and Shea Blvd. Both roads were lined with businesses, but to park you had to pull into the interior which revealed a large open parking lot. The lot serviced all the businesses that lined all four sides of it. It was the size of a city block. Chaz's entrance faced the interior.

All by itself near the south end, a freestanding building stood. It was empty now. At one time it had been a theater where plays and concerts were held. There is something sad and lonely about buildings that had, at one time, been alive and vivacious and were now empty and alone. Locally it was noted for having had dinner theater. One of those was starring Bob Crane when he was murdered. Crane starred in an old TV show called Hogan's Heroes. I don't think his murder was ever solved. Don't ask me how I know stuff like this. I don't even watch television. I do read a lot.

I picked Marianne up right on the dot. She lived in a fourteen hundred square foot home in the Encanto district. It was known as an historic district and the houses were old and had unique architecture. It was facing south with a small carport on the east side. Her vehicle was parked there. I parked on the street and went to the door. It had a doorbell which was obviously not functional. I rapped on the door. A moment later, she opened the door. She looked gorgeous.

She gathered a small, jeweled clutch and I led her to the Mustang. I held the door for her. She slid in, giving me just a flash of thigh. I went around and climbed in.

"Wow, this is some car," she said.

"I like it a lot," I said.

As I fired it up and pulled away from the curb she said, "I suppose you are a fast-cars, fast- women kind of guy."

"Half right. I like fast cars but I'm too shy for fast women. They scare me."

She laughed. "I'll try to take it easy on you."

"Much obliged."

I hit some traffic and began to worry we might not make our 8:30 reservation. I pulled into the parking area with three minutes to spare. I found a parking spot down two stores from the restaurant. As I went around to open her door, I caught a glimpse of a man down by the ex-theater. A fat man. I stopped and looked at him. It wasn't the same guy. I opened Marianne's door. She slid out.

"Something wrong?"

"No. Not at all. I just thought I saw someone I know, but it wasn't him."

The restaurant on the outside wasn't anything special, but once inside it was very classy. There was a maître d waiting just inside. I gave her my name and she signaled a waiter to lead us to our table. All the wait staff wore starched, crisp white long-sleeve shirts and black pants. Our table was against the far wall, which is exactly where I would have picked. The walls were covered with original art. Many were nudes. They all looked expensive. The kitchen was in the open and was a beehive of activity. The bar was the first thing inside the door where, if we had been early, we could have waited and enjoyed a cocktail.

The waiter held Marianne's seat and told us that Michelle would be waiting on us. The waiter asked if we would like a cocktail or glass of wine while we waited. I did, but I looked at Marianne.

"I like wine," she said, "but I don't know what to order."

The waiter said, "Of course. One of the chef's dishes tonight is osso buco. It's a veal shank braised with vegetables and broth, garnished with gremolata and served with dressed polenta. If you choose that I would recommend a Brunello di Montalcino."

Marianne's eyebrows went up. "Is it good?"

"It's delicious," he said. If he were condescending, I would have punched him, but he seemed very sincere.

"Does that also go with beef?" I asked.

"Oh, yes sir."

"Could you bring a bottle?"

"Yes, sir. Right away, sir."

He moved away and Marianne looked at me. "A bottle?"

"I thought I'd better get enough because I don't think I could pronounce it well enough to order another glass."

She laughed. She looked around the room and watched the kitchen with interest. "I like this place. Which of the cooks is Chaz?"

"He's the one that is giving the orders. And be careful who you are talking to. They are chefs and sous chefs, not cooks."

"Oh heavens. Cooks with egos."

"Egos can be healthy things."

"Do you have an ego?"

"Oh, no. I'm way too humble for that."

She put her hand in her chin. "I can see that."

The waitress brought our wine. "My name is Michelle. I'll be taking care of you today." She deftly opened the bottle of wine. She poured a little in Marianne's glass and handed it to her. Marianne sipped it and nodded her approval. Michelle finished filling Marianne's glass then filled mine. There was half a bottle left. "The two entrées today are osso buco, braised with vegetables and broth and garnished with gremolata and served with dressed polenta. The other entrée is a tenderloin of beef, cooked to your specifications and served with a choice of potato and fresh asparagus. Would you like me to put your order in now or would you like to enjoy your wine and each other for a while?"

I looked at Marianne.

"Let's savor the moment," she said.

"Perfect," Michelle said and moved away.

I raised my glass. She raised hers and gently touched mine.

"Cheers," I said.

"Here's to osso buco," she said. "May it be as good as I've been told." We both took a sip of the wine. It was good. A little more dry than I would have liked, but I couldn't complain. If truth be told, I wouldn't know a really good wine if it hit me in the butt.

I watched her look around the room. She studied all the couples, especially the women.

"Tell me about yourself," I said.

"Not much to tell."

"Where are you from?"

"I was born in San Luis Obispo Hospital, and I was raised in a little town called Carpinteria."

"On the coast?"

"San Luis Obispo is, but my little town is inland a little bit."

"They have a high school there?"

"Probably. We didn't stay long enough for that. We moved around a lot."

"College?"

"Two years at USC."

"Why did you leave?"

"I wanted to be a film maker, so I went to CalArts."

"Disney school."

She nodded.

"Did you make films?"

Her gold flecked eyes came up to me over the rim of her glass. "I fell in what I thought was love with another student. You know, the long-haired type. His hair always seemed to be blowing in the wind. Could talk for days about the European impressionists. Then after a while I realized that was all there was."

"Talk?"

"Yeah. We would sit in a Fellini movie and he would criticize it all the way through. After a while I realized he was just full of crap and wouldn't recognize a good movie if it slapped him."

"What then?"

"I found I could sing so I started doing musical theater. I

ended up in Tempe at Gammage and found another boy. When that ended, I got the job at the Casino, then Elena saw me and offered me a job."

"And here we are."

"And here we are."

"You like it here?"

"I'll let you know."

"Ready to order?"

I looked across the room and caught our waitress's eye. I lifted a finger, and she immediately came over.

"Are we ready to place our order?"

"We are," I said.

Marianne stayed true and ordered the osso buco. I asked for the tenderloin rare to medium rare with baked, dragged through the garden, and the asparagus. As she moved away, I poured more wine into my glass. Marianne wasn't ready yet. As Michelle moved away Marianne said, "What about you?"

"What about me?"

"I know you are an orphan. Do you remember your parents at all?"

"Yes, I have memories. My dad was quiet. I remember he had trouble keeping jobs." I looked down into my drink. "My mom was something else. She was lively. She had blonde hair to her shoulders and a wide smile that took up most of her face. She always had a twinkle in her eye. She would bust out singing and dancing out of nowhere. She would grab me and be singing and twirling me around." I stopped talking. I took another drink to hide the fact that I was getting emotional. It surprised me. I hadn't thought of my mom in a long time. Marianne was watching me. "Tell me more about yourself. You said you met Blackhawk in boot camp. I haven't heard how you were orphaned."

I took another drink of wine and looked toward the front door as it opened. A nice-looking couple came in. "My parents were killed in an automobile accident when I was ten. I had no brothers or sisters. I had some distant cousins that didn't want to take me on, so I ended up in a boy's home in Decatur Illinois. I was there until I graduated from high school. Then I joined the Navy."

"And that's where you met Blackhawk, in boot camp?"

"Not really. At the end of boot camp, I was selected to go through Seal training. When that ended, I was selected to join another group and that's when I met Blackhawk." Now I was self-conscious. I normally didn't talk much about myself. She was easy to talk to.

"What kind of group?"

I looked at her. Her gaze was steady. "If I told you, I'd have to kill you."

She cocked her head at me. I shook my head. "Sorry, that wasn't funny." I took a long drink of wine while I thought out my response. Finally, I said, "It was a special group. It was designed for special covert operations and I truly can't talk about it. We had to sign an oath of silence. There were ten of us. Blackhawk was one of them."

"Blackhawk? I've always thought that was an unusual name."

I was silent for another long moment. "Once we were accepted our old identity disappeared. One of the reasons we were picked was because we were orphans with no family. If you checked, you wouldn't find any records of us in the Navy or in

the Seals. We were assigned code names and Blackhawk was his."
She started to say something, and I shook my head. "No, I don't
know his real name. He doesn't know mine."

"Jackson isn't your real name?"

"It is now."

"I asked Elena and she said Jackson is the only name she's
ever heard you called."

Our food came. I ordered a Wild Turkey on the rocks to have
with my dinner. She was looking at me and I wondered if I had
messed up by telling her too much.

She laughed softly. "You sure look like a Jackson. I'd hate to
find your real name is Elmer."

I did my Elmer Fudd. "Th-th-th-that's all folks. No, not
Elmer," I smiled. "Jackson works for me."

38

They brought our food and we settled down to the business of eating. My beef was just right. Marianne didn't seem to have any problem with her osso buco. After a while I asked her, "How is it?"

"Really good."

They brought my drink and I set it aside. I planned on it being my desert. Finally, Marianne set her fork down and leaned back.

"Wow, I'm stuffed. What is polenta anyway? It's delicious."

"I'm no expert," I said. "But I think it is some sort of cornmeal dish. It can be substituted for potatoes. I like it."

"Yes," she said, "so do I."

Michelle appeared tableside. "Our desserts tonight are crème brulee, red velvet cake and two double chocolate brownies."

Marianne said, "I don't know how I'll do it, but I'll take the crème brulee and a cup of decaf please."

"And you, sir?"

"Nothing for me," I said.

They cleared our dishes and moved away.

"You don't like dessert?"

"It's not that I don't like it, it is just that I don't eat dessert much." I picked up my glass of Wild Turkey and tipped it toward her. "This works for me."

"My grandmother would say you are an alcoholic. But then, if you only had one drink she would say you are an alcoholic."

In my best John Wayne I said, "Waaall judge, I ain't had a drink since breakfast."

Marianne smiled. "Who's that supposed to be?"

I laughed and shook my head. "Someone I'll obviously have to work on."

When Michelle brought Marianne's crème brulee and coffee I asked for the check. She was back in a flash and laid it in front of me. "No hurry," she said.

I picked it up and looked at it. I didn't swallow.

"How much was the wine?" she said.

"I'm not sure you want to know."

"Yes, I do."

I smiled. "58 bucks."

"Oh, wow," she said. "Listen, why don't we go Dutch on this?"

"I won't think of it."

She smiled. "Elena is worried about you. She worries you don't have a job."

"This from a woman who sleeps till noon and sings at night. She won't be happy until I'm nine to five at the post office."

She laughed. "Sounds dreadful." She ate her desert. When she finished, she said, "So, what do you do?"

"In regard to what?"

"Making money. Paying your bills? Paying for this."

"I have savings, and I get a small pension because I lost my foot."

"So you don't work?"

"I'm a boat bum."

She was studying me over her coffee cup. "Yeah, that's what Elena says."

39

It was two thirty in the morning before I pulled into my parking spot. After leaving the restaurant we had sat in front of her place, talking. She told me it was too soon to invite me in. I could live with that. We talked for a very long time, then she begged off because she had a rehearsal the next morning. I did get a kiss. It was a long drive home.

I stepped on board, checked the alarm, and stripped down. I thought about taking a swim but decided against it, so I climbed into the king-sized bed and immediately fell asleep. I hadn't pulled the blackout curtains, so I was awakened by sunlight streaming in. I pulled the pillow over my head and went back to sleep. When I woke again, I had a thin veneer of sweat. I felt good.

I swung my legs over the edge of the bed and hopped into the oversized shower stall. I let the water beat down on me until I ran out of hot water. I shaved, brushed my teeth, brushed my hair back and got dressed. I found myself humming some fatuous tune. I had the key I had found still in my wallet. I pulled it out and studied it. Could have matched any Master Lock anywhere.

I decided to go to the marina bar for breakfast. I slipped on my utility foot, put the key in my pocket and stepped out into the sunshine.

Eddie's skiff was tied to his old River Runner, but he was nowhere in sight. I found him manning the grill in the bar. There were a half dozen customers in the place. The garage door- styled windows were wide open and a pleasant breeze wafted through the large room. The windows were so large and so much air was moved, the place didn't have the normal tired beer, fried food and booze odor that most bars have.

There were quite a few empty stools along the bar. Most of the people chose to sit at the tables by the windows. I picked a stool at the bar and slid up on it. A girl named Sherry was behind the bar. I could see Eddie through the large open window to the kitchen. Sherry came down to stand in front of me.

"Hey Jackson. What can I get you?"

"The breakfast menu please."

"Anything to drink?"

"Tall tomato juice please."

She reached under the bar and pulled a menu and placed it in front of me. She moved to the kitchen window and spoke to Eddie. He looked at me and saluted me with two fingers to his cap. A minute later, Sherry brought the juice. I ordered an ordinary eggs, bacon and hash brown breakfast. I swiveled around and watched the people. Boat people are fun to watch. You have two kinds. The serious boatowner; he or she, is usually brown as a nut and has a no-nonsense air about them. The twice a year boaters have a giddy smile and want to talk with everybody. I tried to avoid those.

Sherry brought my breakfast. "Ketchup, Chalupa?"

I shook my head.

"I haven't seen you around much lately," she said.

"You're busy," I said. "I haven't stopped in for a drink lately."

"I get off at ten," she smiled.

"Good to know. If I'm here I'll come buy you a drink."

"I'd like that," she smiled, and moved away.

A few minutes later, as I finished my eggs, Eddie came out. He untied his apron and sat on the stool next to me. Sherry automatically brought him a Pabst Blue Ribbon long neck.

"How's the diamond caper?"

I reached into my pocket and pulled the key. "I broke into the girl's, Annabelle's, house and found this key hidden in her bedroom wall."

He took the key and studied it. "Yale," he said. "Padlock."

"How do you know?"

He shrugged. "Educated guess. I was a cop, you know."

I smiled. "Yes, I know." I finished my breakfast and moved the dishes away from me to signify I was finished.

"How're Father Correa and Mr. Tortelli?" he said drinking his PBR.

"Beat up and sore. Tortelli finally came out of his coma. The girl's gone."

"Isn't that your specialty?"

"What?"

"Finding lost girls?"

"Very funny."

Eddie finished his beer and slid off the stool. "So, what is your day looking like? I'm going up to the mouth of the river. I think the crappie are schooling up there. Want to go?"

Before I could answer my phone chirped.

I thumbed it on. "This is Jackson."

It was Father Correa. "Jackson, it's Father Correa."

"How are you feeling?"

"Recovering. I've got a beauty of a shiner and a split lip. I haven't looked like this since my boxing days."

"You were a boxer?"

"Golden Gloves, a lifetime ago. I called to tell you that Mr. Tortelli is conscious. I think he could answer some questions."

"Probably."

"You'd have to be gentle. Every time someone mentions Annabelle he starts to cry. He's taking this hard. He blames himself."

"Are you at the hospital?"

"I can be."

"I'll head that way."

40

I lied at the front desk and told them I was Mr. Tortelli's nephew.
They had no way to check without bothering the patient, so they gave
me directions and waved me up. Father Correa was in the room when
I got there. He was right. He had a beauty of a shiner. His other eye
didn't look that great either. His teeth were still missing.

Tortelli laid with his eyes closed and tubes in his nose. His
breathing was heavier than normal.

"He's sleeping?" I said softly.

Tortelli opened his eyes. "I'm awake," he said.

I looked at Father Correa. I shook my head. "You sure you
are okay?"

"I have an appointment next week for my teeth. In the
meantime, I'm on an emergency diet. It won't hurt me." He
started to grin, then grimaced.

I looked at Tortelli. His face was misshapen where he had
been beaten. His eyes were bloodshot and moist.

"Mr. Tortelli, I'm sorry to bother you." I looked at Father
Correa. "Has anyone heard anything about Annabelle?"

Tortelli squeezed his eyes shut and tears ran down his cheeks.

Father Correa shook his head.

"I hate to be the one to bring this up," I said. "But I've been thinking of something ever since your assistant showed me the room Annabelle was in when the men came for her."

"What about it?" Correa said.

"It wasn't very far down the hall. Annabelle smoked. I found a cigarette butt under her bed. It had barely been smoked."

"Yes, I hated that she smoked."

"But, there were no cigarettes or lighter, or matches in the room. I've been wondering if it was possible that she heard the commotion when they came in looking for her, and they started beating on you two. If she heard, maybe she ran. There's a back way out of Safehouse, isn't there?"

"Maybe they didn't take her," Tortelli said.

"I'm not trying to give you false hope, but maybe they didn't," I said. "If she ran and she was a smoker, she would have taken her cigarettes with her. If they took her, I doubt anyone would be thinking about cigarettes."

Father Correa was looking at me. "You may be right there, but maybe they did."

"Maybe they did," I said. I turned to Tortelli. "Did Annabelle have any close friends? Girlfriends? Someone she hung out with. Someone she might contact?"

"Not since school. She spent all her time with her boyfriend."

"You know his name?"

"She wouldn't talk about him. I thought maybe things were changing when she came home. But I guess not."

"Do you remember the names of any of the girls she was friends with?"

174

He turned his eyes toward the window. Finally, he said, "No, I can't remember. There was one girl that she would go ice skating with. I think her name was Emily." He looked back at me. "But I'm not sure."

"Ice skating? In Phoenix?"

"Sure," Father Correa said. "Lots of northerners here."

"Every Friday night they would go to the Skateland Ice Rink," Tortelli said. "When she got older and interested in boys, she quit skating."

"What school did she and Emily go to?"

"I'm not positive the name was Emily. It could have been something else. It was a community college. I couldn't afford a university. The school was Paradise Valley Community."

"How long has it been since she went there?"

He thought about it. "Three years, at least." He looked stricken. "You think she escaped?"

"No way to know right now. There wasn't any blood in her room. The cigarettes were gone. We can only hope so."

40

Paradise Valley Community College was a sprawling college located on several acres at the corner of 32nd Street and Union Hills Boulevard. The parking lot was huge. I circled it until I found a *you are here* map. It showed me where the library was. I parked as close as I could get and went inside. There was a scattering of students. The place was pretty large. In the middle of the room there was an information desk. A young woman stood behind it, looking at a computer.

She looked up as I approached. "May I help you?"

"I wonder if you have yearbooks. I'm interested in three years ago." She pointed toward the back of the room.

"They'll be back against the back wall, about halfway up."

I nodded my thanks and went to where she had indicated. I found the yearbooks and selected the one from three years back. I carried it to an empty table. I quickly found Annabelle's photo. There were three Emilys in her class. Of course, the ice skater could have been in the class behind or ahead. I had brought a notepad and a pen with me. I listed the Emilys then looked at the year behind her. Her class was bracketed by a class behind and a class ahead all in the same book. There was one Emily there. I looked in the year ahead of her. Only one Emily there also.

I drove back to the boat. I intended to go watch Marianne perform tonight, so I wanted to get cleaned up. I also hoped Pete Dunn was in residence. He was.

He was sitting on his stern, reading. I stepped on board and rapped on his glass sliding door. I could see through the boat and watched his head appear as he peered through the sliding stern doors. He came to let me in, setting his book on the galley counter. He slid the doors open and stepped back to let me in.

"Eddie said I just missed you this morning."

"I had to go into town. Do you have wifi? Better yet are you on FaceBook?"

"Yeah, but I don't get on it very much. Mostly because my ex-students are on it. They are always putting their work up and expect me to comment. Why?"

"The girl with the diamond has disappeared. She may be running. I've got the names of girls named Emily that she may have been friends with. One in particular she went ice skating with. It's a long shot but Annabelle may have gone to her for help."

Pete stepped over to a table that had a monitor on it. He reached down and turned the computer on. "You have last names?"

It took him ten minutes to find the ice skater. According to her information on FaceBook, her address was on Onyx Blvd. and there was a photo she had put up wearing one of those cute little skirts the ice skaters wear. Thank God young people want the whole world to know all about their lives. Annabelle, on the other hand, didn't have anything at all on hers.

Pete looked at me. "It looks like Annabelle wasn't much of a Facebook girl."

I wrote Emily's address down and stood up. "I'm going to watch Marianne tonight. You're welcome to join me."

"I have a date," Pete said with a grin.

"A date?"

"She's a realtor. Seems like a great gal."

"Bring her around sometime. I'd like to meet her."

"We'll see how it goes," he said.

I found Onyx Blvd. south of Shea Blvd, off of the SR51. Emily's house was small and neat. The neighborhood was older. There was an architectural style that ran through the neighborhood. I pulled to the curb. I walked up and knocked on the door. A small dog began yipping inside. After a minute the door opened just enough to let me see one eye and a small slice of a face.

"Emily Schrimpsher?"

"Y-yes," she said tentatively.

"I'm looking for a friend of yours. Annabelle Tortelli."

"Annie? Is Annie in trouble?"

"We don't know. She seems to have disappeared and her father Is very worried about her."

The dog was a little ball of fluff and was going berserk. "Hold on a minute," Emily said. "I'll put Koko in the other room." She closed the door. The dog stopped barking. A minute later she was back. She opened the door, wider than before. She was pretty, but her hair hadn't been washed lately. She had the slightly grimy, pudgy look of someone who had quit caring.

Someone who rarely left the house. She wore a soiled tee shirt with obviously, no bra. She had on a very short pair of cut-offs. Her feet were bare and dirty.

"I haven't seen Annie in two years. Ever since she started hooking up with that guy," she said through the screen door.

"Do you know the guy's name?"

"Rick the prick," she said.

"You don't like him?"

"He was a prick, but you couldn't tell Annie that."

"You haven't seen her lately?"

"No. I tried to tell her the guy was a loser and it pissed her off. She shut me down. I didn't want to be around the jerk. And since she always was, we stopped seeing each other."

"I hear you guys used to go ice skating together."

"She went a couple of times. I even loaned her some old skates. I never got them back."

I pulled a business card from my wallet. It had been there for a while and was frayed around the edges. It had the El Patron bar phone as my number

"If you see her, please give me a call. I understand you guys used to go to Skateland Ice Rink?"

She nodded. "I haven't been in a while."

"I appreciate your time."

She opened the door wider and smiled. "Would you like to come in for a beer?"

I looked at her. She wet her lips and gave me a look she had learned from bad television but hadn't practiced enough in the mirror. No amount of practice could make it what she thought it was.

"Boy, I'd really like to, but I have another appointment."

Her face changed. "Go to hell," she said and shut the door. Forcefully.

41

I was early for the show, but the place was jammed. I had to tell the pretty girl at the door I had no reservation. She looked very disappointed in me. All the wait staff, except the bartender, were young college-aged pretty girls. They were all dressed in tuxedo shirts and short, black, satin shorts. I told her I'd get a drink at the bar and stand in the back. I said, "If there is any way you can get a word to Marianne? Can you tell her that Jackson is here?"

Her eyebrows went up. "You're Jackson."

I grimaced. "Maybe I should have picked another name."

She waved a waitress over to her. "Go tell Marianne that Jackson is here."

The girl looked at me with a grin. "You're Jackson?"

Right then I was kinda wishing I wasn't. "I'll be at the bar," I said to the pretty maître d.

I could feel their eyes on me as I wound through the crowd to the bar. As a long-time employee of Blackhawk's, the bartender recognized me. His name was Lem. He came over as soon as I caught his eye. "Mister Jackson," he said. "Long time no see. Scotch on the rocks?"

"Boodles on the rocks, with a twist."

"Coming right up, sir."

I turned with my elbows on the bar and studied the crowd. Mostly millennials. An occasional table with four, but mostly couples. Lem set the drink on the bar atop a napkin. I turned and picked it up. "Can I run a tab?"

He smiled at me. "On the house," he said.

"Well thank you, Lem."

"Don't thank me. You can thank Mr. Blackhawk. Standing orders."

I toasted him by raising my glass. I took a sip. Always good. There was a sudden commotion toward the front. There had been a small amount of floor left open for dancing. Four cute waiters asked four customers to stand so they could rearrange the table. They did it expertly, giving the customers as good a seat as they had before. They did this to accommodate another small table. They sat two chairs on either side.

The waitress that had gone back to tell Marianne I was here was back and came over to me.

"Mr. Jackson, your table is ready," she smiled.

Surprised, I followed her to the table. She held my chair as I sat.

"Compliments of Marianne," she said with a twinkle. "Savannah will be providing your service tonight. Would you like another drink?"

"No thanks."

I looked at my watch. It would be a while before the show started. I knew that when Elena had the place remodeled, she had a full-service room with bathroom, dressing mirrors and a couch installed. I figured Marianne was resting. I was wrong.

I noticed a stir of the people between me and the front door. They were looking past me. I turned and Marianne was coming from the back. She was dressed in a red sequined dress slit up to mid-thigh, with white gloves that almost went to her elbows. She had on stilettos. Her hair was perfect. Blond and soft looking. Her lips glistened with lip gloss and she was looking at me.

I got to my feet.

"I've only got a few minutes," she said as I seated her. "Thought I'd come out and say hi."

"I am so glad you did." I glanced around. Everyone was looking at us. Actually, looking at her. "I feel like a celebrity."

She laughed. "I could change and walk through that door and no one would notice."

"So that's why Cher dresses like she does."

She laughed again. "She does like attention. It's part of the job."

"Do you like the attention?"

She laughed, shaking her head. "Not a bit. I'm actually quite shy."

"Take lessons from Elena."

"Oh my God. Isn't she something?"

"She eats the audience up."

"And vice versa."

Marianne's band consisted of a drummer, a piano player and an upright bass player. They came wandering out. They noodled around, playing a little jazz to warm up.

We both watched them for a few minutes. "Who's your band?" I said.

"Joseph, Enrico and Charlie. Joseph on piano, Enrico on bass and Charlie on drums. They are guys I knew from the casino. They are very good."

"They'd have to be."

"What's that mean?"

"If they weren't good enough, Elena would give them the boot."

"True enough." She stood. "I need to go relax. I usually sit in a quiet spot and meditate for fifteen minutes before a performance."

I stood. "Go then. Get relaxed."

She turned and went to the back. I signaled Savannah. I held up my glass and she nodded and moved to the bar. While I waited, I surveyed the crowd. Every table was taken. Two men came in the front door and moved to the maître d station. They were dressed as if they had just come off the golf course. It was too late for that so more likely than not they had just come from the nineteenth hole. I could tell the maître d was explaining she would have to put them on a waiting list. This irritated one of them and his voice rose above the crowd noise. He was middle-aged. Stocky and florid. He looked as if he might have been a handful at one time but it since had gone to belly. He looked half juiced. He was an inch away from belligerent.

I didn't see the signal but the girl that had seated me turned and went out the door. She came right back followed by Ray, the ex-cop Blackhawk had hired to be the bouncer. He came up behind the two guys. The one guy had worked himself up, and now his voice dominated the room. Ray came up quickly. He put a hand on the man's arm to get his attention. The man turned and shoved him. Ray's heel caught on the edge of the station and he went backwards, his arms windmilling.

I was behind the loudmouth in two steps. As he moved forward, looking as if he was going to kick Ray, I kicked the back of his knee and his leg buckled. He went down on one knee. I turned to the other guy and he held a palm out, discretion being the better part of valor. The loudmouth was trying to stand but I had kicked him pretty hard. Ray had regained his balance. He grabbed the loudmouth by the collar and jerked him up. He marched the guy out. His buddy followed, looking sheepish. The crowd began to applaud.

A few minutes later Marianne came out looking like a million dollars and swung right into *Fly Me to the Moon*. She followed that up with *The Lady is a Tramp*, then kept her promise and sang *It Was a Very Good Year*. She was marvelous. Elena got you feeling rowdy. Marianne got you feeling seduced. At least I did. I noticed that most of the guys in the room felt the same.

Marianne was halfway through her version of a Beyonce tune. I knew that because she introduced it. Savannah came to me and leaned down.

"Ray would like to see you outside," she said, just loud enough to be heard.

"Hold my table," I said, downing the remainder of my drink.

Ray was standing outside the front door, facing the parking lot. Two men were standing there beside him. One of them was Emelio Garza.

42

The last time I saw Garza he was bringing me money for doing his boss a favor.

"These guys want a word with you," Ray said. "They insisted that you come out here. You okay with that?"

I nodded. I looked at Garza. I didn't know the other guy. Garza nodded to me, then looked at Ray.

"I can take it from here," I said.

"I'll be close," Ray said. He stepped back inside.

"Long time no see," I said.

"Emil sends his regards," Garza said.

Emil was one of the most dangerous men I'd ever known. He wasn't Blackhawk but he was close. I'd met Emil when I was looking for the granddaughter of His Excellency Jaime Soto Armado Revera the Consulate General of Columbia. His attaché was Santiago Escalona and Emil was Escalona's muscle. They were all connected, in some way, to the Valdez cartel. Emil had helped me with a couple of problems in the past. I had been lucky and returned the girl to her grandfather. At the same time, Blackhawk and I had recovered a large sum of money stolen from

Valdez by a dipshit relative of Elena's and that, and the return of the girl, made them extremely grateful. We could have turned the money over to the authorities but who wants to be looking over their shoulder the rest of their lives? The Italians would call Garza a *capo* in the organization. He had command of a lot of foot soldiers. He was second in command to the one they called *El Jefe*.

"How is my friend Emil?"

"Usually bored," Garza said.

"Are you here on his behalf, or is it just you?"

"No, just me."

I glanced at the other guy. He had taken a step back and was watching the street. "How can I help you?"

"I'm here because Blackhawk's brother has something we want."

I bit my lip to stop from saying Azeed wasn't Blackhawk's brother. "Why don't you talk to Blackhawk about it?"

He smiled. "You are easier to talk with. The last thing we want is trouble with Blackhawk."

I shrugged. "I haven't seen Azeed since he stopped in here a while ago."

"He sold Dos Hemanos fake drugs and took the money."

"Pretty stupid."

"Yeah, pretty stupid. We have Azeed. With persuasion he told us he gave the money to Blackhawk."

"Did he tell you that he and a couple of his goons came here with AR-15s and forced Blackhawk to open his safe? Did he tell you the money wasn't there?"

He looked at me. "Yeah, he told us that, but I didn't believe

Azeed could force Blackhawk to open the safe."

"You're right. But there wasn't anything in it, so why not."

"Maybe he hid it somewhere else."

"That, you'll have to ask him."

"I'm asking you."

I looked at him for a moment. "Someone putting it on you to get the money back?"

He looked out across the parking lot, then back to me. "Saza went to prison. He did something stupid. Now Salvatore Mendez is the new boss. He wants the money. Mostly just to piss Dos Hermanos off. We have Azeed. Something really bad could happen to him if Mendez doesn't get the money."

"Tell that to Blackhawk."

"I have to get the money back or I clip Azeed. Mendez may not stop with him. I'm just asking for your help."

"Are you threatening Blackhawk?"

"I'm just relaying information. Nobody wants this to escalate."

"Where's Azeed now?"

"I can give you the address, but you won't get more out of him than we did."

"Probably not. Is Emil getting twisted by this?"

He smiled. It was a wan smile. He shook his head, "Nobody twists Emil. Not even Mendez."

"Give me the address where I can find Azeed."

"You have something to write on?"

"Just tell it to me. I'll remember." He told me the address. I looked at him. "It would probably be best if Azeed ended up in an alley with a hole in his head."

"That won't stop Mendez from looking for the money." He stared at me for a long moment, then nodded his head toward the parking lot and turned and walked away. His guy followed. I stood and watched them walk to a dark SUV. Emilio's guy turned to look at me before he slid into the vehicle. I shot him with my thumb and forefinger.

43

I went back inside. Ray nodded as I went past him. I peered into Rick's. Marianne was on a break, so I went down the hall and into the main salon. Blackhawk wasn't in the bar, so I went upstairs two at a time. I found him in his office.

I went in without knocking. He had papers scattered across his desk. He looked up.

"I hate taxes," he said.

"Yeah. Listen, you remember Emilio Garza?"

He looked at me frowning. "Yeah. Emil's guy."

"That's the one. He just showed up looking for me. He says Valdez wants the money Azeed gave to you."

"Delbert," he said. He swung around and looked at the array of monitors behind him. He fiddled with his laptop and the monitor that showed the outside front door suddenly began to feed backwards. When it reached Garza standing there, he kept it going until I came out. There was no sound. When Garza and Garza's man and I were in the frame he froze it. He leaned forward and studied the picture. After a minute he looked at me.

"I don't know the other guy."

"Me neither. What do you want to do?"

"Nothing."

"Nothing?"

He shrugged. "You want to give him the money?"

"Not particularly."

"Me neither, but I'm not sure of keeping it either."

I started toward the door. "Your call."

"Where are you going?"

"Back down to watch Marianne finish her set."

He smiled. "Good idea. Elena is watching you two very closely."

"Someone should," I said, sounding more confident than I felt. I left the room and headed back downstairs.

Marianne was in the middle of a Trisha Yearwood song, *The Song Remembers When*. My table was as I had left it. I sat down and Savannah came and asked if I wanted another. I ordered a ginger ale. If possible, Marianne looked even better.

She finished the night with *One for My Baby*. She left the stage to thunderous applause. A few minutes later she came back out. She was in shorts and a flowered blouse. She had scrubbed off her stage make-up. She sat next to me.

I leaned toward her. "You are very good."

"Thank you." She smiled. Savannah brought a cup of coffee and set it in front of her.

I looked at it. She smiled and said "Decaf." She blew across the top then took a tentative sip. Most of the crowd began to file out. Several of them stopped and complimented Marianne. She met them all with a brilliant smile and a thank you. When they thinned out, the band had left and the staff called it a night, leaving only the bartender and one waitress.

She looked at me. "I'm going to head home. Would you like to join me for a nightcap?"

I smiled at her. "I'd be a fool not to."

She was driving a yellow VW bug and I followed her to her place. Once inside she said, "I'm going to shower, can I fix you a drink for while you wait?"

"Scotch, if you have it."

She turned some music on. She went to the kitchen and looked under the sink and pulled out a half bottle of Johnny Walker Black. "This okay?"

"Perfect," I said. I took the bottle from her hand. "I'll fix my drink, you go shower."

"Be right back," she said.

A moment later the water pipes in the kitchen began to hum, which told me she had started the shower. I found ice cubes in a tray in the top freezer of her refrigerator. It was an older model and didn't have an ice maker.

The living room was small, but very tasteful. Small but elegant paintings were on the walls. There was a fireplace with family photos on the mantel. An old photo of an older couple, a young woman and the same woman, older now, with two children and what presumably was a husband in uniform. The woman looked much like Marianne.

I went to the sofa and made myself comfortable. The music was some nice gentle jazz. I relaxed. Ten minutes later she came out. Her hair was damp and pulled straight back. The remaining make-up had been scrubbed off. She wore a soft woolen shirt with the sleeves rolled up. She had put on a pair of corduroy shorts. Elena had said once that a sure sign a woman is comfortable with you is if she is around you with no makeup.

She said, "You look comfortable."

"I am," I said.

"I'm going to get a glass of wine and join you."

"If I knew what you wanted, I would have gotten it for you."

"You don't know where it is."

"True that."

A moment later she was back with a half glass of white wine. She sat on the couch with me, curling her feet under. She raised her glass. "Cheers." I clinked my glass against hers. We both drank. She smelled like a cross between a high mountain breeze and a lilac. I almost whinnied. Or at least pawed the ground.

"The music okay?"

"Just right," I said. We sat in comfortable silence for a moment. For something to say, I said, "Blackhawk says Elena is keeping an eye on us."

Marianne was looking at me. Not just looking toward me but really looking at me. "I hope not right now."

"Not right now?"

She set her glass on the coffee table and slid over. She put both her arms around my neck. Her face was just a couple of inches away from mine. It was definitely lilacs. She leaned in and kissed me. It wasn't one of those wild passionate movie kisses but rather a heart thumping, soft, sweet and soul-wrenching kiss. A kiss to remember. It went on for quite a while. I opened my eyes to find her staring at me. She broke off. She never took her eyes off of mine. She began to unbutton her shirt. She leaned in and kissed me again; this time it was the passionate big screen kiss. With her weight against me I couldn't paw the ground, but I was sure I did whinny.

44

I'm usually an early riser. Saloon entertainers work late and sleep late. I gathered my clothes, all of them since I was naked, and tiptoed into the living room. I quietly dressed, then found a piece of paper and a pen and wrote her a note saying I would call her later. I left my number.

I was driving away when I noticed the red SUV tailing me. I drove out of Marianne's neighborhood, trying to be nonchalant and appear unaware. I wanted them to follow. They did. I wondered if they had been there all night. I wasn't expecting to spend the night, I don't know why they would have.

They were pretty good. I headed north then turned east on Thomas. When I reached Central Ave. I turned north and led them to Dunlap. I turned west on Dunlap and they followed. I turned north on Nineteenth Ave. and they had to run a light to keep up. When I got to Bell Road I waited until the last minute, then slid into the right hand lane and turned right. I knew there was a Fry's grocery ahead and I gunned for it. When I reached it, I turned into the giant parking lot and the guys were way behind and out of sight. I circled the lot and positioned myself at a gas pump, ready to come back out behind them when they went past. That's what I did. A minute later they went ripping by and I pulled out behind them. They went east all the way to State Route 51 then they turned south on it. I hung back far enough that they couldn't recognize me. I followed all the way to the I-10 junction, and I followed them onto I-10. I goosed it to catch up. If I was going to lose them, this is where it would be.

Sure enough, as soon as I jockeyed through the five lanes of packed traffic, they had gained some distance on me and I could see them ahead pulling off onto the Seventh Street exit. By the time I got to the exit it was loaded with cars. I was about tenth in line. By the time I made the turn I had no idea where they had gone. I drove with traffic and began to laugh out loud. I didn't even know who they were. They could have been Azeed and his guys. They could have been Garza's Valdez guys, or they could have been the diamond thieves. I was multi-tasking. I went through a McDonald's drive through and got coffee and three breakfast sandwiches. I pulled to the side of the parking lot and sipped the coffee and munched the sandwiches and thought about what the hell to do next.

I had Detective First Grade Boyce on my favorites list in my speed call. I hit the button and it started ringing. She answered on the third ring.

"What do you want?"

Hey, she still had me in her phone.

"I need a favor. Don't hang up," I said hurriedly.

"Why would I hang up? I have all day to hang around waiting to do you favors."

"I'm being followed, and I don't think it's an admirer. I've got a license number and I'm hoping you could track it down for me."

"You bet your ass it's not an admirer. You don't have any."

I grinned. She hadn't hung up by now. I had a chance. I rattled off the license number and the make and model of the car. Honda Pilot, license ADL45987. Now she hung up.

I finished the sandwiches and got out and tossed the garbage in the can. I reached into my pocket and pulled the key I had found at Annabelle's place. I thought about it. I got into the Mustang and drove to Tempe.

My magic phone gave me the address and directions to Skateland. I found it on a side street west of the SR60 off of Country Club. It was a brick building standing alone behind a large parking lot. There was a smattering of cars in the lot. The bricks had been in their original rusty red state at one time, but someone had painted them white. It was time to paint again. The front sported a two-story swoosh also painted white and also needing a repaint. It was outlined with light bulbs. The original owners had thought they could bring a little Vegas to the scene. In the daylight, it was hard to tell how many lights actually worked. Finding parking wasn't hard so I parked near the front door. The door opened into a foyer with long benches on either side. I presumed it was for skaters to sit and put their skates on. Or off. There was a double glass door on the other side of the foyer. I pushed through it. To the right was a long desk with racks of rental skates. There was a bored teenage girl behind the desk, by the cash register. On the left was a snack bar, unattended at this time of day. There was a handful of skaters gliding round and round. Toward the back of the ice was a group of children getting lessons from another teenager.

Off to the side were two doors spaced fifteen feet apart. One was labeled MEN, the other WOMEN. I walked by the bored teenager, who didn't look up from her phone. I went into the women's locker room.

I called out, "inspector."

No one was in the room. There were five stalls but mostly there were benches and three-foot-high lockers. Another door led to a shower room. Some of the locker doors hung open. A few had padlocks. I pulled the key and started down the row trying each padlock. The fifth one opened. Inside was a dilapidated gym bag. The kind I had in high school. I pulled it out and sat on a bench with the bag beside me. I stared at it. Old ice skates or a fortune in diamonds? Open the door and find the lady or the tiger.

The bag had two cracked faux leather handles with a zipper that ran across the top. The zipper was old and difficult. I got it opened. I stared at the Ziplock baggies of glitter. Diamonds of all sizes. I lifted the bag out and held it up to the light. It was magical. I replaced the baggie inside the bag and opened it to show the diamonds. I pulled my phone and took several pictures. I zipped up the bag. I sat there and thought. I already had Blackhawk's money in my hidey hole. Who would think to look for the diamonds here? Annabelle? She had to have been the one that placed them here. Who else could it be? I went through a mental list of places I could stash the diamonds. None worked. I looked at the lock in my hand. It was about as ordinary looking as was possible. I stood up and studied the other locks that were on the lockers. Mostly like mine. I took the bag and went out and then into the men's room. I put the bag in a locker and locked it with my padlock. I memorized the locker number.

My phone rang. I didn't recognize the number.

"Jackson," I said.

"Captain Newsome," his gruff voice said into my ear. "Thought you might want to know we found a dead girl in a dumpster on Polk Street. She had your card on her. I'm heading that way, but I'm pretty sure it is Annabelle Tortelli."

"Give me the address," I said.

45

Captain Newsome had been given slightly erroneous information. The girl's body wasn't in a dumpster. It was off to the side of the dumpster, leaning against a wall. The dumpster was in an alley behind some block buildings that housed businesses that had been there for decades. The alley was littered with an occasional plastic grocery bag, fast food wrappers and cups, with tufts of scrubby jimson weed and mallow. The only use for the alley was for the garbage truck, once a week.

When I pulled in, I had to park a half block from the activity. There were two patrol cars with lights flashing, a plain clothes car, which turned out to be Captain Newsome's, and a firetruck, sitting large and ominous, blocking the alley. They had covered the body with a tarp.

As I walked up, one of the patrolmen stepped toward me. Newsome waved him off. I went to the body and lifted the tarp. It was Annabelle. I studied her for a long moment. Newsome came over to stand beside me. "That her?"

I nodded. "Annabelle Tortelli. Hooked up with the diamond thieves we talked about."

"You sure about that?"

"Unfortunately, yes. I told you about her father finding the diamond. He owns a dry-cleaning shop on Third street."

"We know that." He was looking at the girl. "Still has the tourniquet and the needle in her arm. Waiting on the ME but looks like overdose."

"No bruises, no contusions." I looked up at him. "No signs of struggle." I lifted her hand and studied her fingers. "No broken nails. No flesh under the nails, in fact they look damned good for a corpse." I noticed something lying against her. I looked at Newsome. "You have a pen or pencil?" He reached into his coat and pulled out a ballpoint. He handed it to me. I slid it inside the empty baggy that was wedged under her hip. I handed it up to Newsome. He studied it, then smelled it. He held it to the light.

"What do you think?" I said.

"Looks like bath salts but it isn't. There's a little bit left in the corner of the bag," he said indicating the bottom of the bag. "Crystalized. It's flakka."

"Flakka?"

He handed me the bag. "Look at the residue stuck in the corner of the bag. See how it's kinda pinkish?"

I looked at it and nodded. I covered her up with the tarp.

"Deadly shit," he said.

"*Crap*," I thought. Her dad's going to be devastated.

Behind Newsome another car pulled in. Detective Boyce stepped out. She walked up to us. She didn't look at me. She nodded to Newsome. "Captain," she said.

She knelt and gently took the tarp away from Annabelle's face. She studied her. She took a pair of surgeon's gloves from her jacket pocket and pulled them on. She pulled the tarp down to the girl's waist and picked up one wrist after the other, studying her hands and arms. She turned Annabelle's face from one side to the other. She stood up and looked at Newsome.

"Not gangs," she said. She finally looked at me. "What are you doing here?"

"I knew her. She had a card of mine on her."

She smiled. It wasn't like a *that was funny smile*, more like a *are you shitting me* smile. "A card? Like a business card? What does it say? Boat bum and all round dipshit?"

"Pretty much," I said. As usual, she could irritate me within seconds.

She looked at Newsome. "Young, pretty and clean. What's she doing here?"

"No other tracks on her arms. I'm guessing this was her first time, at least with a needle. You and I both know this area is notorious for hard drugs. But I think she OD'd somewhere else, and somebody dumped her here."

"Well, she's all yours." She turned to me and said, "I've got that license plate run. When I get back, I'll try to remember to text the name and address to you. Until then, ta-ta." She turned and walked to her car.

"That's a hard woman," I said more to myself than anyone else.

"Hell of a detective, though," Newsome said. "I get the impression you aren't one of her favorite people."

"Yeah," I said, watching her drive away. I looked at Annabelle. What a waste. I went to the Mustang and started it. I sat for a minute, thinking. Hard work for me. I drove away. Two blocks later I saw the red SUV on my tail.

46

I was already aggravated by Boyce. The red SUV didn't help. "If that's the way you want it," I said out loud. Everything in modern vehicles is computerized. I connected to the audio system and asked my magic phone to call Blackhawk. He has caller ID. He picked up on the second ring.

"Yeah," he said.

"You remember the guys that stole the diamonds?"

"The ones that held Jimmy?"

"The very same."

"What about them?"

"They're beginning to annoy me." I told him about being followed early in the morning and again now.

"Where were you that early in the morning?"

"Not important," I said. "You know that house downtown that Azeed tried to…" "Delbert," he interrupted. "Yea, Delbert. That place. Anyway, get Nacho and you guys bring two cars down there and I'll lead them to us."

"And beat on them till they cry wee-wee-wee all the way home."

"That's the idea."

"I'll bring Jimmy. A little payback never hurts."

"Head that way. I'll call when I have them where I want them." He disconnected.

I didn't want them to know I'd spotted them, so I drove as normally as possible back toward downtown. I came off SR51 onto I-10 and took the Seventh Street exit. A little déjà vu for them. This is where they had lost me, but I didn't want to lose them. It took some doing, but I didn't. They followed me south on Seventh. When I turned west on Van Buren I called Blackhawk.

"I'll pull into the driveway of the house. If they pull to the curb, you and Nacho block them in."

"If they don't stop?" Blackhawk said.

"Follow them."

"Roger that," he said.

"How far away are you?"

"Damn near there."

I made sure to miss the next light. I could see the red SUV two cars behind me. I made the turn by the Arizona Center, then turned again into the neighborhood where the house was. The house was as we had left it, bullet holes and all. I pulled into the driveway. A moment later the red SUV pulled past and parked at the curb. A moment later, Jimmy's truck and Nacho's Jeep went by. When they reached the red Pilot, Jimmy suddenly pulled his truck across their bow. Blackhawk and Nacho pulled in behind. I got out and ran toward them, my Kahr in my hand.

By the time I got there, Blackhawk was standing in the road covering the driver. Nacho had a sawed-off shotgun pointed at the passenger.

As I reached the Pilot, Jimmy was leaning down, looking into the vehicle. "Howdy boys," he said.

"Same guys?" I said.

He nodded and grinned, "The driver is."

I leaned down and looked at them. Both guys had been on the back porch with Annabelle.

I looked across at Blackhawk. "Get them out here." He reached down and opened the driver's door. He had his Sig Sauer in his hand.

"You heard him. Everybody out." The guy in the passenger seat was a little overweight and losing his hair. He looked like the guy Captain Newsome thought was O'Malley, the inside man. The driver was, I guessed, Rick the prick. He looked young and slick enough to attract a young girl like Annabelle.

The two men reluctantly climbed out. "Put your hands on the roof." They complied. Blackhawk frisked the driver while Nacho did the passenger. They both found pistols.

"Eject the magazines and throw them on the floor in the back."

They both released the magazines and jacked out the rounds in the chamber. They threw the guns, magazines and bullets onto the floor in the back.

"Give me their wallets." Jimmy pulled the passenger's wallet. Rick the Prick didn't have one. He had no ID at all. The passenger had a driver's license. He was O'Malley.

"Let's get off the street," I said. "Bring them back to the house. Jimmy, move your truck so it isn't blocking the street." I turned to the two men. "Put your hands in your pockets. We are going to the house where I'm parked."

Jimmy headed to his truck and the rest of us walked back to the house. Once inside I told Nacho to go up the stairs and sit on the landing. I had the two men go halfway up the stairs and sit down. I made them do it without taking their hands out of their pockets. It was awkward but they managed to do it.

Once we were all set, I looked at each man. "Tell me how the girl died," I said.

They looked surprised. "What girl?"

"Annabelle," I said.

They looked at each other. Rick the prick said, "We didn't know she died. She got away from us. We've been looking for her."

"You know what flakka is?"

They both shook their heads.

"She OD'd on it. They found her body in an alley this morning."

"She was Elliot's girl," Rick said.

"Who's Elliot?"

"He was on the back patio of the house out north. He was sitting there with us."

I remembered him. He's the one that talked to me.

"Was she in on the heist?"

"What heist?"

I pointed my gun at him. "Don't piss me off."

"She didn't have anything to do with it," O'Malley said.

"Shut up," Rick the Prick said.

"You lost your diamonds," I said.

Now I had their attention. "Where was the girl found?" Rick said.

"Don't be stupid. You know where the girl was found because you dumped her there. Otherwise, why would you be in the neighborhood. I saw you. When I started driving you followed me. Why are you following me?"

They were silent for a while. Finally, O'Malley looked at Rick and said, "I told you Elliot trusted the girl too much."

"She had no diamonds with her," I said.

Rick was looking at me hard. We did that for a while. Finally, he said, "You know about the diamonds?"

"Yes, I do."

He looked at me longer. He was thinking. God help them if he was the brains of the outfit. "You know where they are." It wasn't a question.

"Yep."

"Easy to say," O'Malley said.

I pulled my phone and dialed up the pictures I'd taken of the open gym bag. I held it in front of them. They stared at it.

"What are you going to do now?" Rick finally said.

I smiled. "This is a lot of diamonds. Worth a lot of money. You guys have a buyer lined up. I wouldn't know the first thing as to where to find a buyer. So I figured we'll sell the diamonds to you."

"How much you want?"

"I want half of what you were going to get."

The taller guy thought about that. "We need to talk to Elliot."

I pulled a card out of my pocket and held it toward him. He took his hand out of his pocket and took the card. "Talk to Elliot and call me with a figure. Now, get out of here."

They stood up awkwardly, O'Malley almost losing his

balance. I waggled the Kahr toward the front door, and they went out.

As we watched them get into their car and drive away, Nacho looked at me. "You have a business card?"

I nodded.

"What does it say?"

"Jackson. Boat bum and all round dipshit. Then the El Patron number."

"Sounds right," Blackhawk said.

47

Marianne had picked a good day. Because she worked Saturday nights, she took Sunday and Mondays off. Today was Monday and the sun was shining, the sky had big fluffy clouds, but not too many of them. The temperature was going to be in the upper seventies. We had been talking and she began to ask me about the boat and the marina and what it was like to live on the water. I invited her out for a boat ride and a picnic.

She was an hour late, so while I waited, I prepared a basket of goodies, a cooler of beer, water and soft drinks. I walked them over to *Swoop*, my twenty year-old, twenty-foot Grumman Sport Deck. It took two trips. On my second trip I realized I should have just run *Swoop* over and tied off *Tiger Lily's* stern. I hadn't thought of it because I had a beautiful blonde on my mind. I wiped *Swoop* down. I checked the fuel and oil and fired it up. It had been sitting for a while. While I was letting it idle, Eddie came chugging up in his fifteen-foot skiff. He pulled over when he saw me.

He bumped the rubber bumper on the dock and cut the motor.

"Ahoy the *Swoop*," he said.

"Ahoy yourself."

"You gettin' ready to go out."

"Gotta date," I said.

"Whooee. Be sure and let Maureen know."

"Why would Maureen care?" Maureen was the marina manager.

"We were having an after-work beer and she mentioned she was worried about you. A young virile guy living alone on a boat."

"Virile?"

"Her word, not mine."

"Where are you headed?"

"I'm going to start by the dam, then work the cove north of Scorpion Bay."

"Good luck to you. Maybe we can get out later in the week."

"Anytime," he said, shoving off from the dock.

I turned my motor off and climbed out and folded the canvas cover. I put it in the large Tupperware tote I had bolted to the dock. I put the padlock in place. There was a time when none of us had locked anything, but the world was changing.

I was up top reading when I saw the new shuttle kid drop Marianne at my dock. She was wearing a two-piece swimsuit with a large, flowered scarf knotted around her waist. She carried a large straw bag. I was standing on the bow end of the sundeck. As she came through the gate, she saw me and waved. I waved back. I went down and met her on the bow.

She took my hand and I helped her on board. She looked as fresh as the morning light. I escorted her into the salon. She set her bag on the bar. She turned to me and put her face up. I kissed her, then I did it again. She looked around.

"I'm sorry I'm late. I got a late start, then I drove right by the marina road and was halfway to Wickenburg before I realized it."

"They don't give much warning that the turn is coming up."

"Well, show me your fabled boat."

"Fabled?"

"Fabled to all at the El Patron."

"I think we should start our day with a light cocktail. I took the liberty of making a small shaker of whiskey sours."

"What is a whiskey sour. Will it make me pucker?"

I took the shaker out of the locker and shook it then poured the drinks in a tall glass with ice and a lime twist. "See what you think."

She took the glass and sipped it. "Oh wow," she said. "This is delicious."

"Good."

"Now give me the tour."

I swept my hand, indicating the room. "This is called the main salon, and this," I said pointing, "is the galley."

She smiled. "Not the living room and the kitchen."

"Oh no. Boats are special, and everything has a special name. For instance," I nodded toward the bow, "that isn't the front of the boat, it is the bow."

"And the back is the stern?"

"Now don't ruin it for me. I'm having too much fun educating the poor little small-town girl."

She laughed. "How do you know I'm a small-town girl."

"You told me."

"Oh I did, didn't I." She nodded toward the controls. "That's where you drive the boat?"

"That makes me the captain. The captain is all-powerful on a boat."

"I'll keep that in mind. Show me some more."

"Okay," I said. "Bring your drink."

"I never leave home without it."

"Down here on the main deck I have the salon, the galley, a small stateroom, a closet and the master stateroom with a closet and a full bath."

"Staterooms are bedrooms."

"Only to land lubbers. Follow me."

I led her down the hall. "This is my stateroom," I said. "I did remember to make my bed this morning."

She looked at the king-sized bed. "Is the captain still all-powerful in here?"

"Here more than anyplace. Here is the head and my shower."

"Big bed, and big shower. Why do they call it a head?"

"Are you sure you want to know?"

"Probably not."

"Good choice." I opened the sliding door to the stern deck. "I spend a lot of time out here fishing and reading. Let's go up to the sun deck."

I followed her up. Watching the muscles in her rear as she climbed, I had to behave myself.

I showed her the cockpit and showed her how I could drive the boat from up here. "I'd like to take us on a boat ride in my runabout. I've made a picnic lunch. When we come back, maybe we can sit up here at the cocktail hour and watch the sun go down."

"Sounds lovely."

I went to the bow and said, "Come here. I'll show you my neighbors." She came up and put her arm around me.

I pointed. "That Sunliner down there belongs to Pete Dunn. He's a writer. Made his money in television. He lives there full time unless he's in California on a project."

I pointed across the marina. "That River Runner is where old Eddie lives."

"The River Runner is the old beat up one?"

"Correct."

"Old Eddie?"

"Same thing. Him and the dog Diesel. Eddie is a retired cop from Chicago. He's the marina handyman. He sometimes works at the bar or the gift shop."

She looked. Then looked all around. "Mr. Dunn's boat looks fancier than yours and yours is a whole bunch fancier that Mr. Eddie's."

"Eddie lives a simple life."

"He keeps a dog on that boat?"

"Oh no. The dog doesn't belong to him. The dog doesn't belong to anyone. He usually sleeps on Eddie's boat or on the dock out front of it. Maureen, the marina manager lets the dog stay because it keeps ducks and geese off the docks. They make a terrible mess. Ready for a boat ride?"

"You bet your whiskey sour."

48

We were lucky. Usually, the wind is up by this time of day. Today it wasn't. I took us on a wide sweep of the lake. The beautiful day made up for the fact that the shoreline was brown rock and dirt with occasional desert plants. Not green and lush like eastern lakes, but beautiful in its own right. Marianne sat on the back bench just behind me trailing a hand in the water. Occasionally she would twist around and look at something across the lake. We reached the upper part, where the eagles were nesting, and boats were forbidden. I swung around and went slowly past the Castle Creek area. I spotted Eddie in a cove and pointed him out to Marianne.

On the opposite side of the lake, about a mile straight across from the marina, was a manmade sand beach with ramada tops and picnic tables. At a gentle speed, I headed down past the Lake Patrol building and turned toward the beach.

Because it was Monday there weren't many people on the beach. In good weather, over the weekends the place would be packed. Low priced entertainment for families. I headed for the north end of the beach. Lake Patrol usually kept the beach free of boats when it was busy, but I didn't think they would bother me today. Not unless Barney Fife was on patrol. Every force had a Barney.

I nudged *Swoop* into the sand shore. I stepped off the bow. I grabbed the fifteen-pound anchor and walked it up and buried its flanges into the sand. Marianne waited at the bow until I reached a hand up and helped her off. I climbed up and toted the cooler down, then the basket.

There were ramadas about fifty yards off. She picked up the basket.

"Do you want to grab a ramada, or stay by the water in the sand?"

"It's such a nice day, I don't think it would hurt me to get a little sun. We can build sandcastles here."

"Good idea."

I went back up on the boat and pulled a beach blanket from a locker. She had selected a spot a few feet up and had set the basket down. I carried the blanket and the cooler up to her. She helped me spread the blanket.

I reached into the basket and pulled out a tube of SunSport sunscreen. "Good idea," she said. She sat down on the blanket on her knees. "Would you do my back?"

I squatted down beside her, taking the lid from the tube. "I'll do any part of you that you want."

"Don't be naughty," she laughed.

While I applied the sunscreen, she was watching a group of young men down the beach, working out. They had two large tractor tires that they would heave up and flip over. They had a bench and weights and a couple of them were running sprints to the water and back in the sand. Running in sand is not easy.

I finished with the sunscreen. She rubbed some on my back. When she finished, I pulled two long-neck Dos Equis' from the cooler and popped the tops. We toasted, then leaned back and watched the young guys working out.

After a while she said, "Who do you think they are?"

I pointed back up the grade. "Behind that last ramada. What do you see?"

She shaded her eyes and squinted to where I was pointing. "Oh, I see. A firetruck. They're firemen. Are they off duty?"

"Probably not. They have their radio. If they get a call they'll be out of here in seconds."

She turned to look out over the water. "Not very busy today."

"Monday," I said.

She turned her attention to my foot. I had the waterproof utility foot on. She said, "I knew about that but I never notice it."

"Long pants," I said. I smiled at her. "There was a time the other night you should have noticed."

"I was busy. Does it bother you?"

"Before we leave, I'll have to take it off and rinse it. The sand gets in and irritates my stump. Does it bother you?"

"No, not at all. Tell me again how you lost it?"

"In high school I worked summers in a processing plant. I lost it in an industrial accident. I still get a small disability check every month."

"Can't be enough to make up for the loss of your foot."

"I get around okay."

"Yeah, I noticed."

"Hungry yet?"

"You bet."

While we were eating our lunch, the firefighters got a call and packed it up and were gone in a flash. When we finished and cleaned up Marianne asked if we were going swimming..

"Too cold," I said. "Water's only 65 degrees. You'll freeze your tush off."

"How do you know?"

"I checked before we left."

"Well, what do you want to do?"

I looked at her, holding her gaze until she turned pink. "No way," she said. "Not out here."

"How about a nap then?"

"Sounds good." I lay back and she snuggled into my arm. The sun was warm but not hot. There was a gentle breeze, and the waves made a hypnotic sound on the shoreline. I closed my eyes and dozed off.

I felt Marianne sit up. "Jackson," she said softly.

I opened my eyes and sat up. I looked to where she was looking. Down the shore where the firefighters had been, were three men. They were swarthy men with short, full beards and unkempt hair. They were wearing gray work pants, long sleeved shirts and sandals. They each carried a quart bottle of Colt 45 malt liquor. I saw that the bottles were almost empty. They were looking at us, grinning. They were making comments to entertain each other but I couldn't hear what was said.

"Let's go," Marianne said.

"It's okay. They won't bother us." As they drew closer, I casually stood. I dug into the cooler and pulled another Dos

Equis. I popped the cap and took a swig. Then I turned and looked at them again. By now they were just a couple of dozen feet from us. I waited for them to open the dance.

They were obviously drunk. They were occupied with Marianne. She stood to stand beside me. She seemed composed. Good for her.

"Hey, amigo," one of them said. "Maybe, hey, you give us your beer."

"And the woman," the one on the right said, laughing.

"You can have the beer," I said.

I leaned over and pulled another Dos Equis from the ice. I flipped it to the one that wanted the beer. I made sure it fell short into the sand.

"Hey," the guy said, leaning over to retrieve it. I kicked him in the face. Before the other two could react, I swung around and popped the one with the smartass mouth in the jaw with the base of my beer bottle. He went down like a sack of potatoes. When I turned to the third guy, he was already running toward the parking lot.

Marianne was standing with her hand on her mouth, her eyes wide. I leaned down and retrieved the beer bottle from the sand. I wiped it off on the blanket. I looked at her. "Waste not, want not. You ready to go?"

She picked up the basket and climbed into the boat. I followed with the cooler. I got the anchor while both guys were sitting up rubbing their booboos. I pushed off *Swoop*, jumped aboard and fired her up. I backed us out and swung around.

Marianne was sitting staring out at the lake. Finally, she said, "You didn't even seem scared."

"I was busy."

"They could have had guns or knives."

"They didn't."

"What if they had?"

"I'd have handled it differently."

She was quiet. Softly she said, "handled it," almost like she was talking to herself.

49

By the time we docked the Grumman the wind had come up. Not enough to be a nuisance at the marina but it would make it harder on the water. It was a good time to come in. I had pulled up to the stern of *Tiger Lily* and dropped the cooler and basket. I had offered for Marianne to stay at the Lily while I buttoned down *Swoop*, but she chose to ride along.

While I retrieved the canvas cover, Marianne wiped down the interior with a hand towel I keep in the locker. I snapped on the cover and we walked back to *Tiger Lily*. *Thirteen Episodes* was unbuttoned but I didn't see Pete anywhere. I had to use the head; the beer had gone through me. While I was in there, I took my foot off and rinsed my stump and the prosthetic. When I came out, the first thing I noticed was Marianne's swimsuit lying on the floor. I stepped into the master stateroom and Marianne was lying on the king-sized bed, naked as an egg. She was watching me.

I held up the prosthetic. "You mind if I leave this off?"

"As long as everything else is operational."

We spent a long, slow, sweet hour.

Later, she wanted a shower, so we showered together. This led to another long languid half hour after which we ended up on the sundeck, me with a Boodles martini, her with a Grey Goose cosmopolitan. We watched the fading sun marry the far mountains. As it reached the mountain tops it seemed to elongate, looking for all the world like a flattening red egg. As soon as it was gone, the air turned cool. I had finished my drink and had gone down for another while Marianne had plowed through half of hers, one small sip at a time. I noticed the goosebumps on her arms.

"Let's go down," I said as I came back up. She nodded and stood.

In the stateroom she looked at me. "I didn't bring a change of clothes," she said.

"Let me see what I might have." There was a storage bin built under the bed. I pulled it out and she rummaged through the clothes that had been left behind by various guests. Several months ago I had hosted a house party that had lasted well into the night. Elena had invited several of her girlfriends and there had been a handful of women's clothing that had been left behind. They had all been cleaned. She found a faded pair of red shorts that fit. She pulled them on over her bikini bottoms. She couldn't find a blouse, so I gave her a black tee of mine. It was way too big, but she rolled the sleeves up, tied a knot at the waist and looked cute as hell.

The sun was down now. Marianne said, "I hate to say this, but I'm getting hungry."

"I have some frozen fish fillets and some frozen lima beans and potatoes."

"That sounds like a lot of work. I don't want to put you out."

"Let's go down to the bar. They serve food."

"That sounds easier."

The bar was almost empty. As luck would have it, Eddie was behind the bar. Without many customers, the room looked large and empty. I guided Marianne through the back door and into the bar.

"Table or bar?" I said.

"Bar's fine."

I went halfway down and held her stool as she slipped onto it. Eddie came from the back, sporting a clean shirt and work pants, his face scrubbed, and his hair slicked back and still damp.

"Hey, there," he said. "Who's the young lady?"

"Marianne, this is my good friend Eddie; Eddie, this beautiful and talented lady is Marianne."

"I like this place already," Marianne said.

"What can I get you two?"

"You want a cosmo or something else?"

"I'd like a vodka martini."

"What kind of vodka?"

"Ketel One please."

"I'll take a Bombay Sapphire on the rocks with a twist."

"Lemon?"

"Yep."

"Coming right up."

He fixed the drinks and set them on coasters in front of us. "Are you hungry?"

Marianne lifted her drink and sipped it. "Starving," she said. "Even though this is Monday, not Friday, I've declared tonight all you can eat fish fry night."

"You had a good day."

"We saw you while you were fishing," Marianne said.

"Caught more than I can store, so I have them on ice just hoping you would come in to eat them. I serve them with hush puppies, cole slaw and steak fries. I have fillets of stripers, some crappie and catfish."

"Yum," she said. "I'm in."

"Make it two," I said.

"Great," Eddie said. "I'll be right back."

We watched him go into the kitchen and strap on his apron.

"He likes you," Marianne said.

"It's mutual. I met him my first month here. I had just bought the *Tiger Lily* and I had to overhaul her bottom."

"Sounds racy."

I laughed. "It was summertime, so it was hot, dirty work. I hired Eddie to help me. He's in his seventies but he works harder that any twenty-year-old."

We sat and enjoyed the quiet time between us. In a few minutes, Eddie brought us plates heaped with fish and fries. The hush puppies were nestled in with the fries. The coleslaw was in a separate bowl. He sat the platters in front of us. "Another drink?"

"Be a fool not to."

"How about you, missy?"

Marianne said, "My lips are getting numb, but I can't resist your charms."

"No one can," I said.

We dug into the food like two ravenous wolves. When he set

the drinks up Marianne said, "Jackson says you have known each other since he first came here."

"That be true. Did he tell you how he cleared my nephew of a murder charge and saved a little girl from a murderous gang of jackals?"

Marianne turned and looked at me. "Noooo. I don't think he told me that."

I was looking at Eddie. "Bucket mouth," I said.

"Tell me," Marianne said.

I was silent. I looked at Eddie. "You started this."

He reached under the bar and pulled a long-neck PBR. He popped the top off and took a drink. "First one today," he said, looking at the bottle with a smile.

"Tell me, Eddie," Marianne said. She looked at me. "I need to know more about him."

Eddie opened his mouth and I said, "*Reader's Digest.*"

Marianne said, "What's that mean?"

Eddie said, "You sure she's old enough for you?"

Marianne gave him a frown and a look.

He kept talking to cover up. "I have a nephew, lives in Cottonwood. Name of Billy Bragg. He's a cop up there. Off duty he got in a row with a guy up there who was mouthing off about a girl Billy was sweet on. In fact, Billy and her are married now. But in the heat of the moment Billy told the guy if he said anymore about the girl, Billy would kill him. A short time later, the guy shows up without a head."

"Without a head?"

"Somebody lopped it clean off."

Marianne shuddered. "How awful," she said.

"So I asked Jackson to go up with me and see if we could prove Billy was innocent."

"Did you?"

"Eventually," I said.

"What about the little girl?"

Eddie took two long drinks. "Turns out the bad guys were homegrown jihadists. One night Jackson was taking the fourteen-year-old daughter of a friend from Cottonwood to Sedona, and they ambushed him and took him and the girl captive."

Marianne took a drink and looked from Eddie to me and back. "Okay, you guys are pulling my leg. You probably do this with all the girls Jackson brings in here."

Eddie raised his hand. "Honest to God's truth," he said.

She was looking at me. "You swear this is true?"

"I swear," I said. "On Elena's bosom."

"That's a big swear," Eddie said.

"Now I know you are putting me on. What happened to the girl?"

"Safe and sound," Eddie said.

"What happened to the jihadists?"

Eddie said, "There's a little mystery about that. Their camp was found out in the middle of the desert, but they were never seen again."

She finished the food, wiping the last of the hushpuppies into the last of the ketchup on her plate. "The fish was delicious," she said, wiping her mouth with a napkin. "And the drinks were great, but your story is a little weak, and I don't believe a word of it."

50

The next morning, we slept late, then went to the bar to have hamburgers for breakfast. When we finished, we went back to the boat and used friendly porcelain. I called for the shuttle and we met it across the walkway of the marina. The kid took us up to the Mustang. The Mustang was sitting on flat tires. The rest of it had been vandalized. The seats had been ripped open and the trunk lid was jimmied. The spare tire had been sliced open. Marianne couldn't believe there would be vandals at a marina.

I called an Uber for Marianne and waited with her until it came. She wished me good luck, kissed me goodbye and I walked back down to the marina. While I walked I called AAA. I found Maureen in her office. She was watching a soap on TV. When I came in, she switched it off. On the wall was a bank of monitors showing just about every view of the marina.

"Good morning," she said.

"Bad morning," I said. I nodded toward the monitors. "I know there are surveillance cameras all over, do the ones at the paid-parking work?"

"Something wrong?"

"Someone vandalized my car."

"The Mustang?"

"Yeah, the only one I have."

"Now don't get snippy. Let's take a look." She swiveled in her chair and started typing on her laptop. "It's camera three." She pointed at one of the monitors. "When do you think it happened?"

"During the night sometime."

One of the monitors began running backwards. When I saw some activity I said, "There."

"I saw it," Maureen said. She stopped the feed and paced it backwards. It showed two men in hoodies searching the car. The camera was fastened on an upper beam, so the picture was looking down at the men. With the hoods you couldn't see their faces.

"Can you zoom it?"

"Don't have the budget for that kind of equipment."

"See the guy in the gangster shorts? When he has his back to the camera, stop it."

The image was just a blip, so she had to backtrack twice until she finally got it. She froze it with the guy's back to us. I leaned forward and studied the image.

"Bar codes," I said.

"What?"

"Tattoos. Eddie calls them bar codes. Says they identified many a guy in Chicago by his tattoos. Look at the guy's legs. If you want to stay incognito, don't get tattoos."

"You know this guy?"

"You bet your sweet bippy. Know him and know why he did that to my car."

"Why?"

"They're looking for something I don't have. They searched the boat. Now the car."

"They must want it really bad."

"They're not going to get it from me."

I called a body shop I had used before and had AAA haul it down there. I called Uber and caught a ride to El Patron. It was early enough, even Ray wasn't there yet. Jimmy was cleaning behind the bar. I slid up on my usual stool.

"Doesn't Blackhawk hire cleaners?"

"They never get it clean enough," he said. He threw a bar towel at me. "You can help me out by wiping down the tables and chairs." I grabbed it and started wiping. They kept the tables and chairs lined against the wall. This left the middle open for the dancers. When Elena was on, there were always dancers. One night, after many shots of tequila, I tried it myself. What I recollected, which wasn't much, was I made a complete fool of myself. If I had any skills, that wasn't one of them. Especially while missing a foot. I could snuggle up and dance real slow, but nothing ambitious. I do remember Nacho laughing so hard he was in tears.

When I finished wiping, I sat at the bar and Jimmy poured me a tomato juice. I sat there and watched Jimmy clean while I waited for the place to come alive. Jimmy was very fastidious. He liked it clean. No dusty booze bottles for him.

After about an hour Blackhawk came and sat beside me. I knew he knew I was here. All he had to do was check the monitors, which he did every morning. Jimmy poured him a cup of coffee and set cream and sugar out.

"I didn't see the Mustang on the monitor," he said. "Then I saw you sitting down here."

"I went up the hill to get the Mustang and found it trashed."

"Trashed?" He put cream and sugar in his coffee.

"They slashed the seats and tires and jimmied the trunk lid."

"Who they?"

"Bucky Beaver and Tattoos."

"Who?"

"The two guys that were with Azeed…."

"Delbert."

"Delbert, when they were here. The same ones that searched my boat."

He shifted around. "Searched your boat?"

"I didn't tell you?"

"I would have remembered. Why don't you tell me now?"

So I did.

51

"So what do we do with the money?"

"Who does it belong to?"

"Az...Delbert sold phony drugs to two gang bangers. Belong to Ace Double Deuce. They're hooked up with Dos Hermanos. So, it's drug money. Which means I don't know whose it is."

"Who were the two guys with Delbert?"

"Bucky and Tats."

Blackhawk just looked at me.

"Bucky has a serious overbite and Tats has tattoos."

"Who do they work for? Delbert?"

"Valdez."

"How did Valdez get involved?"

"Evidently a guy named Salvatore Mendez is the new head of Valdez since the other guy went to the slammer. Mendez saw a big bag of cash floating around out there and decided he wanted it. I don't know how Delbert got involved with him."

"If the guy is a dipshit loser, then I have no doubt Delbert's mixed up with him."

Across the square shaped bar Nacho had walked in. He was

carrying a newspaper and sat at his usual stool.

"Salvatore Mendez? Did I hear you talking about him?" he said, looking at us.

I looked across the bar at him. "You know who he is?"

"Yeah. I'm surprised you don't."

"Never heard of him." I looked at Blackhawk. He shrugged.

"You must hang out with the wrong class of people," Nacho grinned.

"High class, you mean?" Blackhawk said.

"Damn straight. If you hung with some low life druggies you'd know this guy."

"Tell me about him."

Jimmy came down to Nacho. "Can I get you something?"

"Coffee made?"

"You bet." He turned away to get the coffee.

Nacho looked at me. "Mendez is a bad dude. When Saza was caught and put away there was an internal war. Mendez came out on top. Two of the contenders disappeared and have never been found. Guys I know tell me that your old friend, Emilio Garza, tipped the balance in favor of Mendez. Garza's in the top tier now."

"He's the one that told me they wanted the money."

"Watch your back. Mendez will squash you like a gnat. Garza won't protect you."

"Do you know where Mendez is?"

"I can find out."

"What do we do when we find him?" Blackhawk asked.

"Tell him where he can find the money."

Blackhawk looked at me, his eyebrows going up. "You're kidding."

"Actually, what I'm thinking is to tell Mendez who has the money."

"And who would that be?"

"Elliot, Rick the prick, and maybe a guy named O'Malley."

Blackhawk was silent for a moment. "The diamond thieves."

I smiled and he began to nod.

52

It was windy and looked like rain. The weather app on my phone showed a front coming from the west. I had the bow and stern doors open and the cross-breeze was slowly turning cooler. The sky looked like the front had already arrived. I was lying on my couch reading a Malcom Gladwell book. Guy is smart. My phone chirped.

"I think we need to get Emil involved," Blackhawk said in my ear without preamble.

"He's Valdez," I said.

"He's anyone he wants to be. Lately it's been Valdez."

"And he probably would have someone inside Dos Hermanos."

"I would, if I was him," Blackhawk said.

"Let me call him," I said.

I was almost too shocked to talk when Emil actually came to the phone. At one time he had given me his cell number but now when I called, the number was disconnected. So, I called the only contact I had for him, which was the Columbian Consulate in downtown Phoenix. When I told her my name, the girl that answered put me on hold. I was trying to imagine what she looked like. I'd only been there two or three times and each time it was a different girl. The ambassador's attaché, Salvatore Escalona, liked his receptionists young, stacked, and good-looking. Unfortunately for them, when they decided they had the married man right where they wanted him, they ended up looking at want ads.

So when Emil came on the line, I was stunned.

"My old one-footed miracle worker," he said.

"How is his excellency's granddaughter?"

"Living in Columbia under the supervision of her mother. And I sense an ask is coming up, otherwise why bring the girl up."

"Ouch."

"What can I do for my favorite boat bum?"

"I'd like to meet."

There was a silence. Finally, he said, "Telephones are not safe?"

"Exactly. Can we meet?"

"I'll send you a text," he said and disconnected.

A minute later a text came across my phone. It gave the address of a yuppie watering hole in downtown and gave me an hour to get there. For extra money I had gotten the Mustang back sooner rather than later. They even delivered. I changed, brushed my teeth, and headed downtown.

The place was in the heart of downtown a half block from a public parking garage. It still took me three floors to find a spot to park. I took the stairs down to the street and walked to the stairs that led up to the bar. It was in an area that had several shops. They all faced an open air patio. When I got there, I realized I had met Emil here before. He was waiting on the restaurant's patio. He had a small table, and I took the only other chair there was.

He had what looked like a mojito in front of him. As I sat, a pretty, young woman came over to take my order.

"Iced tea, no lemon," I said to her. As she moved away, I looked at Emil. He had a quiet competence about him. There was an aura of something I had seen in few men. Blackhawk and some of the others in my old team had it. The colonel had it. Captain Mendoza had it. It was almost a shimmering of dangerous and at the same time, a quiet confidence. We waited until she brought my tea. Emil ordered a platter of nachos. She looked at me and I shook my head. She turned to go get his order.

Emil looked at me. Finally, he said, "And so?"

I paused, then said, "Salvatore Mendez."

He was surprised. "What about him?"

"And a guy calls himself Azeed Muhammed. Real name Delbert Smith."

"He still alive?"

"As we speak, I don't know. Was a couple of days ago."

"Matter of time."

"Good old Delbert sold phony actiq to a couple of Dos Hermanos dudes and absconded with the money."

"Absconded? You been reading again?"

"Not enough," I said. "Salvatore Mendez wants the money. I understand he'll be cutting hands and legs off to get it."

"You understand correctly, but Mendez isn't Dos Hermanos."

"Yeah, I know he's Valdez, but I'm told he wants the money anyway."

"He's greedy."

I didn't say anything.

"Why bring him up?"

"I'm told Mendez is the new, uh, what's the word...Padrino?"

"Godfather. We don't use that term. To Valdez he is El Jefe."

"Are your people happy about that?"

"It is what it is."

"Can he be trusted? If he gives his word, I mean."

"No."

"Not maybe. Not possibly?"

"No."

The waitress brought Emil's nachos. "Anything else I can get you gentlemen?"

"Chalupa," he said. "The hotter the better."

"Right away," she said.

After she was out of earshot, I said, "You don't like him."

"No."

I leaned back and studied him. I took a drink of tea.

He looked back and sipped the mojito. "What's this about?"

"I think I can find the money Delbert took. My decision is what to do with it."

"Buy a new boat."

"Yeah, that's what everybody says. But if I did that, I'd have to live the rest of my life looking over my shoulder waiting for you or Garza to show up."

"There is that."

"If I did find it, and I gave it to Mendez, what would he do with it?"

"More prostitutes, more cigars, faster cars."

"What if I gave it to you?"

He looked at me for a long moment. "Does Blackhawk have it?"

"No."

"Do you have it?"

"No."

"Under no circumstances do you give it to me."

"What about Garza?"

"He'd have the same dilemma as you."

"Why wasn't Garza made the new El Jefe?"

"I wish he had been."

"But they didn't ask you."

"They never ask me."

"I would like to contact Mr. Mendez. Can you give me his number?"

"No." He leaned back and thought. "I can call him and tell him to contact you. You may have knowledge as to where the money is. I will tell him you are a special friend to the ambassador. He will call you."

"And then?"

"And then you watch your ass. This man is crazy."

53

I was lying on Blackhawk's couch in his apartment thinking. Elena was taking her nap. Blackhawk was still wrestling with taxes at his dining table. Nacho came bursting through the door.

"Oh good," he said. "You're here."

Blackhawk looked up, disgust on his face. "Don't you know how to knock?"

Nacho was shocked. "It's not like I'm gonna catch you and Elena in here doing the nasty."

"It's common curtesy," Blackhawk said. "Common decency. Civility. Manners. It's what your mama taught you."

"I'm sorry," Nacho said. I swear he ducked his head like a child getting a scolding.

"Go back out and try again," Blackhawk said.

Nacho turned and went back out, closing the door behind him. A moment later there was a rapping at the door.

"Who is it?" Blackhawk called.

I fell off the couch laughing.

Then I laughed harder when I heard Nacho say, "Uh…, it's Nacho."

"Well come in," Blackhawk said. Nacho came slowly through the door. "What are you doing, standing out there?"

Nacho hesitated, then grinned when he realized Blackhawk was putting him on. He said, "I found out where we can find Salvatore Mendez." He looked at me. "Why are we looking for him, anyway?"

"I thought I wanted to give him some money, but I changed my mind," I said.

Nacho handed me a piece of paper. It had an address on it.

"I talked to a couple of old cronies that are still connected to Valdez. They told me where this guy is. They advised me to stay clear of the guy. Said he's crazy."

I looked at the paper. The address was on Seventh Street. I went over to a small desk Blackhawk kept a laptop on. I pulled up the county assessor's site and searched for the address. It turned out to be a small restaurant bar. The owners name wasn't Mendez. I didn't recognize the name listed as the owner.

I looked over at Blackhawk. He was absorbed with his paperwork.

"Hey," I said. "You want to go to lunch with Nacho and me?"

"Better than taxes," he said pushing the paperwork away.

The place was in a strip mall between Missouri and Camelback on the east side. It had a pole sign out front with the name *Milano's* on it. Parking was in the back. We were in Nacho's Jeep. He was driving. We all had a pistol. I had the Rugar LCP .380 with the infrared sight, Blackhawk had his Sig Sauer in his pocket and when Nacho stepped out, he took a Glock from under the front seat and stuffed it in the back of his pants.

We walked around to the front entrance. The place had several rooms. The entrance was on the left side of the bar. The hostess seated us in another room and toward the back. A girl brought us menus and took our drink orders. We all had beer. The place was old school. Nothing fancy, old paintings of Italy on the walls. The waitress was wearing jeans and a tee shirt. She looked clean, but not done up. I sat with my back to the wall and Blackhawk and Nacho were on either side. I didn't see anyone in the place that looked like cartel guys. Most of the customers were sitting at the bar. They looked like day laborers stopping for a beer.

Blackhawk said to Nacho, "You sure you got the right place?"

"No. But it is the place they told me about. Milano's."

Blackhawk looked at me. "What do you want to do?"

"Eat lunch," I said. "See what happens."

When the waitress came, we all ordered hamburgers. They had fries on the side, I had a side salad. A different girl brought our food. Blackhawk ordered another round of beers. Finally, when we were finished, the first girl came to clear the table and to see if we wanted anything else.

"Is Mr. Mendez in today?" I asked.

She stopped and looked at us. "Who's asking?" she said.

"I'm a friend of His Excellency Ambassador Revera. He asked me to say hello to Mr. Mendez."

"Who?"

"Ambassador Revera," I repeated.

"I'll see if there is anyone here named Mendez."

It was quite a while, but it wasn't the girl that came back. It was Emilio Garza. He came into the room, moving in that easy way of his. He came over to our table. Blackhawk shifted slightly, making his pocket more accessible. Nacho hitched forward in his chair.

When Garza got to our table, he stopped and looked at me. His face was impassive, then he smiled.

"Have you come to give me more money?"

"Not yet. Care to join us?"

"Mr. Mendez says he will see you." His posture was composed and relaxed.

I stood. So did Blackhawk and Nacho.

"Just Jackson," Garza said.

He turned and walked away, assuming I would follow. I did. He led me back past the front entrance, past the bar and then down a short hallway. There were restrooms on one side and an unmarked door toward the end. At the end was a door with an exit sign above it. He led me through the hallway door. The room on the other side of the door was spacious with a large desk facing out from the back wall. There were two chairs and a leather couch on the other side. A man sat behind the desk. He was smoking a cigarillo.

The man had longish, wavy dark hair and was tall even sitting down. He had a burly chest and prison tattoos on his neck. He wore an expensive dark sport jacket. His biceps stretched the fabric of the jacket.

"This is Jackson. The guy I told you about," Garza said. The guy waved a hand toward one of the chairs. I sat down.

His dark eyes showed me nothing. He rarely blinked. Like a rattlesnake sizing up a mouse. I sat quietly, waiting.

Finally, he said, "I'm told you can find the money Azeed

Muhammad stole?" He looked at Garza, who had leaned against the wall. "Emilio told me you returned stolen money to him and you returned Revera's granddaughter. He says you can be trusted to keep your word."

It didn't sound like a question so I didn't say anything.

He leaned forward. "I think you know what happens to people that don't keep their word to me."

I smiled.

He continued. "If you find the money and keep it, everyone you hold dear will die a terrible death. You will not be able to run far enough. If you find the money and return it to me, I will give you ten percent."

"Generous enough," I said.

He looked at Garza, then waved his hand in dismissal. I stood and followed Garza out. Short and sweet.

54

It was nearing midnight. I was in the main lounge of the El Patron. Marianne was due to finish her show at midnight and had told me she would join me for a nightcap. Elena's show always ran until 1 AM. The place was packed, the dance floor full. Blackhawk and Nacho were helping Jimmy behind the bar. All three were really busy. I'd offered to help but Blackhawk said they could handle it. I was sitting on the opposite side of the square bar from the bandstand. Elena had made the bandstand oversized to accomodate her large band.

I was nursing a Dos Equis watching Elena, and the beads of condensation ran down the cold bottle. It was my second. To my right I saw four men come through the main door. They were dressed like they were from out of town. They had on pressed, long-sleeved shirts, creased dress pants and shiny black wingtips. All the other guys in the place had on multicolored shirts, blue jeans and boots. I recognized two of them. Rick the prick and O'Malley. One of the others must be Elliot.

There were no tables available, so they moved to the bar. There were only a couple of barstools available, so they stood until Nacho came to take their order. He recognized them at once and looked down at me. I nodded at him. They were looking at Jimmy, Blackhawk and when they saw Nacho look at me, they turned and looked at me. I winked at them.

They stood there until Nacho filled their order. They all ordered beer. Nacho brought it in longnecks. When Nacho handed them their beers, Blackhawk came over and said something to them. I'm sure he said the beers were on the house, but I couldn't hear anything above the band and crowd noise. Jimmy was looking at me. I beckoned him over. I leaned toward him.

"Without them seeing, I want you to get pictures of these guys."

"What about the surveillance cameras?"

"They are at too high of an angle. I want good facial recognition photos. Just don't let them see you."

"You got it."

I picked up my bottle of beer and slid off my stool. I went over to them. They stepped away from the bar and watched me. If they were carrying, I couldn't tell it. None of us had weapons except for the sawed-off shotgun Nacho kept behind the bar for emergencies. He'd had it there ever since men had come in and took Elena. Turned out to be a really bad move for those guys.

I came up to the guys. They were watching me and I saw Jimmy off to the side, with his phone out, taking pictures. As I reached them, the band brought the song to an end. The crowd applauded enthusiastically.

"You boys looking for me?"

There were two of them I'd not seen before. One of them I

immediately assumed was Elliot. He said, "I'm looking for my property." He wasn't especially tall, but he looked fit. He looked like a runner. I guessed he was about forty. What made me think of his age was he was completely bald. One of those guys that, after fighting the oncoming baldness finally one day said screw it, and shaved it all off.

The other new guy looked straight out of the military. Blond hair cut in a crew-cut. Young and muscular. He started to move around me, to get on the other side. I held up a hand to stop him. He didn't like that, but he stopped.

Blackhawk and Nacho had moved over to where we were. Jimmy had put his phone away and was hustling drinks.

"What'll we'll do," I said, "is I will talk with one of you." I looked at Elliot. "Which I assume will be you. The other three can go back and wait in the car, or you can go down the hall to the Electric Slide, which is our country bar. The other place, closer to the front door, Rick's American, just closed. No sense to stop there."

They stood looking at me. Then one by one, they looked at Elliot. He nodded. "Go on," he said.

"You can't take the alcohol out of the building," Nacho said.

None of them had taken a drink. They set the bottles on the bar.

"Go on," Elliot said, his eyes on me. They filed past me. As they got to the door, Marianne came in. She looked around, then spotted me and started forward.

I looked at Nacho. I nodded toward Marianne. "Go take care of her, would you please."

When I turned back to Elliot, he was looking at Marianne.

He watched Nacho intercept her and guide her to Elena's table by the bandstand. It was kept clear for Elena's breaks. Marianne looked toward me, and I turned away.

Blackhawk went to the end of this side of the bar and asked two guys to move down. They didn't hesitate. He nodded at me.

"Let's sit down here," I said to Elliot. We both carried our bottled beer down to the newly vacant stools and slid up.

Elliot took a drink. "I want my diamonds."

I smiled. "I like a man that gets right to the point."

He turned his eyes to me. He wasn't friendly. "What do you want for them?"

"Why did you kill the girl?"

He looked at me. After a moment he shook his head slowly. "We didn't kill the girl."

"She died."

"Yeah, she did. Damned shame. At first the girl was a lot of fun. I probably spent too much time with her, but like I say, she was a lot of fun. Then she began to party. Harder and harder. She became addicted."

"There were no tracks on her."

"Pills. She hated needles. She was afraid of them. I was gone overnight, and she OD'd. When I got back, I went to check on her and she was gone. It must have just happened. I had the guys take her out to the doper neighborhood. I called 911. Sweet girl, but stupid." He looked at me. "You ever do drugs?"

"Scotch."

"Yeah, stick with that. Drugs are dumb."

I shrugged. "The cops say the diamonds are worth $300 million dollars. I'm thinking $500 thousand should be about right."

"You can't sell them." This was not a question.

"No, I can't, but you can. You'll probably get $100 million. Even if you get half that, $500 thousand is pocket change."

"If they can be sold. Which isn't as easy as it sounds. The bad news is I don't have a half million dollars lying around."

"Most people don't. But I'll bet you thought about it."

"Having a half million lying around?"

"How to pay me."

"Yeah." He put an elbow on the bar and looked around the room. He watched Nacho come back from talking with Marianne. "Here's how it will work. You give me half; I sell that and that gives me the money to pay you for the rest."

"Or you take off. Half is better than zero."

He looked at me straight on. "I'm much too greedy to do that. Why should I leave half on the table.?"

"I'd find a buyer eventually."

"You wouldn't live that long."

"Well, you've told me one thing I believe."

"And that is?"

"You don't have the $500 thousand."

"Do we have a deal? Half, I sell it, pay you and you give me the rest."

"I need to think about it."

"Don't take too long."

55

After Elliot and his buds had left, I went over and sat with Marianne. Jimmy had brought her a Sprite. He looked at me. "You want the photos sent over now?"

"Sure," I said. "Sorry I didn't come watch you," I said to Marianne before she could ask what photos Jimmy was talking about. "I just got here about an hour ago."

"It looked like you were ignoring me," she said. The gold flecks in her eyes picked up the lights in the bar and reflected them back to me.

"Yes. I'm sorry." I looked up, watching Elena for a second. We had to talk a little louder because the music was louder here. "I'm afraid she'll end up with hearing problems."

"Occupational hazard," Marianne said.

I looked back to her. "The guy I was talking to is a jerk. I was afraid you would come over and I would have to introduce you. I didn't want to do that."

"What were you talking about?"

"A girl I knew that died of an overdose. He was dating her." I told her about Annabelle and her father and Father Correa. I left out the diamonds and the beatings. Which meant I had to do a little tap dancing, which I didn't want to do. You start lying in a relationship and soon there is no relationship. At the same time, I knew she wasn't ready to know about people in my life like Elliot and his gang. Maybe I was afraid she'd start learning who I was. I didn't want to scare her off. I was really starting to like her. A lot.

We sat there, enjoying Elena through her last number. To thunderous applause, which we took part in, Elena took her bows, then came down and sat with us. Jimmy brought her a club soda and a shot of tequila. He looked at Marianne and she shook her head. Blackhawk came over to join us while Jimmy and Nacho were policing the bar. They gathered the glasses and bottles and swabbed whatever mess was left. The musicians packed their instruments. They went to the bar and Jimmy gave them all the drink of their choice. Blackhawk was carrying a tall glass of ice, soda and I guessed Glenlivet. He set a rock glass of ice and Ballantine's in front of me.

"Great show," Marianne said.

Elena took a sip of tequila and a drink of club soda. "Thanks, baby. I never get to see your show."

Blackhawk said, "That would mean either Marianne plays until 2 or you quit at eleven."

"I'd prefer the latter," Marianne said.

"Me too," Elena said. "But once I get going, I can't stop. When the band is on it and I'm feeling it, it's like heaven on earth."

"Better than sex?" Blackhawk said.

"With anyone but you, baby."

"Wisely put," I said.

Across the room the bar phone rang.

"Probably a wrong number. Late for a phone call," Blackhawk said.

Jimmy went over to it. "El Patron," he said. He listened a minute then turned and looked at me. "It's for Jackson," he said.

Everyone looked at me and I shrugged. I stood up and went to the bar. Jimmy handed me the receiver. "Jackson," I said.

It was Emil. "You know who this is?"

"Of course."

"I got a call from Garza a minute ago. Mendez and four of his goons are heading your way. He thinks he can shake or shoot the location of the money out of you. He's had someone inside the club all night."

"Thanks," I said. He hung up. I looked across the room. Everyone was watching me. I gestured to Blackhawk. He got up and came over to me.

"Mendez is on his way. He thinks he can make me tell him where the money is."

"What's the plan?"

"Get Elena upstairs. Send Marianne home and have Nacho follow her to make sure she's safe inside. Get Jimmy and everyone else out of here. You and I will meet them outside."

"What then?"

"Up to them."

The musicians were filing out. Jimmy was packing it up and the girls and Nacho were watching us. We walked back over to them.

Elena stood up and unknowingly helped us out. "I'm tired. I

think I will turn in. Maybe read a little." She looked at Marianne. "You can stay here tonight, if you wish."

"No thanks," Marianne said. "I just want a hot shower and my own bed." She looked at me.

I said, "Blackhawk and I have some stuff to take care of." I looked at Nacho. "Can you make sure Marianne gets home, okay? Then come back here."

"Why is he coming back here?" Elena said.

"Business," Blackhawk said.

"Monkey business," she said. She yawned. "I'm going up."

Marianne stood and so did Nacho. "Goodnight all," she said and turned toward the door.

"See you tomorrow," I called after her.

Without her hearing me, I said to Nacho, "Make sure she's in and locked up, then get back here as fast as you can. Make sure Ray locks up."

"Trouble?"

"Mendez," I said.

He looked at me, then turned and hurried after Marianne.

56

I stood outside watching Marianne drive away. Two seconds later Nacho's Jeep followed. The night was cool with a slight breeze. The LED pole lights that formed the perimeter of the parking lot cast an eerie, almost greenish glow to the asphalt. I stood in the shadows holding Nacho's shotgun. A minute later Blackhawk came out. He was carrying two pistols. He handed me one. It was a Smith and Wesson .38 caliber snub nosed revolver. Great for close work.

"What's the plan?" he said.

"You go around that corner," I nodded at it. "I'll go around this one. I figure Mendez is arrogant enough he'll come straight at the door. When they are out of their cars, we'll step out and have them in a cross-fire." Blackhawk reached into his jacket pocket and pulled another pistol. It was a Glock. He handed it to me. "Backup to the backup," he said. He turned and walked around the corner. I noticed he now had a pistol in each hand. I turned and went to my corner. I leaned against the shadowed stucco wall and waited. I could almost hear the movie music in my head. I felt loose and confident. With Blackhawk on the other side these poor suckers didn't have a chance.

I had hardly started waiting when the bright lights of a big vehicle turned into the lot. When it went under one of the pole lights I saw it was a black Suburban. I was right, it came straight at the front door. I kept myself out of sight until I heard the car doors slam. I looked around the corner. There were four of them. They all had automatic rifles. The headlights stayed on, illuminating the front entrance. Mendez was the biggest man. I could hear their low voices but couldn't make out what they were saying. Mendez gestured to one of the others. He went to the back of the Suburban and opened the cargo doors. He pulled out something that appeared heavy. He had his back to me, so it was after he turned that I realized it was a battering ram. Anyone that watched police shows on TV would have recognized it.

He carried it around to the front. Another one of the guys leaned his rifle against the car and took the other side of it. They walked up to the front door and prepared to batter it down. I stepped around the corner. I had the shotgun in my hands and the Glock in my belt with the .38 in my hip pocket.

"It's unlocked," I said easily.

They froze. They all turned to look at me. They were all illuminated, not only by the car lights but also by the overhead light above the door. I knew I was just a black silhouette pointing a shotgun at them. Blackhawk stepped out from the other corner.

"You could just ring the bell," he said.

Mendez started to move his hand. "This is a ten gauge. It'll blow you in half from here," I said. He stopped moving.

"I have a rat," he said, mostly to himself.

"We saw you on the security cameras," I said.

He looked at the cameras that were mounted on the two corners. "I just wanted to talk," he said.

"Great," I said. "Just have your guys drop the ram and their rifles on the ground. You can take your pistol out and drop it also."

Nobody moved until he nodded. Then they all complied. I stepped closer keeping the short barrels pointed at Mendez.

"So talk."

He looked from Blackhawk to me. "I was thinking that you might get greedy and try to keep all the money. I want to sweeten the deal. I'm willing to offer you fifteen percent of the money if you recover it. How's that sound?"

I thought, *sounds like you don't expect to give me anything but a bullet to the head.* "That's great. We need to get something straight though."

"What's that?"

"I'm the only one that has an idea as to where it is. No one else has a clue. You can threaten them, you can beat on them, you can threaten their babies, you can shoot them. It would be no use. They don't know."

"So why don't you just get it?"

"Easier said than done. Certain elements have to be in place, or I can't get it. Here's what I will do. There are other guys involved. They don't know about you. Soon I will call Garza and tell him when those guys have the money, and better yet, where they'll be. That okay with you?"

"No funny business."

"No funny business." I pointed the shotgun at the guy that had retrieved the battering ram from the back. "You, collect all the guns and put them in the back of the Suburban."

He looked at Mendez. Mendez nodded. He gathered them up and put them where I had told him.

Nacho's jeep pulled into the lot, splashing light over us. He pulled up several yards behind Mendez's vehicle and when he stepped out, he was holding a shotgun.

"Time to go," I said, waggling the barrels of my shotgun. The lights caught the barrels as they moved.

"Don't come back here," Blackhawk said. "None of you. Ever."

"No problem there," Mendez said. "Place is a dump." He turned and climbed up into the cab. The others followed.

As they drove away Blackhawk came over by me. "Dump?" he said.

"He had to save some face," Nacho said.

57

I got back to the boat about three-thirty. I pulled the blackout curtains with every intention of sleeping till noon. My phone chirped at ten. It was Marianne.

"Hey," I said.

"Hey, yourself," she returned. "I thought I'd see if you wanted to come down for a home cooked meal?"

"I can't resist that. Unless you want to come up. I can open a can of chili."

"So tempting," she laughed. "This is my grocery shopping day. Anything in particular you would like?"

"I like it all," I said. "Whatever suits you tickles me plumb to death."

"How about a kielbasa orzo salad?"

"Sounds great. Whatever that is."

"You've never had it?"

"If I have, I didn't know what it was. What time?"

"Come at 5."

"Done deal," I said. "I'll spend the day looking forward to it."

"See you then," she said and hung up.

I swung out of my bed and hopped to the head. I took care of business, then hopped to the galley and started coffee. I changed into my swimsuit and attached my swim foot. I went to the stern and lowered myself into the chilly water. I kicked out toward the buoy.

On my third trip I stopped and hung on to the buoy. The lake was alive. The ramp had two boats being backed into the water. One guy was struggling and was making multiple attempts to back it straight in. I smiled when I saw the other boat go straight in, easy peazy. I watched as the driver of the second truck step out and shake out her long blond hair. I treaded water while I watched the woman go over to the struggling driver and talk to him. She turned and started back to her rig. He tried it again. It was worse this time. He stopped and he must have called to her. She stopped and turned and went back to him. He stepped out of the cab of his truck and she slid in. She expertly backed the boat into the water. She stepped out of the cab and talked to the guy. She went back to her rig. They were a long way away, but I could see the guy pausing to look all around. Probably happy not to have witnesses. Just wait until it was time to take the boat out of the water. Backing an empty boat trailer is infinitely harder than one with a boat.

I did three more laps, then pulled myself up out of the water. I toweled off. I was covered in goose bumps. I stripped and hot showered and put on fresh clothes. I put on my utility foot. I drank another cup of coffee then stepped out on the dock. Pete's sliding doors were open. I leaned down and called, "Hey, Episodes. Are you home?"

Pete came out on the bow. "Morning partner," he said shading his eyes.

"I'm going up for breakfast. Care to join me?"

"Sounds good. I've got a couple of things to finish, I'll be up in a minute."

The marina was quiet. It was early. Eddie was sitting at the bar eating sausage and eggs. He was reading yesterday's *Arizona Republic*. I slid up beside him.

Sherrie was behind the bar. She looked down at me. "Coffee?"

I nodded. Eddie looked at me. "Morning, sunshine," he said.

"Morning. What's going on in the world?"

He shook his head. "Different day, same bullshit. Murder, mayhem, life, death, politics and all the news fit to print."

"I heard that a record number of newspapers have gone out of business."

"World's going to hell in a handbasket."

Sherrie brought the coffee. Without being asked, she laid some pink packets of Sweet'n Low next to it, then set a small pitcher of cream next to them. "You eating?" She looked at me with a smile. Pretty girl.

"Yes, ma'am," I said. "Two eggs over medium, sausage patties, hash browns and an English muffin."

"Yes sir." She grinned and saluted me. "Coming right up."

Eddie watched her walk away to place the order then turned and looked at me. "Better keep your guard up."

"One at a time," I said.

Pete came in and sat next to me.

"Good morning, young man," he said, leaning over to look at Eddie. Eddie was mopping up egg yolk with a piece of toast.

"How old are you when you dream?" Eddie said.

Sherrie came over and Pete said, "Good morning, gorgeous."

"Good morning, Hollywood," Sherrie said. "Breakfast?"

"You betchum," he said. He looked at me, "What'd you order?"

I told him. "Same for me," he said to Sherrie. He looked at Eddie. "What was it you said?"

"How old are you when you dream?"

"That's easy. I'm forever nineteen." Sherrie wrinkled her nose. "That's when I lost my virginity."

"Interesting question. I don't know," Pete said watching Sherrie's rear end as she moved away. "Probably thirty-five for me." He turned to me. "How about you?"

The cook was quick today. Sherrie came back with my breakfast. She set it in front of me. She stood there waiting for my answer.

"Probably however old I was just before I lost the foot. Losing a foot isn't as bad as a young maiden losing her virginity. How about you, Eddie?"

He looked at Sherrie. "Bring me a PBR, would you hon?" He hitched around to me, "I've thought about it. I'm forty, forty-five. I could still run like the wind. Now I have to call ol' Diesel to lean on so I can get off the floor. Bad knees."

"Someone once said, old age ain't for sissies," Pete said.

"Whoever said it, got that shit right," Eddie said reaching for the PBR as Sherrie set it in front of him.

58

I wasn't planning on leaving for Marianne's for a couple of hours when she called. Her voice sounded worried.

"What's up?"

"It's probably nothing," she said. "A guy came to the door with a package. He was looking for an address."

"What? UPS or something?"

"No, like a private courier. A normal car was at the curb. A red SUV. He was looking for 2309. I'm 2308. On either side is 2306 and 2310. Across the street is a double lot. It's 2307. The next one on that side is 2311. There is no 2309."

"Honest mistake?"

"I would think so. But the guy looked familiar. It finally came to me after he had left."

"Yeah?"

"He was talking to you last night at the club."

I paused. Then I said, "I honestly don't know why the guy would come to your house. I told you he was a jerk. I want you to lock all your doors and have your phone in your hand. If he comes back, call 911. I'll see if I can't find Nacho and have him come sit out front until I get there."

"You're scaring me. What's going on?"

"There is probably a simple explanation. Like I said, the guy is a jerk. He's been known to harass women. I'll be there as soon as I can." I didn't want a conversation to get started so I said "bye" before she could react and hung up. I speed dialed Nacho. At first when it rang, I thought he wasn't going to answer, then he did.

"Yeah," he said. He sounded like he had just woken up.

"It's me." Without preamble I said, "You remember the guys that came in last night to see me?"

"Yeah."

"One of them just came to Marianne's door pretending to deliver a package with a bad address."

"She's sure?"

"Sure enough. Can you run over there and sit out front until I get there? I'll text her address and phone number. Take a weapon."

"Always. Give me ten minutes."

"Thanks. I'm leaving now."

It was the time of day for the three o'clock rush to get home from work. I'd always thought that rush hours were at five. Not in Phoenix. Rush hour started at three. I never could find anyone that could explain it to me. Luckily, I was driving the other direction.

I took the Carefree Highway across to I-17, then south to Bethany Home. Once off the freeway, I wound my way through neighborhood streets until I pulled into Marianne's neighborhood. I always admired how neat and prim her neighborhood looked. I spotted Nacho's Jeep and pulled in behind it. As I approached, Nacho leaned over and opened the passenger door. I slid in.

"Thanks," I said.

"Sure," he said. "Why are they bothering Marianne?"

"They saw me talking to her at the club. They're probably trying to figure out how to use her for leverage."

"For the diamonds?"

"Yeah. You know about that?"

"I'm Nacho the Magnificent. I know everything."

I smiled. "I appreciate you coming. I'll take it from here." I opened the door and stepped out. I looked up and down the street. Nothing. I leaned down. "See you."

Nacho started his Jeep. I closed the door and he drove off.

Marianne was standing at the door. She was in an embroidered blouse with sleeves that flared out to just between her elbows and wrists, and a pair of shorts. She was barefooted. I left the Mustang on the street. If Elliot came back, maybe he'd see it and be put off. She held the door for me.

I kissed her. She put her arms around my neck and held me tight. I hugged her until she let go.

"Come on into the kitchen. You can help me put the salad together."

I reached behind me and locked the screen door. I followed her into the kitchen. It was small but serviceable. It did have a butcher block in the middle of the floor. On the butcher block were different colored peppers. A jar of Kalamata olives, a red onion, a jar of roasted red peppers with a carton of cherry tomatoes and a chopping knife.

"If you could chop that stuff up?"

"What is orzo?"

She picked up a box from beside the sink. She held it toward me. "It's pasta. It looks like rice."

"Oh," I said.

She stood looking at me. She reached over and took my hand. "But before you get started, I have to show you something." She pulled and I followed her through the living room and into the bedroom. Once in the bedroom she turned and put her arms around my neck once again. She kissed me with her mouth open. We kissed for a very long time.

She stepped back and unbuttoned her shorts and let them drop. She kicked them off. She pulled the blouse over her head. She had no bra. She stood looking at me, little red spots had appeared on her cheeks. She hooked her thumbs into her skimpy panties and pulled them off. There was a little wisp of proof she was a true blonde. She took my belt and unfastened it. She unbuttoned my pants and helped me get them off.

"I always was a dessert first kind of guy." I said, thickly.

59

Later that night, I followed Marianne to the club. She wanted to be there an hour and a half before her show was scheduled. I parked beside her and walked her in. I told her I had errands to run, and I'd be in touch tomorrow. She kissed me. Ray was trying hard not to look.

There is a sprawling shopping center on I-17 at Happy Valley Road called Noterra. It was on the way to the lake, and it had a gigantic *Dick's Sporting Goods* store there. I guess I could find what I wanted at a Walmart or a Target, but I was sure Dick's would have it.

It was nine-thirty, and I was sure they were open until ten. I was right. As I walked in, you could tell the clerks were ready to close down. Rather than wandering around looking, I stopped the first clerk that came by and they directed me to the workout section.

I was looking for a gym bag. Like one that the diamonds were in. It didn't have to be exactly the same. Something distinct and memorable in its design. And I wanted two of them.

I picked a dark blue one with bright red piping. There was its twin right next to it. I got them both. I paid, but as I started to drive away, I saw the all-night Walmart on the other side of the complex and turned toward it. It had a few cars in the parking lot. When I got inside, I couldn't find any help in the electronics section. I finally had to go to the registers and ask. The gal got on the intercom and announced that I needed help in electronics. There was no one around, but I supposed she wasn't supposed to leave her station.

I went back and waited. I was almost ready to go back to the registers when a harried little guy came rushing up. He had an Assistant Managers badge and was bald except for the side of his head where he had let the hair grow. This he had combed over the top of his head, then lacquered in place with hair spray. No comment.

He did what I wanted him to do. He sold me a burner mobile phone and I bought 500 minutes. I thanked him and left. Twenty minutes later I was walking down the hill to the dock. Once on the boat, I went topside and called Blackhawk.

"Hello," he said. His voice was very noncommittal.

"It's me," I said. "I bought a new burner. Keep the number. I've got some ideas on what to do about Delbert, the money and the diamonds."

"We're packed," he said. "Can it wait till tomorrow?"

"Tomorrow and tomorrow and tomorrow, creeps in this petty pace from day to day, to the last syllable of recorded time."

"Jesus Christ, I'm busy," he said and disconnected.

60

The next day I had three cups of coffee and a bagel and I drove down to El Patron and picked up Blackhawk. I had to persuade him to come with me, but once I told him the plan he came along. We drove downtown to the Columbian Consulate offices to pay a surprise visit to Emil.

We parked in a public parking garage and walked the three blocks to the building the consulate was in. It was on the third floor. The receptionist lived up to Escalona's standards. As usual she had never heard of an Emil.

I did the talking but she was looking at Blackhawk. Sometimes it bruises the ego. But I was somewhat used to it.

Finally, when I quit talking Blackhawk leaned over and looked deeply into her eyes and asked her to check in the back to make sure there were no Emils. She flushed and got up and went to the back. I think there was just the slightest little extra back-end action because she knew we were watching. I say we; she didn't care if I was watching or not.

She came back and said, "Why don't you gentlemen sit?" She waved toward two expensive looking leather chairs. "I have someone looking." As we sat, she went back to her place behind her desk. Blackhawk pulled his phone and began messing with it. I watched her. She couldn't help herself; every few seconds she would glance at Blackhawk.

After several minutes, her phone buzzed. She picked it up, "Yes sir?" She listened then said, "Yes sir." She stood and moved around her desk. "Right this way, gentlemen," she said with a bright smile. We followed her to the back. We passed Escalona's office, or at least where it had been at one time. The door was closed and there was nothing on it to indicate it was Escalona's.

She led us to the last door in the hall, rapped on it and opened it. She stepped aside and indicated for us to move past her. We stepped in.

It was a rather plain room. There was a couch and a large TV with soccer on it. There were chairs and small tables with lamps. There was nothing on the walls. No photos, no paintings, no nothing. Pretty drab.

Emil was sitting on one of the chairs smoking a large cigar.

"Sit down," he said. He took a drag and blew the smoke to the side without inhaling it. He nodded to Blackhawk but put his attention to me.

"I've already done you a favor. Your quota's up for the month."

"Blackhawk's so-called brother...,"

"He's not my brother."

"Are you certain?" Emil said.

Blackhawk looked at him. "I used to be indecisive, but now I'm not so certain."

Emil laughed. He looked at me. "Is he still alive?"

I shook my head. "Right this minute? I'm not sure. He calls himself Azeed Muhammed. He sold phony drugs to two Dos Hermanos guys."

"I heard."

"I have their names. Freddie Venezuela and Mickey Ebert. The question is, are they still alive?"

"Shouldn't be but are."

"I want to talk to them."

"What about?"

"Getting their money back to them."

Emil took another long drag on the cigar. The odor was heavy in the room but I kinda liked it. He looked at Blackhawk, then back to me. "Is that what you are going to do?"

"No."

He smoked some more. He nodded his head. "If you get the money, what are you going to do with it?"

"Give it to you."

"I told you I don't want it."

"I don't want Mendez to end up with it."

"I don't either," he said. "Your two Hermanos pricks hang out at a joint on the west side. Called the Hi Low Club."

I waited for more. There wasn't any. He just puffed on his cigar and looked at me. I pulled the burner phone out of my pocket. "Put this number in your phone. It's the one I'll use to talk to Mendez."

He took it from my hand. I couldn't see what he was doing but his thumbs moved very quickly. I didn't know how his thumbs kept from covering two letters at a time. When he finished he handed me back my phone. "Got it," he said.

I stood. Blackhawk followed. "Thanks."

He shook his head. "You go in there, be prepared. The place is a Dos Hermanos hang out."

"We'll be fine," Blackhawk said. Emil looked from Blackhawk to me.

"I think Dos Hermanos is spoiling for a war," I said.

"Bad decision," he said. "War is not about who's right. It's about who's left."

I looked at him, shaking my head. "You two should go on the road."

61

Blackhawk had trouble pulling Hi Low Club up on his phone until he discovered it was Ilya's Hi Low Club. It was at the end of a Safeway complex on the westside off Thunderbird Road. It rested next to a travel agency. Its sign was not large, just above the door. A sign on the door said *No Firearms Allowed*. Blackhawk and I looked at each other and smiled. Really? A Dos Hermanos place? No firearms allowed?"

There was a small foyer as you came into the door. You were met with a chalkboard with the specials listed for each day. We moved left to enter the bar area. The first thing I noticed was the similarity of the actual bar itself to the main salon at El Patron. The bar was a long rectangle with bar stools on three sides. The back of the rectangle was a place for the cash register and a staging area. There was a walkway between that and a wall that had a long window into the cooking area. The window had a wide flat area on the bottom where the cooks set the food as it came up.

First thing in the bar area were two small pool tables. The kind that took a quarter then released the balls. In the corner was an electronic golf game and an electronic dart board. Besides the bar in the middle, on the left was a series of high-top tables, each with two chairs facing the wall and a stuffed bench behind that ran the length of the wall. On the right side of the room there were tables with four chairs each.

The place was half filled. I headed to the high-tops and Blackhawk followed. The two on the end, closest to the door were empty. I slid up on the bench and Blackhawk turned a chair to face outward and sat down. Through the kitchen window I could see two cooks. There were two barmaids, one servicing the rectangular bar and one taking care of us outside the bar. Carrying a tray filled with beer bottles and brimming mugs, the waitress came by us in a hurry.

"I'll be right there," she said as she hustled past.

I started to say, "No problem," but she was already past. She was tall, slim, and middle aged. Her hair was pulled back in a ponytail, with no thought of looks and every thought about function. "Working her ass off," I said.

"She has no ass."

"So observant. You hungry?"

"Is a fat dog lazy?"

True to her word, the waitress was back as soon as she dropped her load at her destination. She brought two laminated menus with her. "What can I get you to drink?"

"What's on tap?" I said. She turned and looked at the array of tappers. She opened her mouth to start the long list and I said, "You know, never mind. I'll save you the trouble. Gimme a Bud Lite."

She looked at Blackhawk. "Make it the same," he said.

271

"Beautiful," she said.

"You're pretty yourself," he said without hesitation.

She laughed out loud. "That's a good one. I'll get your beer while you decide what you want to eat."

"Thanks," I said.

She moved away. Blackhawk began to study his menu. I studied the room. Across the bar to the far side, there were five men gathered around one of the tables. I couldn't see what they were doing, but by their motions and body language I could tell they were playing cards. Two of them were Azeed's buyers, Freddie and Mickey. I had taken photos of them at the park with a long lens. I had since transferred the photos to a file in my phone. I pulled it out and started scanning until I found them. Venezuela and Ebert. I watched them for a minute, then quit. We were strangers in here. I didn't want to appear to be staring. We were just a couple of guys in for a beer and burger.

Blackhawk set his menu aside. I was still deciding. A minute later she was back with the beer.

"Have you decided?" she said as she set the beers down.

Blackhawk said, "I'll have the Rueben and a side salad. Ranch on the side if you have it."

"You got it," she said. "How about you, sir?"

"Cheeseburger and fries," I said."

"Great," she said.

"I'm not beautiful?"

"You are just fine, hon. How would you like the burger cooked?"

"Medium well," I said.

She gathered the menus and moved to put the orders in.

I took a drink of beer.

"Some of us have it, and some of us don't," Blackhawk said.

"Make a good title to a book."

"What?"

"To have and to have not."

"I think it's been taken."

"We need to talk to those two guys. Make them an offer they can't refuse."

"Jesus. Are you on a movie kick? Let's eat first."

We just nursed the beers, and they were half empty when the waitress came with the food. While I was waiting, I studied the other people in the bar. Some looked like regular customers. Some looked like Dos Hermanos. Most of the Dos Hermanos guys had tattoos. Most of those who I thought were just customers didn't.

The place reminded me of the SanDunes, a bar Cicero Paz ran his opioid empire out of before Captain Mendez shut him down and threw him in the slammer.

I was smiling, remembering Detective Boyce being undercover as a bag lady. She had been instrumental in Paz's downfall but had been discovered by one of Paz's guys after she had taken a tumble and he saw her pristine white panties. Too clean and white for a bag lady.

"What are you smiling about?"

"Detective Boyce's panties," I said.

He just looked at me. "You are one weird white man."

I saw the waitress bringing our order. I drained my beer. Always be prepared. She set the plates in front of us.

"Can I get you anything else, gentlemen?" she said. "Another beer?"

"Be a fool not to," Blackhawk said.

"That's my line," I said as she moved away.

The cook had arranged my plate with all the fixings separate. The tomato, onion, pickle, and lettuce separated. I squeezed the mustard onto the meat, arranged the tomato, onion and pickle on the patty and ignored the lettuce. I took a bite. Perfection.

62

The waitress was right back with the new beers. Blackhawk and I ate in silence. Finally, he said, "How's the burger?"

"Everything a burger should be. How about the Rueben?"

"Ditto," he said.

"Too bad this place isn't closer. I'd eat here more often."

We finished the meal and slid the plates toward the front of the table to signal we were finished. Blackhawk pulled a clipped wad of bills from his pocket and selected a fifty. He laid it on the table where it could be seen.

"Let's go over and slip a horse's head under those guys' bed covers," I said.

"Is everything a movie to you?"

"Sure. Isn't it to you? Don't tell me when we were on an op racing up a river or climbing through a jungle, you didn't hear music in your head. Dun dun, dun dun…"

"If you weren't so plain crazy, I'd have you checked for dementia."

The waitress came over and collected our plates. She balanced them on one arm and picked up the fifty with the other hand.

"Would you gentlemen like anything else? Dessert?"

"No thanks," I said.

"I'll be right back with your change."

"Keep the change," Blackhawk said. "Anyone that thinks I'm beautiful deserves a nice tip."

She beamed. She leaned forward and looking him in the eye, said, "Honey, you are beautiful."

As she moved away, I said, "You undertipped her. Let's go talk to Fudd and Rabbit."

We moved around the bar to the other side. The five guys had adjusted the chairs to accommodate the four-sided table with the five of them. The other three guys could have belonged to the same Hispanic hillbilly family. Mickey Ebert had a very white name but a very Hispanic face and body. The difference was, he was red headed and freckled. The uniform of the day was multi-colored short-sleeved shirts opened all the way down, revealing ribbed wife-beater undershirts.

Blackhawk moved past them and stole a chair from another table. I took one from a table on the near side. At the same time, we set our chairs and sat down like we were watching the game. They didn't want anyone watching the game. They all set their cards down and looked at us. It wasn't friendly. There was no money on the table. They were playing with poker chips. Just a friendly game, officer.

They couldn't decide which one of us to look at. I made the decision for them. I looked at the other three, one at a time.

"We'd like to speak to Freddie and Mickey in private. It will just take a minute, so if you gentlemen will excuse us."

The one across from me said, "What the fuck are you talking about?"

I looked at Freddie. "We carry a message from Delbert Smith."

He cocked his head. "Who the fuck is that?"

I said, "You know him as Azeed Muhammed."

He stared at me for so long I didn't think he was going to say anything. Finally, he did. "You guys give us a minute."

The three guys reluctantly stood. Freddie waved at the other side of the bar. "You guys go over there and have a beer."

One of the guys said, "I know how much I have on the table."

"I don't want your fuckin' money, just go get a beer," Venezuela said. Honor among thieves.

They moved away and Blackhawk and I occupied two of their chairs. I saw our waitress watching us with a puzzled look on her face.

"Is Azeed still alive?" Venezuela said.

"The last time we saw him, he was."

"When was that?"

"A couple of days ago."

Mickey said, "I'm surprised. Dos Hermanos has a price on his head. Them with a Dos Hermanos price on their head don't last very long."

"Dos Hermanos wants their money back," I said. "That's why we're here." Now I had both of their attentions.

"What I know is," I said, "there will be a time and place where Azeed will be at a certain location and he'll have the money with him." I pulled my burner phone and held it for them to see. "I need you to give me your phone so I can put my number in it."

"Why?"

"So you know it's me when I call."

"Who are you?" Mickey said.

"My name's Jackson. Here's the deal. There will be a very short window of opportunity. When I call, or someone calls from this phone you will be given instructions. If you want the money back, and I'm sure that getting the money back for Dos Hermanos will probably save your asses, you must follow the instructions to the letter. You will get the call in the next four days. Don't leave town. You won't want to be late when the time comes."

"Late to where?"

"I don't know yet. When you get the call, we will know."

They were looking at me like you would look at a python at the zoo. Finally, Venezuela handed me his phone. I put my number in. I put his in the burner then thumbed it. His began to ring. I disconnected and handed it back.

"The word is, Azeed lost the money. He doesn't have it," Freddy said.

"Trust me. He has it back," I said. "At least a friend of his has it. Wait for the call. You guys get it back and we get fifteen percent. Dos Hermanos will figure that it's better to get 85% back and not have two dead soldiers."

"What if we get it back and we stiff you. Maybe our guys won't want to pay you a dime."

"Fifteen percent is better than a hot piece of lead in the back of your head. You know how easy it was to find you two?"

Mickey said, "I'm not afraid of you."

Blackhawk and I stood at the same time. "That's the stupidest thing you've ever said in your life," Blackhawk said.

63

The next night I was at Rick's American, sitting toward the back and watching Marianne having the audience eat out of her hand. She had changed her set-up a little and added some rockabilly tunes. Her second set she went through a half-hour history of rock and roll. She started with *Rock Around the Clock* and ended with Springsteen's *Born to Run*. They ate it up. For someone with such a sultry voice, she could rasp out a rock song.

When she finished, I waited around until she had shed her make-up and changed into regular clothes. The usual, blouse, jeans, and boots. She said she wanted to go down and watch Elena finish. We sat at Elena's table again.

Marianne watched Elena like she was mesmerized.

She leaned over. "You see that?" Not taking her eyes from Elena. "See that move. It looks so natural, but you know she has practiced it over and over." She glanced at me. "You said she had no desire to go to Vegas."

"What she says."

She shook her head slowly, "She has so much talent. Do you think she doesn't go because of Blackhawk?"

"Could be. But I think she gets everything she wants right here. Guy named Roger Miller wrote a song about *Kansas City Star, that's what I are.* In these circles, Elena is a star. And they appear to have enough money to make them happy."

Still watching Elena, Marianne said, "I went shopping with her a while back. She didn't blink buying an eight-hundred-dollar pair of shoes."

I chuckled. "The same with Blackhawk. He wears those two-thousand-dollar suits and I wear a tee shirt and a pair of jeans."

"How much do your prosthetics cost?"

"Don't know. I get them through some kind of Government program."

"Even the swimming one?"

"They don't ask, and I don't tell."

We sat and watched Elena until she closed her act. The crowd was slow to leave this time, so it took a few extra minutes for Blackhawk to join us. He was followed by Jimmy with a tray of drinks. He placed a drink in front of each of us. Elena had her tequila and club soda on the side, Blackhawk had a rock glass with one cube of ice and two fingers of a very dark brown liquid. Jimmy had a cosmo for Marianne and a Dos Equis for me.

"Whatcha drinking?" I said to Blackhawk.

"Crown Royal Black," he said. "Too much scotch will stunt your growth."

"That's why Jackson is so short," Elena laughed.

I leaned back and looked at my friends. I looked at Marianne. I looked across the bar at Jimmy and Nacho as they got the bar ready for tomorrow. I thought about how lucky it was for an orphaned boy who joined the Navy to have what some folks would say is an extended family. Extended from what, I didn't know, but was glad to have them.

When Marianne finished her Cosmo, she said she was ready to get home. She looked at me. I stood. "Me too," I said. Elena and Blackhawk looked at us, smiling.

The night was cool. I kissed Marianne in the parking lot.

"Come have a nightcap," she murmured, her lips against mine.

"Be a fool not to."

I followed her. Without traffic it took no time to get to her place. She pulled up into the carport and I parked on the street.

She had the key in the lock and turned it. She opened the door and screamed. I flew the final few feet, up onto the porch and grabbed her shoulder. I pulled her back. I could see inside. The place was turned upside down.

I pulled her back. "Go get in your car," I said. She didn't move. I tugged on her. "Go get in your car," I said with more urgency. This time she moved, down the steps and toward her car. I leaped off the porch and was in the front passenger door of the Mustang in a second. I pulled the appropriate knob and the tray slid out. I took the .38 caliber and checked the loads as I raced back to the door. The whole thing didn't take five seconds.

I went in the house at an angle. The living room was a total mess. The couch and chairs were upside down. The dining table was on its side. The kitchen drawers were spilled all over the floor. I went through the rest of the house. I didn't rush. I wanted to be sure. There was no one. I slipped out the back and made my way around the house in the dark. I studied the street. I started toward Marianne's car when I saw Marianne was at the front door. I came up behind her. Her eyes were wide, and she had a hand to her mouth. We went in.

"No one's here," I said. Then I noticed she was staring at the pistol in my hand. I shoved it into my hip pocket.

She was shaking her head in disbelief. Finally, she looked at me for a very long time, then said, "Who did this?"

My turn to shake my head. "Don't know," I lied.

She stared at me. She started in and stumbled. I helped her to a chair which was still upright. I got her seated. She buried her face in her hands. I stood there for a couple of minutes, neither of us moving.

Finally, I turned and began to straighten the furniture. I started in the living room and set everything upright. I went from room to room, working on the big stuff. They had dumped all the drawers onto the floor. I didn't know what to do with that stuff. I didn't know which drawer went where, nor what belonged in it. When I got to the point I needed her direction, I went back into the kitchen. She was as I left her. Head in hands.

I reached over and put my hand on her shoulder. She jumped sharply, then pulled away. "No, don't touch me!" She wouldn't look at me.

"Why don't you come out and spend the night on the *Tiger Lily*. I can put you up in the extra stateroom. We can fix all this up in the morning."

She was shaking her head. "No. No, you better go."

"If you want to stay here, I can stay with you."

She was still shaking her head. "No, you go. I want you to go!"

"Will you be okay?"

"Just go!" she screamed. Looking at me wildly. "Don't you understand? I want you to go! I don't know who you are. I know the man that I saw you with did this. The man that had the phony delivery. I just don't know why. I should have known at the beach. I was told you are dangerous. Who always has a gun? I don't know you. Just go! I've made a bad mistake."

I stood there. My heart in my feet. Finally, I went to all the windows and doors and made sure they were locked. I went to the front door. I turned and looked back at her. She was as before, head in hands, only now I could hear her sobbing.

"If you need me, all you have to do is call," I said. She didn't move, just sat sobbing.

I made sure the front door was locked, got in the Mustang and drove away. I got to the boat and laid on the bed staring at the cheap ceiling in the dark. Finally, I got up and started swimming. I swam for a long time. The water was really cold. I finally climbed out, showered, and laid down on the bed again. I had been trained to sleep at a moment's notice. Not tonight. Finally I dozed off. The last thing I remembered was it beginning to get light.

64

It was a week later. There had been a cool spell and it had actually rained twice. Marianne had told Elena she wanted time off to go back and visit her parents. Elena and Blackhawk knew something was wrong, but they didn't ask. Elena hired a four-piece jazz band that included a trumpet player that played a pretty mean Miles Davis. So I was told. I had not been in Rick's since the night Elliot and his dipshits had ransacked Marianne's house. I knew they were looking for the diamonds and I should have anticipated it. If they had known who Marianne really was, they wouldn't have bothered. Truly my bad.

Yesterday I had wandered out to Skateland, went by the distracted teenager and retrieved the gym bag with the diamonds. I took it back to the boat and transferred the diamonds into the black and red bag I had bought at Dick's Sporting Goods. I had taken a photo of the diamonds in the opened new bag, ensuring nothing identifiable showed in the background

I carried the bag with the diamonds over to Eddie's scow. I put a foot on the bow and rocked the boat. "Hello the River Runner," I called.

A moment later Eddie came out from below. He didn't have his cap on, and I realized that I don't think I'd ever seen him without a cap on. There was a line across his forehead where the top was lily white, and the bottom of his face was leather brown. Over the years he'd lost a lot of hair and what he had left was sticking out in wispy bunches.

"Sorry I woke you," I said.

"Just meditating," he said. "Knew an old guru in Chicago, said it was good for you." He squinted up at me. The sun was high. "Come on down for a cold one. Got some PBR on ice."

"Don't mind if I do." I followed him back down into the belly of the boat. It was small. Just large enough for a bed and a fold down tabletop. There was a hot plate on it, with an old coffee pot. Old Diesel, the grizzled grey and black, marina dog was curled up on the bed. The dog lifted his head and looked at me. When he saw who it was, he rested his head on his paws again. Eddie popped the top on two Pabst Blue Ribbons and handed one to me. He sat on the bed next to Diesel. He pointed his bottle at a lawn chair, folded in the corner. I pulled it out and opened it and sat. It was one of those aluminum ones with the plastic strips woven back and forth. I saluted Eddie with my bottle. He saluted back.

He looked at the gym bag. "Going someplace?"

I shook my head. "I'm going to ask you to watch this for a couple of days."

"What is it?"

I took a drink, then set my bottle aside. I opened the bag and showed it to him.

"Holy crap," he said. "Those real?"

"If they weren't, I'd dump them in the lake and be rid of them."

"Oh, no. Don't do that. Not good for the fish. Fish'll think they can eat them and it'll kill'm."

"No, I wouldn't do that. These are real. Did you hear about the big diamond heist in New York a while back?"

He shook his head. "Don't keep up with New York," he said. "Chicago is about all I can handle."

"Well, this is them. Lotta people looking for them."

"Hell, yes there are. How did you get them?"

I told him about Annabelle. How I found the key and how she used to ice skate. How I found the diamonds at the skate rink. "Just by accident," I said.

"Accident my ass. That's using the old noggin. What are you going to do with them?"

"Right now, give them to you. I've already had my boat searched. Nobody that's looking knows about you. I've got a plan to get the diamonds back to the cops, but I want the diamond thieves' asses while I'm at it." I told him how Annabelle died and about Father Correa and Annabelle's father getting beaten up.

"Bastards," he said. He looked around. "This ain't a very big boat. You got ideas as to where I put them?"

"I think you could put them right next to Diesel there and no one would look here for them. But I do have an idea."

"You wouldn't be Jackson if you didn't."

"Put the bag in a submersible bait bucket. Hang it over the side. These are all city boys. They don't even know what a bait bucket is."

"What if something goes wrong?"

"Then you have choices. You keep them, or you get them to Captain Mendoza or you cut the rope."

"What are you going to do?"

I emptied the beer. He pulled another one and popped it and handed it to me. I took a long drink. I looked at Diesel, who had decided to watch me. Maybe he knew what was coming. I looked back at Eddie.

"When I was a kid there were two guys in my neighborhood. Mean guys. They each had a dog. One a rottweiler and the other a pit bull. Now both of those breeds are nice, sweet breeds unless they're taught to be mean. These two assholes taught their dogs to be mean. They rarely put them on a leash. Both of those dogs would chase me on my bike while the guys laughed. I waited until one day both of those guys were out on their porches with the dogs. I rode up on the lawn of one and teased the dog until he chased me, then I led that dog right over where the other dog was. It was the damnedest dog fight you ever saw. Both those jerks got bit a number of times trying to separate them. I sat a half block down the street and laughed my ass off."

"So that's what you are going to do?"

"I've got two bad packs and I'm going to sic them on each other."

As I stepped off Eddie's boat he said, "Hey, what ever happened to that pretty little blond girl you were having out?"

I stood looking at him. I shrugged. "I screwed it up."

"You need to stop doing that," he said.

65

It was late. Really late. The El Patron was closed up tight. The parking lot was haunted by the distant LED perimeter pole lights, and the colorful sign over the main door. The main salon lights were out except for the night lights inside, the ones under the edge of the bar. It was so quiet I could hear the ticking of the building as it settled. There were overhead fans, slowly circling. You had to quit breathing and listen hard to hear them. They hung from the ceiling, two stories up.

Blackhawk and I sat at the bar. Our rock glasses sat empty in front of us. They had held Scotch earlier. It had been so long, they had dried. Blackhawk was staring into his glass, deep in thought when we both heard the same noise. We looked at each other.

The noise had come from the back room which had an outside door. We had heard that door open. We turned slightly to face that direction. We were on the opposite side of the bar from the doorway that led to that room. We could hear the footsteps of two men as they came through the stockroom.

Azeed came into the bar first, followed by Nacho. The light

was low enough it caused Azeed to hesitate. Nacho shoved him.

Blackhawk stood, "Over here."

Azeed was moving hesitantly, uncertain as to why he was here. Nacho shoved him again. Azeed stumbled over to us. Blackhawk waved at a stool, one removed from him. "Sit down," he said.

Azeed's eyes were adjusting. He looked from me to Blackhawk, then climbed up on the stool. Nacho went to the end of the bar, lifted the gate and went inside. He poured himself a drink. He downed it, then poured another and came back to us.

Azeed was looking at Blackhawk. He tried to look confident. "What's this all about?"

"How'd we know how to find you?"

"Hell, I don't know. I didn't think anyone knew where I was."

"Salvatore Mendez and Emilio Garza know where you are. If Freddie Venezuela and Mickey Ebert find out where you are, how long would you last?" I said.

"What do you want with me? You have the money."

"I want to get something straight," Blackhawk said. "You are not, and never have been my brother. If I hear you spreading that bullshit again, I will shoot you myself."

"We have the same mother," he whined.

"My father married your mother for a very short period of time after you were already born. Your birth father and mother are different from my birth father and mother. There has never been any blood between us. But that's not why we brought you here."

"Why did you bring me here?"

Blackhawk waved a hand, indicating the room around us. "I

SAM LEE JACKSON

have a very good business here. It is very successful. I am happy here. Elena is happy here. If I were as footloose as you, I would be gone with the money. Under these circumstances that much cash is just a pain in my ass. I don't want it."

"I'll take it."

"I know you will," I said. "But we don't trust you. I don't want Dos Hermanos to come busting down the doors. I don't want anything to do with Salvatore Mendez nosing around, trying to get information as to where you are, or where you went. So here's how we are going to do it." I reached my hand out. "Give me your phone."

He hesitated.

"Give it to him," Blackhawk said.

Azeed pulled his phone from his back pocket and handed it to me.

I took the phone and put the number of my burner phone in it. I handed it back.

"Within three days you will get a call from this number. It may be Blackhawk, it may be me, or it may be someone else. Whoever it is, they will give you instructions. You have to follow the instructions to the letter. If you don't, you won't get the money and you may die. If you do, you will get the money. You understand?"

He nodded.

"Good. Now get out of here."

He looked at Nacho, who was ignoring him. "How am I supposed to get back?"

Blackhawk said, "There's an all-night gas station two blocks down. Lots of light. You can get a beer. Take your phone down there. Call someone who gives a shit."

290

66

I had spent the night in Blackhawk's spare bedroom. When I awakened the apartment was quiet. It was just after ten. I knew Elena wouldn't be up yet. Blackhawk would be, but he wasn't here. I made the bed, military style. I took a quick shower in the guest bathroom. There was a toothbrush still in the store packaging and a tube of half-used toothpaste. I found a bagel and some hard-boiled eggs in the refrigerator and made a breakfast out of it.

I found Blackhawk in his office, engrossed in the business of doing business. I told him what I was going to do, and he told me to take Nacho with me. Nacho wasn't going to be in for a couple more hours. I went down and let myself out. I drove the Mustang down to the gas station that Blackhawk had directed Azeed to and bought a large cup of coffee and a newspaper.

I went back to El Patron and sipped the coffee and read the paper and by the time they were both gone Jimmy was in. Nacho followed about a half hour later. I was going to visit Emilio Garza at Mendez's hangout. Timing was everything. It was still too early. The cleaners were in now and were sweeping and mopping and wiping and all the things you do to make the bar friendly. I helped Jimmy load the beer lockers and move in fresh kegs. Nacho took his turn with coffee and the paper. After a while Blackhawk came down the stairs. He poured himself a cup of coffee.

"You still here?"

"I decided it was too early. I don't want to show up and no one is there yet."

He carried his cup over to the cash register and counted the money. He took it all out except for the seed money for today's business. He counted off some bills and handed them to Jimmy. Jimmy nodded and put them in his pocket. Blackhawk went down to Nacho and gave him a handful of bills.

He came and sat next to me. "Uncle Sam know you are doing this?" I said.

"Fair is fair. Their share of the tip money."

"How do I get a job here?"

"You're unreliable," he said.

I waited another couple of hours, then gathered up Nacho and headed for Milano's. We lucked into an open parking spot in front. Nacho stuck a 17 round Glock in the back of his belt. I had the Ruger in an ankle holster and the Kahr under my arm, hidden by my unbuttoned shirt. Why would Marianne worry about me having a gun?

We went in. There were only a handful of customers. Two were at the bar. There was an open table by the door. I nodded toward it and Nacho took a seat. He shifted in the chair so the Glock was available. I went to the bar and sat. The bartender was the lady I saw waitressing the last time I was in here. She placed a coaster in front of me.

"What can I get you?"

"First beer you put your hand on," I said with my winning smile.

A moment later she set a Coors in front of me. She looked across at Nacho. "Can I get you something?" she said to him. I could see him in the mirror. He shook his head. The bartender gave me a look and started to move away.

"Can you tell Mr. Garza that Jackson would like a word with him," I said.

She stopped and looked at me. "Don't tell me there's no Mr. Garza here," I said. "Just go tell him."

She gave me a hard look and turned and left the room. A minute later she was back but she didn't look at me. I waited.

After a long enough wait to put me in my place, Garza came from the back. He surveyed the room. He saw Nacho and nodded to him. Nacho gave him an imperceptible nod back. Garza came around the bar and sat next to me.

He looked at me, then at the beer I hadn't touched. "Ready for another one?" he said.

"Haven't touched that one," I said.

"You don't like Coors?"

"I don't drink when I'm dealing with lions and tigers and bears."

"Oh my," he said. He hitched around to look at me directly. "So, what are we doing?"

"I want to move to that corner table." I nodded at it. "Then I want to tell you a story."

I picked up the Coors and moved to the table. I didn't look but I knew he was following. Once we got settled, he said, "Okay, tell me a story."

I smiled at him. "There once was a nitwit that sold fake drugs to two rival gang members."

He shook his head. "I know this one, tell me something I don't know."

"Okay. Once upon a time there was a little girl that was given a fifteen-thousand-dollar diamond by an international jewel thief."

When I finished, I had told him the whole story including what I wanted him to do.

"I like this story," he said.

67

It was before dawn and it was blustery and drizzling. It was cold and I was trying to somehow keep the rain from getting behind the collar of my leather flyboy jacket and down my neck. I had a wide-brimmed straw Stetson on, and it was getting soaked. It's not supposed to rain in Arizona. I had the Ruger strapped to my ankle, the Kahr under my arm and a Mossberg pump loaded with 4-gauge rounds in my hand hanging down by my leg. There were extra rounds in my jacket pocket.

Blackhawk stood in the next doorway about ten feet from me. He had his Sig Sauer. I know he did even though I couldn't tell. Hanging down from his right hand was a 9mm pistol caliber carbine. Looked like an AR-15 but it wasn't. The parking lot behind the store fronts on Scottsdale Road and Shea Boulevard were empty this early. All of the businesses faced both ways. Toward the streets and toward the parking. I knew Nacho was sitting in his Jeep on the street on the southside, waiting for Blackhawk's call.

Blackhawk was watching me. I looked at my watch and figured it was time. I keyed up the photo of the opened new gym bag with the diamonds and sent it to Elliot, along with a text stating the bag would be sitting in the middle of the parking lot in front of the old theater playhouse at the southeast corner of Shea and Scottsdale Road. I told him to be there no sooner than one half hour from now. If he showed earlier, it would screw the deal.

I keyed up the photo of the other gym bag. It was open and revealed the cash. I sent this along with separate specific messages to Mendez, Freddy Venezuela, Mickey Ebert, and Azeed. I told each of them the same thing, again stressing not to play funny. It would screw the deal.

I then sent texts to Captain Mendoza, Captain Newsome and Detective Boyce, along with the photo of the diamond bag. I said the diamonds would be changing hands in the middle of the parking lot in thirty-five minutes. I told them both sides had surveillance on the site and if they showed too early, they probably, not only, wouldn't catch anyone, they wouldn't get the diamonds. Of course, this from my anonymous burner phone. When I finished, I waited to make sure the messages had gone then I took the sim card and smashed it. I did the same to the phone. I dumped the pieces in two separate dumpsters. One of which was Chaz's restaurant. Nobody would want to dig through all that goop. It was delicious on the table but not after being scraped into the large garbage bags. Even if they did find the phone, there was no way to identify me. I looked at Blackhawk. He was watching.

"Call Nacho," I said.

He pulled his phone and called Nacho. A minute later Nacho came walking in from off the street carrying the two bags. Each had an airline lock on them. He carried them to the front of the dinner theater and set them ten feet apart out on the open asphalt where they would be obvious. He turned and hustled away. Now it was time to wait. My greatest concern was the cops would show up too soon. I soon found out I had other concerns.

I walked over to Blackhawk. Even the cold rain didn't disturb him. "Nothing left to do," I said. "You want to stick around for the grand finale?"

"Wouldn't miss it for the world," he said.

We hunkered back under an overhang and waited behind a dumpster.

68

There was still five minutes to wait when Blackhawk and I heard a scuffling noise behind us. We spun around. Azeed and his two buddies, Bucky and Tats stood, each with a AR-15 pointed at us.

"Howdy boys," he said with a cocky grin.

Yeah, we were surprised. "You had the club staked out," Blackhawk said.

"Duh. And they say you was always the smart one," Azeed said. "We took turns. When you and Nacho left so early this morning, I knew you were up to something, so we followed you." He waggled the rifle at us. "Put your guns on the ground."

We complied. "Now the pistols," he said. I lay the Kahr beside my shotgun. Blackhawk did the same with his Sig Sauer. I still had the ankle pistol, but they seemed satisfied with what they got. Azeed's mind was elsewhere.

"So, why the two bags?"

"Door number one, or door number two," Blackhawk said.

"Let's go look," Azeed said.

"Let's just do them here," Bucky said.

"What if the money's not in the bag," Azeed said with disgust. "Let's go look." At least that told us how much time we had.

At his prodding, we started across the parking lot. Halfway to the bags Elliot and Rick the prick came strolling out from the neighborhood that bordered the east side stores. They were focused on the bags. At the same time Mendez's Suburban came rolling in from Scottsdale Road. Two seconds behind the Suburban another SUV followed and I thought it was more Valdez guys. Then I recognized Freddy Venezuela at the wheel. Hooray, the gang's all here.

Elliot and Rick froze. Elliot brought his pistol up and began firing. Salvatore Mendez had driven right up to the nearest bag and came out of the Suburban firing a pistol at Elliot and Rick. Elliot was hit in the leg and went to one knee. Rick was firing at Mendez, which made him duck. The guy with Mendez came out on the other side of the Suburban but didn't have a shot. Rick grabbed Elliot's arm and with Elliot hobbling, the two jumped behind the nearest dumpster. Using it as cover, and as quick as Elliot could move, they raced back into the neighborhood.

Then it was like synchronized dancing. Bucky and Tats were distracted. Without even looking at the other, Blackhawk and I swiveled. We swung our left arms over the top of the AR-15 barrels and clamped down, pinning the barrels to our bodies. We both punched our guy in the mouth and nose with the heel of our hand. Then slapped them hard in their ear. We followed with a hard punch to the solar plexus. They both sagged. We yanked the rifles away and smacked them in the head with the rifle butt. They were out of the game.

Azeed had gone nuts. He was running toward the bags and at the same time began firing at Mendez. By now Freddy Venezuela had popped out of his SUV and emptied his pistol at Azeed. Azeed's momentum got him to the bag then he was down, his chest covered in blood. I could hear sirens in the background. With our confiscated weapons Blackhawk and I fired a burst at Freddy and Mickey. They jumped back into their SUV and burned rubber backing out of there. Mendez had joined his guy on the other side of the Suburban.

Blackhawk and I were committed now and were out in the open. I had that old feeling. I felt cold and hard and ready. I was seeing everything and taking everyone in. I knew precisely where everyone was, how far away and how to take them down. It was like being in slow motion. Blackhawk and I moved with the precision of years of experience. I was firing Bucky's AR-15 at the front end of the Suburban. Blackhawk split away and both of us raced to the Suburban, firing all the way, keeping Mendez and his guy ducking for cover. I took the front, Blackhawk the rear. Then, Mendez came up over the hood and pointed his pistol at me. It was then Bucky's AR-15 decided to run out of ammo. The idiot had brought only a third of a clip. I guess he figured that would be enough.

I was still in the open and Mendez had me, but I was moving. I dove to my left. There was a huge explosion from a half block away and Mendez's head snapped backwards, a mass of blood and brains. I hit and rolled. I could hear Blackhawk firing from the rear of the Suburban. I crawled quickly under the vehicle. I could see where the shot had come from. Emil and Garza were standing by a black Escalade that was pulled sideways across the entrance to Scottsdale Road. Garza was holding a large rifle. From the sound and concussion, it had to be a .50 caliber. I slowly got to my feet. Emil waved. I was too stunned to respond. They climbed into their vehicle and drove away. Mendez and his guy were lying on the asphalt, the rain gently washing the blood and gore off them. I looked for Blackhawk. He was standing out in the open, holding one of the bags. Delbert lay at his feet.

"Let's go," he shouted and began to run.

We sprinted out of the complex. Nacho saw us coming and had the doors open. We dove in and he sped away with the doors still open. The sirens were close now.

Blackhawk was in the back seat.

"Which bag did you grab?"

"I don't know," he said.

69

The nightly newscast reported the police had recovered the stolen diamonds in an elaborate government sting. The thieves had been caught in Scottsdale after a shoot-out with known local drug dealers. The diamonds thieves' ringleader was arrested after trying to get medical help for a gunshot wound. It was speculated that the drug dealers were trying to steal the diamonds from the diamond thieves. An Associated Press reporter said he had information that the police had an inside man that had aided in breaking the case.

O'Malley turned state's evidence and ratted out Elliot, Rick, the military kid and the other one, whose name I didn't know until then.

I spent the week fishing with Eddie. Spent a night of cocktails with Pete and Eddie talking about the merits of their favorite movies. Pete said the greatest of all was *Citizen Kane*. Eddie called bullshit! He said the best movie ever was *Rooster Cogburn and the Lady*. I read three books, all Spenser novels by Robert B. Parker. You could read them as easy as drinking a glass of water. I watched a long Ken Burns documentary about baseball with Eddie, on Pete's television.

Both weekend nights I spent at El Patron watching Elena. The second weekend I did the same thing, but I left early on Saturday night. As I was leaving, I heard a familiar voice in the hallway. I felt my heart constrict. I stopped in the hallway to listen. A sweet-sounding voice singing a beautiful song. I stood there for a while listening, then ducked my head and walked out. I drove back to the boat.

It was midweek. I was up top with a Dos Equis that had gotten warm. I was reading a Jon Meachum biography of Andrew Jackson. I was having a hard time liking the guy. Jackson not Meachum. The marina had been busy so I didn't pay attention to foot traffic on the dock.

Then I heard Blackhawk's voice, "Ahoy the *Lily*."

I climbed up out of the chaise lounge and hopped over to the bow. Blackhawk, Elena and Marianne stood below me. Each was shading their eyes. You could have knocked me over with a feather.

"Uh….come on aboard."

"We'll come up," Blackhawk said.

I become aware that I was only wearing an old set of trunks and my stump was bare. "Grab some drinks," I said.

I heard them move through the boat. I heard the locker door shut. In a few seconds they were coming up the steps. Elena led the way with Marianne behind and Blackhawk taking up the rear. The girls each had a bottle of beer. Blackhawk carried two.

Elena grabbed three more lounge chairs and placed them in a semi-circle so we could talk but still look at the lake. I glanced at Marianne. She looked uncomfortable. I'm sure I did too. Blackhawk handed me my beer.

"Sorry. I wasn't expecting company," I said as they sat.

"Just family," Blackhawk said.

There was an awkward silence.

I looked at Marianne. She was looking out across the lake. I took the bull by the tail, "Look," I said to her. "I'm really sorry I frightened you." She turned her head to look at me. "I was foolish to think that guy wouldn't cause a problem," I continued. "I am truly sorry I got you involved. I am truly sorry I didn't anticipate his reaction."

She took a drink of her beer, looking at me over the bottle. "Did I ever tell you I was a Marine brat? I grew up going from base to base."

"I don't think so. If you did, I've forgotten."

"My Dad was a career Marine. He was a lieutenant colonel."

"I should have remembered that."

She shrugged. "Doesn't matter if you don't. I went back to see my parents. My Dad isn't doing well. Physically, I mean. Just getting old, I guess."

"I'm sorry about that."

"You are sorry about a lot," Elena said. Blackhawk reached over and patted her knee.

Marianne held my eyes. "I told my parents about you. I told them everything I knew about you. I told them how you handled those three guys on the beach. I told them you got choked up when you talked about your mama. I told them that you and Blackhawk are orphans and I have never seen a closer bond between two men."

"Might as well be married," Elena said. Blackhawk patted her again.

I was silent. I couldn't hold her gaze. I looked down at my stub and began unconsciously to rub it.

"I even told him that your names were not your names."

"Oh, but they are now," Blackhawk said.

She nodded. "Yes, they are now." Her gaze was intense, I couldn't keep it. Her eyes were glistening.

She took a swallow of beer, her beautiful adam's apple working in her wonderfully slender neck. "When I finished telling them all this, my dad told me to quit acting like a pussy. He said he'd like to meet you someday."

THE END

Did you enjoy
The Man with the Lightning Scar?

If you enjoyed this book, and you are customer in good standing with Amazon, please let us know what you think. After you get on Amazon.com, search for the book then click on the reviews and leave one. Thanks for reading.

You can go online to leave a review at the address below, or for more Jackson Blackhawk reading adventures.

www.samleejackson.com

Ever wonder how Jackson lost his foot? Join the El Patrón Club and learn this and more behind the scenes information about Jackson and Blackhawk. Also, be included in upcoming notifications for new novels and new behind the scenes content. Have questions about Jackson, Blackhawk and the gang? Leave an email at sam@samleejackson.com and we'll put the answer up on the El Patrón Club.

Go to the following url.

samleejackson.com/elpatronclub